# The Parrot Man Mystery

Also by Kathy Pelta,
starring Margaret Drusilla Kinkaid
THE BLUE EMPRESS

# THE
# Parrot Man Mystery

## K·A·T·H·Y  P·E·L·T·A

### Illustrated by Karen Ritz

HENRY HOLT AND COMPANY • NEW YORK

Published by Henry Holt and Company, Inc.,
115 West 18th Street, New York, New York 10011.
Published in Canada by Fitzhenry & Whiteside Limited,
195 Allstate Parkway, Markham, Ontario L3R 4T8.

Library of Congress Cataloging-in-Publication Data
Pelta, Kathy.
The Parrot man mystery / written by Kathy Pelta ;
illustrated by Karen Ritz.
Summary: While operating a pet-sitting business, eleven-year-old
Margaret Drusilla and her friends, Wil and Denise, uncover a parrot-
smuggling operation in Malibu, California.
ISBN 0-8050-1130-7
[1. Mystery and detective stories.  2. Smuggling—Fiction.
3. Pets—Fiction.  4. California—Fiction.]  I. Ritz, Karen, ill.
II. Title.
PZ7.P367Par   1989
[Fic]—dc20        89-33671

First Edition
Designed by Victoria Hartman
Printed in the United States of America
1 3 5 7 9 10 8 6 4 2

With thanks to Bill Dusel
of the U.S. Fish and Wildlife Service
for his help and encouragement
—K.P.

# Contents

1 • NOTHING BUT TROUBLE  1

2 • A BIG MISTAKE  12

3 • THE SHERIFF ARRIVES  23

4 • A SECRET AND A CLUE  34

5 • A MYSTERIOUS PHONE CALL  49

6 • A STARTLING DISCOVERY  54

7 • THE LETTER FROM BRAZIL  62

8 • ON THE TRAIL OF EVIL EYES  68

9 • SPIES ON THE PIER  77

10 • THE PROMISE  90

11 • THE MESSAGE IN THE MARGIN  100

12 • A CRISIS!  107

13 • CAUGHT IN THE ACT  114

14 • A SECRET VISITOR  121

15 · WHERE IS WB? 125

16 · THE ZERO HOUR 130

17 · LOOKOUT FOR SMUGGLERS 136

18 · TRAPPED! 143

19 · A PRISONER 147

20 · CONTRABAND 153

21 · TWO MYSTERIES SOLVED 159

# The Parrot Man Mystery

# Nothing but Trouble

I raced into the pet shop.

"Mr. Willy-Bones! I need puppy biscuits for Hilda." I slammed a quarter on the counter. "As many as this will buy."

The old shopkeeper was at his bulletin board, tacking up a notice. I was too far away to read all of it. But I couldn't miss the two words in big letters at the top: BIRD SMUGGLERS!

"What's *that* about?" I asked.

"Bad guys," he said.

"You mean *here*? In Pacific Cliffs?"

"Yah, could be," he said, his double chins wobbling. "Up the coast by Malibu."

I knew about the smugglers in Texas who stole my aunt's necklace. I even helped catch them. But I knew *nothing* about bird smugglers from around here. I hoped

1

they wouldn't make off with Mr. Willy-Bones's valuable birds—*especially* Ringo, the parakeet I wanted to buy.

As the shopkeeper dropped the puppy biscuits into a paper bag one by one, he counted to himself in Swedish—*"ett, tva, tre, fyra."* It didn't look like twenty-five cents' worth. But then Mr. Willy-Bones gave me a wink and slipped one more in the bag.

"Five!" he said—in English this time. Only, with his accent it sounded like "Fife!"

Grabbing the bag, I dashed for the door. No time to find out about the smugglers now. I was pet-sitting and had to rescue Hilda, Mrs. Eastley's dachshund, from the next-door neighbor. As far as I was concerned, that nasty man and his mean-tempered parrot were the *real* bad guys. Not some parrot smugglers—who probably didn't even exist! If Hilda left the house and wandered into that Parrot Man's yard . . . it could be the end of her. I shuddered at the thought and ran the entire ten blocks to Mrs. Eastley's.

Fortunately all was quiet when I got there. No sounds came from the other side of the hedge, where the Parrot Man lived. Then I heard Hilda's bark, from Mrs. Eastley's kitchen.

"Hilda?" I called. The flap of the doggy door moved, and the little sausage dog waddled out. She wiggled and yipped as I petted her. I gave her one puppy biscuit.

"More later," I promised. "After your walk."

I snapped the leather leash to her collar, and we started across the yard. Suddenly a voice squawked, "Bad dog!"

The words came from somewhere high up the thorny hedge. When Hilda began to yip, the scolding grew sharper.

"*Bad dog!* Bad. Bad. BAD!"

Hilda barked even louder. She strained at the leash. I held tight. Would the old dog attack the voice or run from it? Then Hilda lunged. I tried to hold her back, but a ninety-pound, eleven-and-a-half-year-old girl like me was no match for a ten-pound, aging but determined dachshund.

Near the top of the hedge flashed a fan of red feathers.

"Hilda!" I screamed. "Come away."

But the dog froze. A red parrot bore down on her like a jet fighter. Its huge beak cut through Hilda's leash. Two inches closer and it would have slashed the dachshund's neck. Screeching and snapping, the bird circled for another attack.

I swung my pack to fend it off. "Leave Hilda alone!"

With a shriek the parrot vanished into the top of the hedge. Hilda staggered under the hedge and crouched, trembling.

The day Mrs. Eastley hired me to look after Hilda, she warned me about the man next door. "Stay clear of that trouble-maker," she'd said. "And don't ever tangle with that nasty-tempered bird of his." She wasn't kidding.

I grabbed for Hilda. She acted scared and confused, and scrambled farther back.

"Not *that* way!" I yelled. "That's where the parrot lives."

Too late! Already Hilda had vanished into the yard next door.

Drat! That parrot could turn the sausage dog into *real* sausage. Dropping pack and leash, I tore across Mrs. Eastley's front lawn to the street. But when I came to her neighbor's yard, my steps slowed.

That man with the parrot had the only yard on this side of the street with a chain-link fence. Not very friendly! And ivy grew so thickly over the fence that I couldn't see in. Worse than unfriendly—it was scary!

At the gate I stopped. Plastic strips were woven through the gate's steel links. I couldn't see in. What was that Parrot Man hiding in his yard? I like playing detective, but being here didn't seem like such a good idea after all.

As I backed away, a white Mercedes splashed through a puddle, spattering mud on my white shorts and purple T-shirt. Dumb driver!

I glared after the sports car, then once more faced the Parrot Man's gate.

"*Bad!*" Now the squawk came from behind the fence. I paused, remembering Mrs. Eastley's warning about the parrot's temper. Instead of barging in, maybe I should wait for Hilda to come home on her own.

But what if she didn't? What if I was too late already?

My mind was a jumble. Should I go into the Parrot Man's yard, or retreat? Hilda's frightened yip made the decision for me. I couldn't let that dog become parrot chow.

Taking a deep breath, I opened the gate and stepped inside. The yips and squawks ceased. I looked around the dusty yard. No Hilda, no parrot, but cracked flowerpots and rusting tools lay everywhere. The yard seemed messy, not sinister. Was that the man's secret: He was a junk dealer?

"Hilda? Where are you?" I peeked under a faded sofa. It was missing two legs and most of its stuffing. Hilda wasn't there, nor was she behind the splintered wooden crates stacked against the fence.

In a vegetable garden a spindly scarecrow stood guard. Its black hat flapped in the sea breeze. But no dog crouched among the beans and tomato plants. Suddenly from behind me came a loud squawk and Hilda's frantic yips. I whirled around.

Was she in the Parrot Man's cottage? Thick vines and tropical plants hid the porch from view. Maybe the yard was only junky, but the house was sinister. It gave me the creeps. From a safe distance I called, "Hilda? Are you in there?"

The dog tore around the corner of the cottage, chased by a man in baggy red swim trunks and a white T-shirt. On his shoulder rode the parrot.

"No-good mutt!" the man yelled at Hilda. "Get outa here!"

*"Outa here! Outa here!"* echoed the parrot.

As fast as her stiff hind legs would allow, Hilda streaked past me into the garden. She began circling the scarecrow. The man gained on her, his stringy gray ponytail flapping in the wind. He snatched up a garden hoe.

"*No!*" I cried.

The man spun around.

"*Don't hit her!*" I raced over to grab Hilda.

The man threw down the hoe. "I told that old witch . . ." He waved a skinny arm toward the hedge separating his yard from Mrs. Eastley's. "I told her if her mutt came in my garden again I'd call the authorities. And by Jupiter, I will. I mean it."

"*Mean it! Mean it!*" screamed the parrot.

"Please," I begged. "Don't call the police. It wasn't Hilda's fault. When Mrs. Eastley's gone, she gets nervous—"

"And my Casper gets nervous when that mutt's around, so we're even." His bony fingers stroked the bird's bright feathers. Then he scowled at Hilda. "Now get that pest outa my yard. *Scoot.*"

I grabbed Hilda and dashed out the gate, not stopping until I sank, gasping for breath, on Mrs. Eastley's back step. Hilda whimpered. Her heart still thumped wildly.

"Don't have a heart attack, Hilda. How would I ever explain it to Mrs. Eastley?"

While soothing the trembling dog, I kept glancing at the hedge. But no red macaw lurked, ready to pounce. For a long time I stayed with Hilda. Though I now had a half dozen clients to care for, she was my first. I felt loyal to the little wiener dog.

"That was a close call," I said, stroking her velvety ears. The soft fur reminded me of the many pet hamsters I'd had in my life. "If I lost you, Hilda, my reputation as a pet-sitter would fizzle. Nobody in town would hire me. I'd *never* earn enough money to buy Ringo."

Ringo was the beautiful green-and-yellow parakeet at Mr. Willy-Bones's pet shop. I started my pet-sitting service to save enough money to buy him. Of course, I liked all kinds of pets. I wouldn't be in this business if I didn't. But I wanted a pet that could talk. Ringo wasn't like that mean red parrot, though. Ringo was a gentle bird.

The morning sun was high in the sky. "Have to go," I said, putting Hilda down. She whined to be held. "Sorry, old girl. Other clients are waiting. Also, I have to buy you a new leash."

I unhooked the stub of strap at her collar and dropped both parts of the leash in my pack. "To know what size to buy," I explained.

Too bad! A real leather leash would use up more than a week's pet-sitting profits. But Mrs. Eastley would be sure to notice if I got cheap plastic. I'd have to pay with my savings, too. All the money she'd left me was a few quarters to buy puppy biscuits. Then I had an awful thought. What if she didn't pay me back?

I jumped up. "Hilda, I need more customers. And from now on, they have to pay in advance. And I won't ask a quarter a day. I'm charging a dollar."

I gave the old dog a nudge. "Time to go in."

She waddled across the porch, her old nails scratching the wooden floor and her sagging tummy nearly scraping bottom. At her doggy door she stopped. Lifting the flap, I urged her in.

"It's okay, Hilda. You'll be safe in your very own kitchen."

I pushed two puppy biscuits in after her, then left.

Passing the Parrot Man's ivy-covered fence, I got mad all over again. It wasn't fair that *I* had to buy that leash. The parrot had trashed it. Its owner should pay. I ought to tell him so. In fact, I would—right now! Before my mind could flip-flop, I flung open the gate and charged in.

"Hello?"

No answer. I walked across the man's trashy yard. Then I spotted him, the bird on his shoulder. He stood on the roof of a shed by the back fence, waving two red flags. It looked like he was signaling somebody on the beach or in a boat. Strange! I moved closer.

*"Sir?"*

At my shout the flags clattered on the roof, and the man spun around. "What're *you* doing back here?"

I showed him the cut leash. "Your parrot did this."

"Eh?" He cupped a gnarled hand to his ear. "Speak up."

*"Your parrot did this."*

"No need to bellow." The wiry old man hopped down the rungs of a ladder. I noticed the telescope mounted on the shed's flat roof. What was this guy up to?

"Since your bird cut up Hilda's leash . . ."

The parrot's sharp talons gripped the man's shoulder.

With unblinking eyes it stared at me. I stepped back.

"I just think . . ." I went on ". . . you should . . . buy a new one."

Taking one of the pieces of leather, he rubbed it between thumb and forefinger. "Mighty thin." He tossed it back. "Musta been wore out already."

My jaw fell. Wasn't he going to do anything about it? "The strap was fine till your bird bit it. I was walking Hilda—"

"Eh?"

"*Hilda*. Mrs. Eastley's dog," I yelled. "You see, I have this pet-sitting business, and—"

"What kind of business?" The man's eyes narrowed.

"I sit pets."

I handed him one of Mom's cards. I'd drawn a line through her name and title, "Ellen Kincaid, Commercial Pilot," and over them I'd written, "M.D.K., Pet Specialist."

"What's *that* s'posed to mean—'Mighty Dumb Kid'?"

"They're my initials." I glared at him. "My name's Margaret Drusilla Kincaid."

"Humph." He gave back the card. "Got a permit? Need a permit to run a business."

When I shook my head, he waved an arm. "Scram!" he snapped. "I'm busy."

"But . . . but . . ."

"Go away—before I call the authorities."

Would he really do that, and ruin my business? As I backed off, I looked at him. Was that a wink beneath those bushy gray eyebrows? No way! Not from that grouch. He was just squinting at the bright sun. Suddenly the parrot sprang from his shoulder.

"*Away!*" it screeched, diving at me. "*Go away!*"

I ran!

# 2

# A Big Mistake

Once across the street I felt safe. I sank to the ground, gasping for breath. The parrot's screeching had stopped. Over the thudding of my heart in my ears there was only the far-off sound of waves slapping the beach. It was soothing. After a while my heart no longer felt like it would jump from my chest.

I looked at the blue Pacific. The sky was so clear, you could almost see Hawaii. For sure I could see up the coast to Malibu. . . .

Malibu! I jumped up. That's where the smugglers were. I wished I knew more about them. Maybe their hideout was in those cliffs near Malibu Beach. When I went back to the pet shop, I'd ask Mr. Willy-Bones.

Now, though, I had to get going. Darn that Parrot Man! He made me waste half my morning. I'd be lucky to finish my rounds by five—with hardly any time left to look for new clients.

Grabbing my pack, I started down Edgecliff Road. A silver Rolls-Royce glided by. It paused at the entrance to Edgecliff Estates, and then the guard waved it through.

That gave me an idea!

Why not detour through the Estates? I could look for new customers now. It wouldn't take long. And with just a few rich clients from here, my money worries would be over.

I hurried to the entrance. Putting on what I hoped was a convincing smile, I strode up to the guard. He wasn't fooled. He knew I didn't live here.

"Hold it, young lady." He eyed the mud spots on my clothes. "Visiting somebody?"

I nodded. "A friend."

"Name?"

"The name of my friend, you mean?" I tried to think. Did anyone in my sixth-grade class live here?

"Well, she's not really a friend." I was stalling for time. "She's more like an acquaintance." My mind was a blank. All I could think of were my friends from the east side of town.

A Mercedes 350SL slammed to a stop—the same car that had splashed mud on me. The guard waved him by. The driver was Floyd Barker, host of *Uncle Floyd's Kiddie Brigade* on TV—and also Denise Barker's stepdad! What luck! I'd forgotten about Denise. She'd skipped a year, so she was younger than the rest of our class. And smarter, too! But we *did* know each other. And she lived in the Estates!

I grinned at the guard. "Denise Barker," I said. "That's who I'm visiting."

With a grunt he motioned me through.

I'd never been to Denise's house. Maybe she wasn't even home. Who cared? I was here! Now to find a movie star or rich banker walking a poodle with a diamond-studded collar. But after circling three blocks, I met no one. This detour was a mistake. Then something soft rubbed my ankle. I heard a faint meow. It was a tabby—but too skinny to be an Estates "fat cat."

As I stooped to pet it, someone called, "Margaret!"

The cat skittered up a tree, and I looked around. Denise was waving at me from the yard of a huge, Spanish-style house next door. "What brings you here?" she asked.

"Looking for customers. For my pet-sitting service." I pointed to the tabby in the oak tree. "Is it yours?"

Denise shook her head. "I *yearn* for a cat. But Floyd *refuses* to permit one in the house." She wrinkled her nose. "Allergic!"

Then she smiled and fluffed her shiny black bangs. "Describe your service. Is it fun?"

"If you can call getting attacked by a parrot fun."

"You must be referring to that scarlet macaw." She nodded. "A real menace! Its wings ought to be clipped. It perches on the shoulder of an ancient bicyclist who rides past here sometimes. A very peculiar individual."

"Mean, too." I was wondering how the Parrot Man sneaked past the gatekeeper.

I reached into my pack. "Here," I said, handing Denise one of my cards. "In case you hear of someone needing a pet-sitter."

Wrinkling her nose again, Denise studied the card." 'M.D.K.'?"

"My new nickname. From when I was visiting in Texas."

She smiled. "I read the newspaper account of your exploits. A detective enterprise would seem more appropriate, considering how brilliantly you outwitted those criminal types."

I groaned. "Dictionary Denise" was at it again! "Tracked the smugglers, you mean? Pets seem a more sure way to make money," I said. "Except not lately. . . ."

"Obviously your business needs a motto." She cocked her head. "How about, 'Sit Your Pet? You Bet!'?"

I grinned. "It might help. I'll try it. Thanks."

Denise twisted a strand of hair. "What varieties of pets do you sit?"

"All kinds. Birds. Raccoons. Rabbits. Cats—"

Her black eyes lit up. "I have always *longed* for a cat."

"Not Conrad. No claws—but he bites."

"Undoubtedly lonesome," she said. "He craves attention. Do you play with him?"

"No time. I'm too busy with—"

"Let me," she broke in. "I would love to take care of Conrad for you. I *adore* felines."

Suddenly I had an idea—a way to finish today's rounds in a hurry, and find the new clients I needed besides.

"Want to be my partner for the day?" I asked.

"Hmm." She wrinkled her nose. "All right. It might be fun."

I grabbed her hand. "It's a deal."

Denise nodded solemnly. "I must tell Floyd." She slipped past the Mercedes parked in the drive and ducked into the house.

When she came out again, she carried a tennis racket. Floyd stormed behind her. His frown vanished when he saw me. He brushed thin wisps of hair over his bald spot, as if the TV cameras were about to roll, and flashed a big smile, his gleaming teeth matching his white patent-leather shoes.

That phony grin didn't fool me.

He got in his car. With a squeal of tires he blasted off.

"Where's he headed in such a hurry?" I asked.

"To our beach house." Denise rolled her eyes. "Preparations for yet *another* stupendous fishing trip." Grinning, she tossed the tennis racket into a geranium patch. "I had to tell him we were playing tennis so he would let me join you today."

"Where's your mom?" I asked as we started down the drive.

She shrugged. "At the country club. Losing, as usual."

"Losing what?"

"At bridge."

With Denise to help, I breezed through my rounds. And it was fun having someone to yak with, even if she did use lots of big words. We talked about my pet clients. In school Denise acted like she was too much of a brain to mix with the rest of us. She kept to herself. Now she wasn't stuck-up—though she still talked like an encyclopedia with legs.

But that was a good thing. Denise knew a lot about bird smugglers! She told me that they bring birds *into* the United States—not take them out. What a relief! Ringo wouldn't get whisked away after all.

Denise said that in order to sneak past the border guards, smugglers stuff baby parrots into nylon panty hose and hide them under the floorboards of cars or in spare tires. It sounded awful.

"Countless birds suffocate," she said, "before they ever get here."

I felt sick. "How could *anybody* do that to a baby bird?"

"Money," said Denise. "Those rare parrots are worth a fortune. People will pay thousands of dollars for one. Although I fail to understand why *anyone* would want a talking bird."

"I do," I said, and I told her about Ringo. "He's the reason for my pet-sitting business. I need money fast."

"Why such haste? Is he about to fly off?"

"Not fly off. Get sold. If anyone wants him, Mr. Willy-Bones will have to let Ringo go—unless I can come up with the money."

"Bones?" She squinted. "What kind of bones?"

I laughed. "He's the pet-shop owner. He's from Sweden, and his name is Wilhelm Bjornson. It's hard to say, so he lets us kids call him Willy-Bones."

"So how expensive *is* your parakeet?" Denise asked.

"Seventy-five dollars."

"Excessive!" Again she rolled her eyes. "That much, for an ordinary bird?"

"Ringo is a rare Indian ringneck. Wait'll you see. So far I've saved thirty-two dollars." I bit my lip. "I still need forty-three more."

Maybe to a rich kid like Denise it didn't sound like much. But all she said was "I prefer cats. You can play with cats."

"Only they can't talk." I laughed. "But I have to get Ringo away from the pet shop soon or he'll have a Swedish accent."

"Floyd once owned a cockatoo that said '*Buenos días.*'"

"What else did you teach it?"

"Me?" Denise looked disgusted. "Floyd would never allow *me* near his precious birds. Not that I minded. Soon he got bored with birds anyway," she went on. "So he purchased tropical fish. He tired of those and bought a boat. Now he is into deep-sea fishing in Mexico."

"Does he go often?"

"Not often enough. I wish he would go down and *stay.*"

The way she said it, I almost felt sorry for her. At least I missed my folks when they were away.

We worked so fast that by one o'clock we were down to my last two clients—Puddy Kenilworth's goldfish and Kim's tortoise. Denise had even had time to play with Conrad, the clawless cat, who didn't try once to bite her.

We went to Kim's first, where her tortoise was sunning on the back patio. He didn't look up when I shook the lettuce and apple pieces into his food pan. He didn't even peek out when Denise tapped his shell.

"Ugh!" Denise rolled her eyes once again. "I should have stayed with Conrad. . . . Let us go feed the fish."

"Let's save feeding the fish until after lunch," I said. "I'm starved. And Puddy lives on the steepest hill in Pacific Cliffs."

"Good," said Denise. "I despise hills. Only—I brought nothing to eat."

"That's okay. Have a peanut-butter sandwich. Shirlee made three."

Denise took it and nodded thanks. "Who is Shirlee?"

"A friend of my mom's from Texas. She's sitting while my folks are gone. Mom is flying charter for some politician," I explained. "And Dad went to Oklahoma on a business trip."

Denise bit into the sandwich and made a face.

"A decided and *unmistakable* taste of chili."

I nodded. "You get used to it. Chili is Shirlee's specialty. She cooks *gallons*. More than we can ever eat. And it seems to get into everything she fixes."

"What does she do with so much chili?"

"Good question. I'm not sure."

Denise took another bite. "I shall *definitely* bring tuna fish tomorrow."

It sounded like we were partners for more than just today. I was glad. She'd be a real help. She had been this morning. Now we'd have the whole afternoon to find new clients.

As we climbed the hill to Puddy's house, Denise stopped to catch her breath. "I have a brilliant suggestion. If you feed the fish by yourself tomorrow, I will walk that dachshund for you."

"That *is* brilliant! Getting over to Hilda early enough is really hard," I said. "I live so far away."

"It is no problem for me," she said. "I live very close." She pushed her bangs back from her sweaty forehead. "Anyway, to avoid this agonizing climb, I would do *anything.*"

As soon as we got to the garage where Puddy kept his fish, Denise rushed to the laundry sink. She turned the tap on full and splashed her face.

Meanwhile I tried to scoop out the fish so I could clean its bowl. "Guinevere, stop wiggling," I ordered.

"Denise, I need help! Can you take the bowl and pour out the water?"

"But the fish is still swimming in it."

"Don't worry," I said. "I'll catch her and hold her— while you refill the bowl."

Denise frowned. "Chlorinated water will kill the fish."

"Never mind," I snapped. "I have drops to put in so it won't. Now just pour, will you? But *slowly.*"

Denise slicked her wet hair back from her face with both hands, then took the bowl.

"Slower," I said. "You're pouring too fast."

"The bowl is wet . . . *difficult* to hold . . ."

"Denise! It's slipping—"

". . . *can't hold it* . . . WATCH OUT!"

The bowl shot past my open hands. It smashed onto the bottom of the sink with a crash.

*"Guinevere!"* I screamed. The water gurgled down the drain as I gingerly lifted bits of broken glass. But it was too late!

"Oh my gosh," Denise gasped. "The fish . . ." She pointed at the drain.

I felt like crying. "What will I tell Puddy?"

"A pity that that eccentric with the parrot lives

so far away," said Denise. "You could always say the macaw swooped down, grabbed the fish, and swallowed it."

I glared at her. "Very funny." I peered into the sink. "Talk about money going down the drain. Poor Guinevere. Hope she makes it to the ocean."

"Possibly Floyd will catch her when he goes down to Baja tomorrow," Denise said.

I didn't bother to answer. After we carefully picked up the pieces of broken glass and dumped them in the trash, I stormed out.

Denise hurried after me. "Where are you going now?"

"To the pet shop. To buy another fish. *And* a fishbowl. *And* a leather leash for Hilda." I didn't even want to think what this would do to my savings. "I just hope Mr. Willy-Bones lets me charge them all."

"M.D.K., I am *dreadfully* sorry." Denise ran along beside me, trying to keep up. "It was really stupid not to wipe my hands before I reached for that bowl."

I didn't answer. Maybe taking Denise on as a partner was a *big* mistake.

# 3

## The Sheriff Arrives

"Sorry." Mr. Willy-Bones shook his head. "I have no more goldfish." His accent turned "have" into "haf."

"This morning you had *lots*," I said. "Where'd they all go?"

"A teacher bought every one . . . for prizes at a school carnival." The shopkeeper poured himself a cup of coffee from a blue enamel pot, then returned the pot to the hot plate behind the counter and gave me a big smile. "I get more next week."

I looked at Denise. "The Kenilworths get back tomorrow. If I don't find a fish for Puddy, his mom will blab what happened to the whole town . . . and *ruin* my reputation."

Her eyes lit up. "Where is the carnival? Perhaps we could go and win back one of the fish. I am *terrific* at ring toss—"

"That's dumb, Denise! Besides, what if we didn't win?"

She moved to the fish tank. "You could always substitute a tropical fish."

"But Guinevere's a *goldfish*!"

"Merely explain to Puddy how you gave her such excellent care that she changed. He will never suspect."

"For a three-year-old, Puddy's pretty smart," I told her. "He'll know. So will his mom." Still, what choice did I have?

"Okay," I told Mr. Willy-Bones. "I'd like your cheapest tropical fish—and one bowl."

With a small net he scooped out a shimmering red fish with brilliant purple markings.

Denise nodded. "Definitely more attractive then Guinevere."

"Also smaller," I said. "Puddy'll know it's not his."

"Simply tell him she molted—and shrank," Denise said. Then she went to the bulletin board.

When Mr. Willy-Bones gave me the bill along with the fish in its bowl of water, I gasped. "Twelve dollars? For one fish?"

"The others cost even more," he said.

I was hoping Denise might offer to pay. She didn't.

"Can I charge it—till tomorrow?" I asked Mr. Willy-Bones. "Now that I have a partner, I expect to get lots of new clients this afternoon. And I'm asking them to pay in advance."

"So you have the money tomorrow?" The old Swede's

eyes narrowed over the tops of his wire spectacles. "For sure?"

I nodded.

"Yah, well." His blue eyes sparkled. "All right."

"Thanks!" Clutching the fishbowl, I hurried to the back of the shop. "Denise—want to see Ringo before we go?"

I pressed my face against the bars of his cage. The green parakeet fluttered to me. His red hooked beak almost touched my nose. "Hi, Ringo," I said.

"Hi!" he piped. "Hi!"

"Sorry. No time for a lesson today," I told him. "But are you practicing how to say 'good-bye'?"

"Good! Hi!" he said.

"No. Not 'hi.' 'Bye'!"

"Not! Hi! Bye!" Ringo repeated, blinking his black eyes.

"Forget it," I said. "See you tomorrow."

As I turned from the cage, Mr. Willy-Bones came toward me.

"Margaret," he said. "I have bad news."

It was hard to keep my lips from quivering. "About Ringo?"

"Yah. A man from the bird zoo at Thousand Oaks wants him. I must let him know by Saturday."

I stared at Mr. Willy-Bones. "That's only . . . five days. I'll never have the money by then."

"You know our arrangement." His voice was gentle. "Such a rare bird I cannot keep forever. Every day he

loses me money. He takes up space . . . food . . . my time. . . ." He paused. "Your mama and papa maybe could help?"

"They're not even here. Dad's in Oklahoma. And who knows where Mom is by now? The Oregon border maybe."

With pudgy fingers the shopowner stroked his white goatee. "Maybe that nice Texas lady who's visiting you?"

"Shirlee Alabama . . . the sitter?" I snorted. "She's too tightfisted to lend me five cents."

Denise edged past us to look at Ringo. "You are right, M.D.K. He is *definitely* handsomer than Floyd's cockatoos."

The shop owner's eyebrows shot up. "You have cockatoos?"

"Not me. My stepdad," Denise said. "But he sold them."

"Ah. I would like to meet your stepfather some day."

They discussed Floyd and his cockatoos; I blinked back my tears. Five days! How could I ever earn enough to pay for Ringo in that short time?

"Yah," Mr. Willy-Bones was telling Denise. "Cockatoos are beautiful birds. Worth a lot of money."

She shrugged. "Floyd never said anything about that."

Watching her, I tried to imagine how it would feel to be so rich, you didn't care what things cost. Denise was lucky. Suddenly she grabbed my arm, nearly knocking the fishbowl to the floor.

"Speaking of money, M.D.K.—come and see this!"

She pushed me toward the bulletin board and pointed to the notice. " 'Five-hundred-dollar reward!' " she said. " 'For information leading to the arrest of the smugglers.' What do you think?"

# BIRD SMUGGLERS $500 REWARD!

"I know. They're the ones I told you about. But we'd never find them." I frowned. "Denise, we don't stand a chance."

"We *do*," she insisted. "Look. It says, 'Operating in Southern California, possibly Malibu.' Practically in our very *midst*!"

Mr. Willy-Bones hurried over. "No, girls. That is not for you. To pursue those smugglers is a dangerous business."

"But *somebody* has to catch them," Denise said.

"Not you two." Mr. Willy-Bones shook his head. "You children should not get mixed up with those bad guys—"

"But they are so mean to those parrots," interrupted

Denise. "They drug them to keep them quiet. They tape their beaks shut—"

"Yah, yah." Mr. Willy-Bones nodded and gave Denise a funny look. "How do you know so much about this?"

"Floyd subscribed to *stacks* of wildlife magazines when he was raising cockatoos," she said. "They contained dozens of articles about bird smuggling."

"I could use the reward," I said, still studying the notice. "But where would we start looking?"

"I won't have it!" Mr. Willy-Bones stomped his foot. "You must *not*—" A ringing telephone stopped his lecture. Still shaking his head, he went to answer.

"It is imperative, first of all," Denise said, "that we devise a strategy to trap these criminal types."

"Like what?" I asked. "Setting up a roadblock? How can the two of us do that, Denise? It's crazy."

As Mr. Willy-Bones talked on the phone, he was still watching us and shaking his head.

"Not all smuggling is done with cars," Denise said. "We could stake out Santa Monica Airport, just south of here. Isn't that where your mother keeps her plane?"

"Sure—except Mom's not here. Besides, if these guys are breaking the law, they're not going to land at a public airport." Denise might be a brain, but she didn't know everything. "They'll land out in the desert or in an empty field someplace."

"True," she agreed. "Perhaps a wiser strategy is to check out various pet shops—and nab them as they try to sell the birds."

"It'd take forever," I said. "Let's stick with pet-sitting. Now let's get this fish up the hill before it dies on us."

This time Denise kept up with me climbing Puddy's hill. The reason was that I had to go slow to keep from spilling the water out of the fishbowl. Halfway up the hill she smiled and reached out for the bowl. "Want me to carry that for a while?"

"Thanks, but no thanks." I held tight to it. Another round of buying fish and glass bowls and I'd be broke.

By about four thirty we had delivered Puddy's fish and were heading back down the hill. Again Denise tried to persuade me to hunt the smugglers.

"It would be such a challenge," she said. "And with your *vast* experience outwitting those smugglers in Texas—"

"I also got kidnapped, don't forget," I reminded her.

"It would be much more exciting than changing kitty litter."

"Tending Conrad the Clawless Cat isn't my job now, anyway," I said. "It's yours."

Then Denise said something really strange.

"It *is* peculiar," she said, "how reluctant the shop owner was to discuss the smuggling operation. *And* the way he discouraged us from becoming involved."

"Mr. Willy-Bones just doesn't want us to get hurt," I said.

"Perhaps."

"Denise, you're not accusing *him* of smuggling?"

"Not exactly. But we should remain alert to all possibilities. The smuggler could be *anybody*—one of your customers, even." She ran a hand through her thick dark hair. "Did any of them go to Australia? Or South America? Those countries are the source of most smuggled exotic birds."

I began to laugh. "Mrs. Eastley's in Iowa, visiting her sister," I said. "Kim's at camp. The Kenilworths's—"

Denise acted hurt. "I merely suggested we keep our eyes and ears open."

"Tell you what," I said. "If you promise to help me find more pet clients—I promise to *think* about hunting the smugglers. But *after* I get Ringo paid for."

Denise cocked her head like she was deciding. Then she smiled. "Agreed," she said.

So we stopped at every house we passed with a dog or cat in the yard. I gave out business cards with my new motto to the owners. People were friendly. But no one needed our services.

We had no better luck at the park. All we found were kids playing soccer. We stopped to sit on the library steps. But here all we saw were kids with books.

"A smuggler hunt would produce more results," said Denise.

"Produce! I almost forgot." I jumped up. "Mr. Parducci, the produce man at the market, is saving carrot tops for me, for the rabbit. I have to pick them up." I started toward downtown. "What time is it?"

Denise glanced at her orange Swatch watch. "Almost six."

"Forget the market." I spun around and headed the other direction. "I'm going home. I promised to be back at six."

As I hurried toward my house, Denise ran after me. "But there are *hours* of daylight remaining. . . ."

"You don't know Shirlee Alabama. That woman's a . . ." I searched for a Denise-type word. "A menace! If I'm home late, she'll have the police out searching."

"You must be kidding. Nobody would call the police."

"*She* would. Her name may be Shirlee, but she's a Nervous Nellie."

"Wait, M.D.K. ! Tomorrow . . . when I walk Hilda . . . what about her leash?"

Drat! I had forgotten all about buying a new leash when I was at the pet shop. Denise would need one. "Use rope."

"But I have . . . no rope." Denise tried to keep up as I hurried ahead. "And what about her food?"

I stopped to wait. "Maybe you'd better come home with me," I said. "We have clothesline rope. And I can give you puppy biscuits and write out the instructions—"

"Is it *that* complicated?" she said. "Maybe I should not—"

"Oh, no," I said quickly. I didn't want her to back out now. "It's just to— to make sure you know what to do. Why not stay for dinner? I can explain then. That is, if you don't mind chili. That's about all Shirlee ever cooks."

Denise grinned as she started walking again. "I dislike it only with peanut butter."

"You can call your mom from my house," I said.

"Mother seldom worries . . . about my whereabouts." Denise stopped to catch her breath. "Anyway . . . she will be at the club . . . until late . . . and Floyd will be . . . at the beach house."

As I waited, I wondered what it would be like to have parents who didn't care what you did. Might be fun. And I could certainly use a sitter who didn't worry so much "about my whereabouts."

Then I heard the clock in the schoolhouse tower, far below. It chimed six. I broke into a run. "Hurry!"

"I can scarcely *walk*," she gasped, "let alone *run*."

So we covered the last three blocks at a slow crawl. When we got to my block, I saw a black-and-white police car back out of our driveway. No, not the police. It was the county sheriff!

"Your sitter did it," said Denise, fixing her eyes on the black-and-white. "She really *did* call the police."

Then she gripped my shoulder. "You are in for it now, M.D.K.!"

# 4

# A Secret and a Clue

In the doorway Shirlee Alabama crisscrossed her arms. I stared. Who was she signaling? I glanced around. Already the black-and-white car was halfway to the corner. If her signal was for the sheriff—too bad. But no, the skinny arms still flapped.

"She must be waving at *me*," I told Denise. "And she's *smiling*!"

"Hurry—we're just fixin' to sit down," Shirlee called. "There's company for supper."

Then I saw Wil Bradley behind her. I grabbed Denise's arm and started to run. "Come on—it's Wil, my friend from Texas!" When we rushed in, Will gave me that slow, friendly grin of his.

"Howdy, M.D.K.," he drawled.

"Wil! What are you doing in California?"

He hadn't changed. Still a skinny thirteen-year-old with those same knobby knees. And he was wearing California-style surfer shorts! He ducked his head. "My dad had this meeting—"

"Law officers' convention," bellowed Sheriff Bradley from the E-Z lounger. "In Anaheim," he added importantly.

Wil nodded. "I'd never seen the Pacific Ocean—so Dad brought me along."

The sheriff eased himself out of the chair and stood, thumbs hooked in his belt. "All it cost was young Wil's ticket . . . since we're staying with my cousin Pete."

Wil nodded. "Pete's in law enforcement too."

The sheriff broke in. "Well, tarnation, Pete lives in Santa Monica—so close I could almost *smell* Miz Alabama's chili. So I decided to call up and wangle a supper invite."

Shirlee beamed. "I told 'em to come right on over."

That explained the black-and-white squad car.

"I'll tell you one thing, young lady." Sheriff Bradley winked at me. "Riverbank, Texas, hasn't been the same since Shirlee Alabama left. We miss that good Tex-Mex of hers."

"Wilson Bradley, the *way* you *talk*." Shirlee patted her flaming-red topknot, then nudged him and Wil toward the dining table. It was set with Mom's linen tablecloth and china, plus her best silverware, which we bring out only for holidays and birthdays. If Mom knew, she would have kittens!

"You-all set yourselves down," Shirlee said. "And do your talkin' while you eat." Clamping her thin lips into a smile, she turned to me. "Sweetie, if your friend's stayin', find her a chair—" Suddenly the sitter's sharp nose quivered. "*My lordy*, the biscuits." With a shriek she flew to the kitchen.

Wil grinned at me from across the table. "What're you doing these day, M.D.K.? Solving more mysteries?"

Denise looked at me and began bobbing her chin up and down.

I ignored her. "Mostly earning money to buy a parakeet."

Wil smiled. "No more prairie dogs?" Then his face clouded. "Sorry to hear about ol' Gertrude passing on."

"Geraldine the Third *was* old for a hamster," I said. "But now she's up in hamster heaven, with Geraldines One and Two. For a change I'm getting a bird. One that talks!"

"An Indian ringneck parakeet," added Denise. I remembered that I hadn't introduced her to everyone, so I did.

"Do you live around here, honey?" Shirlee asked, breezing in. Without waiting for Denise's reply, she plopped a basket of steaming biscuits on the table, saying, "Help yourself. Plenty more where these came from." Then she shoved the Crockpot in front of the sheriff. "There's more chili, too, so dig in."

For the rest of the meal Shirlee, the sheriff, and

sometimes Wil gabbed about Texas with accents as thick as the sorghum they slathered on their biscuits. My only chance to talk with Wil was when Shirlee left to load up the biscuit basket and refill the Crockpot. Denise was too busy gulping water between bites of the fiery chili to talk at all.

"Don't worry," I whispered to her. "When Mom and I went to Riverbank and I tasted Shirlee's Tex-Mex for the first time, it took three quarts of iced tea to get through the meal!"

Dessert was pecan pie. After finishing off a second slice, Sheriff Bradley pushed away from the table, burped, and patted his belly. "You're one mighty fine cook, Miz Alabama."

Then he winked at me. "How soon you gonna let this lady come back to Riverbank to open up her café again?"

"In a couple of weeks," I said. "When my folks get home."

Shirlee dabbed her lips with her linen napkin. "I may not go back to Texas," she said. "I may stay here."

The sheriff stared at her, the only time I'd seen him speechless.

Wil wasn't shy about speaking up. "If I lived this close to the ocean," he said. "I'd stay too—take up surfing!"

I looked at Denise and giggled. I could just see Shirlee Alabama on a surfboard.

Then Shirlee pursed her lips like she had a great

secret. "Oh, it's not the ocean." But that was all she would say.

I jumped up from the table. "I want to show my bird cage to Denise and Wil."

When Wil stood, the sheriff rested a beefy hand on his shoulder. "Look fast, son. Pete's pickin' us up at nine."

"That reminds me," I told Denise. "Don't you want to call your folks? The phone's in the kitchen."

Denise scooted her chair back. "What time should I tell them to pick me up?"

"Nine's fine," I told her. After she left, I said to Wil, "Did you ever watch *Uncle Floyd's Kiddie Brigade* on TV?"

"Sometimes."

"Floyd's her stepdad."

"No kidding?" Wil scrunched his nose. "It's kind of a dumb show, though."

Shirlee stopped scraping plates to listen. "I've seen that program. It was kinda clever, I thought." She gave a twittery laugh. "That Floyd is *so* funny. And to think that sweet little girl's his daughter!"

When Denise came back, we started for my room. But Shirlee blocked the way. Now she made up for not paying attention to Denise earlier. "Why, honey," she cooed, "I had no *idea* that darling Uncle Floyd on the TV was your daddy—"

"Stepdad," Denise said.

Shirlee pursed her thin lips. "It's my very favorite show."

Denise shrugged. "They are all reruns. It has been *years* since Floyd did a new show."

"Don't matter. He's still funny." Shirlee's eyes were about to pop out of her head. "Will your daddy be pickin' you up?"

"My mother, probably. Floyd had to prepare for his fishing trip tomorrow."

Sheriff Bradley's voice boomed from the living room. "You say your stepdaddy's goin' fishin' tomorrow? So are me and Pete. We're goin' over to Catalina."

"Floyd is going to Baja California," Denise said. "It is a part of Mexico."

"What's he usually catch?" the sheriff asked.

"Usually nothing," she said.

Denise trailed Wil and me down the hall. "M.D.K., how could you call your sitter a 'menace'?" she asked. "I think she is *quaint*. And that pecan pie was *fabulous!*"

"First time she's made anything besides baked apples for dessert," I said. "She's just on her good behavior because of her Texas friends."

I kicked aside some old jeans and one slipper in the doorway to my room and led Wil and Denise in.

Wil frowned. "Wonder why ol' Shirlee decided not to go back home?"

Denise giggled. "She may have acquired a California boyfriend."

"*Her?*" I said. "She must be past seventy."

"Perhaps the boyfriend is too."

"If she stays, it won't be in *my* house," I said. "The

minute Mom and Dad get back, she goes."

As Wil started to sink into my beanbag chair, I pulled at his arm. "First take a look at Ringo's cage." Then I explained, "That's my parakeet's name."

Wil ambled to the ornate metal cage that covered half of my dresser top. "It's fancy all right. Old Jingo'll love it. Where'd you get it?"

"At Goodwill. After I give it a good scrubbing, it'll look even better."

Denise wrinkled her nose. "A new paint job will definitely improve it."

"Oh, *no!*" I said. "You *never* paint bird cages. The paint might be poisonous. If your bird pecked at it, he could die."

Denise stuck her nose in the air. She seemed hurt that I knew something she didn't. "Anyway," she said, "I don't believe in caging birds. *I* think wild creatures should remain in the forest, where they belong."

"Is your parakeet wild, M.D.K. ?" Wil asked.

"Maybe his ancestors in India were—but Ringo's tame." I looked at Denise. "And he doesn't mind being in a cage at the pet shop."

"How can you be *sure?*" Denise demanded.

It was hard to answer her—because I *wasn't* sure. "At least nobody smuggled him into this country in some woman's nylon stocking," I said. "Like they do with baby parrots."

"Nevertheless, I suspect his captors—"

"Ringo didn't *have* a captor," I told her. "Mr. Willy-

Bones told me that practically all Indian ringneck parakeets are raised in this country now—including Ringo."

Denise sniffed and went to the windowsill where I keep my shell collection.

"So what's ol' Ringtail look like?" Wil asked me.

"Not 'Ringtail.' *Ringo!*" I pretended to be angry, but I knew Wil was only teasing. "And he's not mine till he's paid for. Want to see the picture I drew?" I reached into the cage for my sketch of Ringo. "Don't mind the smudges," I said. "But he looks like this. Only prettier. The feathers make a ring around his neck."

Wil whistled through his teeth as he studied what I'd drawn. "You're still a good artist, M.D.K.!" He smiled. "Remember that picture of old Gladys you sent me? I've still got it!"

"Who is Gladys?" Denise asked, coming over to look.

"He means Geraldine the Third. He has this problem with names."

I made a face at Wil. He just stood there, grinning.

Denise gave me a kind of half smile like she wanted to be friends again. She nodded toward the sketch. "That *is* good, M.D.K. Instead of sitting pets, you should do pet portraits. You would have Ringo paid for in no time."

"What's this Marvelous Mingo cost?" Wil asked.

"Seventy-five dollars," I said.

He whistled. "This must be one *rare* bird."

"Come back tomorrow and you can meet him," I said.

"Only promise you won't teach him a Texas drawl."

Wil shook his head. "Tomorrow my cousins are showing me around L.A." Then he grinned. "Want to come along?"

"Can't. We have pets to care for." I started to list them.

"But no more fish, remember?" Denise said as she

went back to examining my shells. "The Kenilworths return tomorrow."

I nodded. Both Denise and I began talking at once as we told Wil about our troubles with Puddy's goldfish. Then I told Wil how the Parrot Man's pet macaw had attacked Hilda.

He laughed. "Sounds like this pet-sitting is a mighty dangerous business."

"At least now I have a partner," I said. "That will help."

Denise shuddered. "Now *I* must cope with the Parrot Man."

I looked from Denise to Wil. Suddenly I got this great idea. If one partner was good, two might be even better. "Want to come with us, Wil? With you along, we'd finish even sooner. And you could help us find new customers."

He rubbed his chin. "I was hopin' to see the sights of the big city tomorrow. My cousins made all these plans."

"Be realistic, M.D.K." Denise waved a sand dollar. "Even with three of us, we *still* might not find any new clients. If it is like today, we may not find any."

I hated to admit it, but she was right. I put Ringo's sketch back in the cage. Was a picture of him all I'd ever have?

Denise cocked her head. "What *I* think your friend should do is assist us in finding the parrot smugglers. After all, you two did manage to track down those criminal types in Texas—"

"Did you say parrot smugglers?" Wil's brown eyes lit up.

Denise nodded. "And there is a five-hundred-dollar reward for finding them."

"All *right!*" Wil's whole face was one big, toothy grin. "After we find 'em, M.D.K., you take part of the reward and buy your talking Bingo. On what's left we'll all go to Disneyland!"

"What do you mean, '*after* we find them'? Who says we will?"

"I'll bet we can do it!" he said.

"Of course we can." Denise looked over at me. "With three of us working on the problem, we are bound to succeed."

I stared into the empty cage. I remembered what Mr. Willy-Bones had told me: only five days to come up with the money for Ringo. I sighed. It looked like the reward was my only chance.

"All right," I said.

"*Stupendous!*" Denise shouted, waving her arms. Then her elbow knocked against the box of seashells. Down it fell.

"Oh, M.D.K. I'm *dreadfully* sorry."

I fell to my knees to examine the damage. "At least my favorite star shell survived," I said. I felt bad about the broken sand dollars. But it was my own fault. I should never have let Denise get near those shells. I should have aimed her toward my stuffed-animal collection. It would have been safer.

Wil stood by the bird cage. He looked like his dad as he hooked his thumbs over the waistband of his surfer shorts. "If y'all want to get that reward," he drawled. "We'd better get started."

Denise sat sedately on the edge of my bed, hands in her lap. I perched beside her. "It's okay about the shells," I whispered. "I had too many anyway."

"So what clues do you have so far?" Wil asked.

I shook my head. "None."

"Yes, we do." Denise turned to look at me. "For one thing, we know they are operating in this area. And also the pet-shop owner is *definitely* a suspect."

I snorted. "Not Mr. Willy-Bones."

"He did attempt to prevent us from getting involved."

I jumped up. "Denise! He was only afraid we'd get hurt."

"He may have *said* that. But how do we—"

"Hold on!" interrupted Wil. "When my dad's on a case, I do believe he puts *everybody* on his suspect list— to start with, anyway. And every clue. We should too." Wil looked at me. "Got that famous notebook of yours, Detective Kincaid?"

I went to my desk to grab a colored pencil and my sketchbook. "So what do I write?"

"Under suspects: Mr. Wilhelm Bjornson," said Denise.

I glared at her.

"Won't hurt to put it down just for now," said Wil.

So I wrote "Willy-Bones"—but lightly, so it would be easy to erase. I knew *he* wasn't involved with those bad guys.

"Now," said Wil. "What about this dude with the nasty-tempered parrot?"

"He *could* be a suspect," I said, and I wrote "Parrot Man" in my notebook.

Wil walked back and forth. It was fun being a detective with him again. And Denise was going to make a terrific partner too. But even with three of us on the case, would we ever solve it?

Wil still paced, thumbs hooked on his waistband. "Any idea how the smugglers are getting here?" he asked.

"If they come from Mexico," Denise said, "it could be by car or bus or truck."

I wrote as she talked.

"Or airplane," I said, writing that down too. "Or boat."

Then I stopped scribbling. I slapped my sketchbook closed. "This is impossible. How can we cover every airport and boat landing and road and bus station around here?"

"Perhaps a better scheme is to capture the criminals when they unload their contraband."

"Talk normal, Denise!" I said.

"What I *mean*," she said, "is when they sell the baby birds through newspaper ads or to pet dealers."

Wil nodded. "It'd be a cinch to stake out pet shops. Then when the guys deliver the birds, we nab them."

"Not that easy," I said, "Lots of places sell pets. Besides Mr. Willy-Bones, there's a store in Malibu. And dozens in Santa Monica. We can't cover them all. I *do* still have my own pet clients to feed, you know."

Suddenly I remembered the greens for the rabbit. I turned to Denise. "I *knew* we should have picked up those carrot tops this afternoon. By tomorrow Mr. Parducci will have thrown them out."

"We could go to the market now," Denise said. "My mother will not come until nine."

"So let's go!" I grabbed my pack. "C'mon, Wil."

We dashed for the front door. But Shirlee stood before it, blocking our way.

"It's after eight," she told me. "Can't let you go out so late. Your mama wouldn't approve."

"Just to the market," I protested. "It's not even dark yet. And with three of us we'll be safe."

From the E-Z lounger the sheriff said, "Miz Alabama, you worry too much. Let 'em go. But remember, son," he warned Wil, "you be back here by nine."

Shirlee reluctantly moved away from the door. We ran out and raced down the hill. When we burst into the storage room at the back of the market, Mr. Parducci was talking on the phone. He pointed toward a couple of grocery bags overflowing with greens that rested against a stack of wooden crates.

I nodded thanks. Wil helped me stuff the bags into my pack while Denise wandered among the boxes of fruits and vegetables. When we were on the street again, she grabbed my arm.

"Did you notice what was on those wooden tomato crates?"

"I didn't see anything," I said.

"Me neither," said Wil.

Denise looked all around. "I have reason to believe," she whispered, "that we have located our smuggler."

# 5

# A Mysterious Phone Call

Climbing up the hill took three times as long as it had racing down it. Wil, with his long strides, had no trouble, but Denise kept straggling behind. Every two blocks we stopped to wait. Each time she caught up, she again tried to convince Wil and me that old Mr. Parducci was the smuggler.

"But those crates from Mexico . . . It's *obvious*," she insisted. "What better way to smuggle baby parrots?"

"Or ship tomatoes." I glared at Denise, wishing she'd skip the detective nonsense and hurry up the hill.

"That Puccini guy looked harmless to me," said Wil.

"*Furtive*," Denise said. "That is how he appeared to me. Did you *notice* how he covered the receiver when we came in? Undoubtedly phoning his cohorts."

"But you have no proof," I said. For a smart kid Denise sometimes was really dense. Not until we reached

49

home could Wil and I persuade her that Mr. Parducci wasn't a parrot pirate.

The grandfather's clock that my dad built struck nine as we burst through the front doorway. Shirlee stood waiting.

"I was about to send for the po-lice," she said, "I was so worried." Behind her the sheriff chuckled.

A car horn sounded, and Denise bounded back out, saying, "That will be for me."

I followed her to the white Mercedes that had pulled into the drive. Shirlee trotted after me, but returned to the porch when she discovered it was Denise's mother and not Floyd at the wheel.

"Hurry up, Denny," Mrs. Barker called.

As Denise jumped into the front seat, I said, "The dog food's in a metal can by Mrs. Eastley's back door." Then I shrieked, "Wait! You forgot Hilda's leash."

I raced to Dad's workshop for a hank of clothesline rope.

"This'll have to do!" I told Denise, thrusting the rope at her through the open car window. "See you in the morning."

When I hurried back to the house, Wil and his dad were on the front porch. "But, Dad," Wil was saying. "I'd rather help M.D.K. feed her pets tomorrow."

"Suit yourself, son," the sheriff replied. "It's your vacation. But how are you gettin' up here from Santa Monica?"

I broke in. "There's a bus every half hour." I smiled at Wil, hoping he had not told his dad too much about our plans. The sheriff might not mind, but Shirlee would. If she knew I was on the trail of smugglers, she'd have a conniption fit.

A black-and-white squad car pulled to the curb. As Wil slid into the squad car with his dad, I told him, "Take bus number fifty-six. . . . It goes along Sunset Boulevard. Get off at Ocean Street. I'll meet you there at ten."

After Shirlee and I went back into the house, she settled in front of the television. But I went into my room and closed my door. So much had happened today, good and bad, that I needed to sort it out. The bad news was the man from the bird zoo wanting to buy Ringo on Saturday. Today was Tuesday. That didn't give me much time to earn enough to buy the parakeet myself.

I took off my mud-spattered T-shirt and shorts and slipped into my nightie. Then I brought Sinclair, my dinosaur bank, from his hiding place on my closet shelf. Settling in my beanbag chair, I began to add up my savings. I counted the coins and the bills three times, but the answer always came out the same: $32.28. And out of that had to come twelve dollars to pay Mr. Willy-Bones for the fish and bowl, and maybe another five for Hilda's leash.

I'd be lucky to end up with fifteen dollars. Denise was right. My only hope was to go for the reward.

Wil's arrival was definitely good news. With his help maybe we *could* find the smugglers.

But Denise was another story. It was unfair to call her bad news, but losing Puddy's fish down the drain

wasn't what you'd call helpful. Neither was spilling my shell collection. Still, she did have some good ideas. And anyway, sand dollars are like four-leaf clovers. The fun part is finding them.

I yawned and pushed myself out of the beanbag chair. After putting Sinclair away, I switched off my light and climbed into bed. I lay in the dark, outlining plans to catch smugglers, but the more I planned, the dumber the idea seemed. How could we find the smugglers in three days? We didn't even know where to start looking. And if the best suspect we could come up with was Mr. Parducci, we ought to give up. I should forget about Ringo and settle for another hamster.

I squeezed my eyes shut, and to make myself fall asleep counted hamsters jumping over a Lincoln Log fence. It didn't work. Finally I got up. A piece of Shirlee's pecan pie and a glass of milk might make me sleepy.

As I padded along the hall, I heard the television blaring in the dark living room. Had Shirlee forgotten to switch it off when she'd gone to bed?

Under the kitchen door a light shone. When I put my hand on the door to push it open, I heard Shirlee's voice. She was talking on the phone—but not with her usual loud cackle. Her voice was soft. Was she worried I might hear?

Instead of barging in, I hesitated. Her quiet tone made me curious.

". . . I'll be ready . . . Friday at twelve . . . and don't you forget the extry containers!"

Containers? For what?

Abruptly Shirlee said, "All righty, Jerome. Talk to you tomorrow." I spun around and raced to my room before she caught me eavesdropping.

But who was Jerome? And what was happening Friday at twelve?

# 6

# A Startling Discovery

The next morning I was waiting at the corner of Sunset and Ocean as the clock in the school tower bonged for the tenth time. The bus from Santa Monica eased to the curb. The door hissed open. First I saw Wil's knobby knees beneath oversized cutoffs, then the rest of his skinny frame as he leaped onto the sidewalk.

That big grin spread across his freckled face. "Find the smugglers yet, M.D.K. ?"

"Hardly. I've been feeding pets since seven. And I'm still not done."

"Guess it helped for your friend to walk that little dachsie."

I nodded. "And now she takes care of Conrad the cat, too. She 'a-dooooores' cats."

Wil scratched his head. "*And* high-powered words.

Doesn't she know any with one syllable?''

"A few."

Wil smiled. "So when do I get to see ol' Gringo?"

"When we get to the pet shop. And his name's Ringo."

As we walked, Wil held out the paper bag he carried. "Want a doughnut?"

"Thanks." I reached into the bag. "All I had for breakfast was a gulp of milk and an orange."

"Doesn't ol' Shirlee insist you eat your morning oatmeal?"

"Shirlee wasn't even there when I got up," I said.

"Where'd she go?"

"No idea. It's too early for the market or the Senior Center. They're the only places she ever goes."

Wil snickered. "Maybe she really does have a secret admirer."

"She's got a secret *something*," I said, and I told Wil about the mysterious phone call. "She talked about 'containers.' And what kind of a meeting do you think it would be on Friday with this Jerome, whoever *he* is?"

Wil shrugged. "No idea." He offered me the last doughnut, but I shook my head.

"That phone call can't mean much," he went on. "Shirlee's a good ol' bat."

"It might have to do with her staying here," I said. "Instead of going back to Texas."

"Could be." Wil stuffed the doughnut into his mouth and crumpled the bag.

"In the next block there's a trash can," I said. "In front of Delia's Beauty Parlor."

The pet shop was a half block beyond Delia's. As we approached, Denise ran toward us, waving her arms.

"Catastrophe!" she screamed. *"Catastrophe!"*

"What's wrong?" I yelled as we raced to meet her.

"It is too dreadful," she gasped. "Hilda is missing!"

"Wasn't she there this morning?" I asked.

Denise nodded, tears streaming down her cheeks. "It happened after I fed her. . . . I tied the rope to her collar . . . we started walking . . ."

"So how'd she get away?"

"I forgot to replace the lid on the food can," said Denise. "After tying Hilda to a bush, I went back to cover it. . . . When I returned . . . she had disappeared! Oh, M.D.K., I am *devastated*. How can you ever forgive—"

"Forget the flowery apologies," I snapped. "We've got to find that dog."

We raced west along Ocean Street to Edgecliff Road, where Mrs. Eastley lived. When we reached her yard, I turned to Denise.

"Where, exactly, did you last see Hilda?"

Denise pointed. "Next to that oleander bush."

"She must have gone into the Parrot Man's yard," I said.

"But I called through the hedge," said Denise. "There was no answer. So I investigated in the tall weeds around Mrs. Eastley's house. I searched for an *hour*."

Wil strode toward the open field in back of the house. "How far away is the beach?"

"Just past the cliff edge—and two hundred feet straight down," I said.

"Is there a path to the beach?" asked Wil.

I nodded. "A *steep* one."

"How absolutely *dreadful!*" Denise wailed. "If she ran down to the Coast Highway, with all that traffic she would *never* survive."

I glared at her. That's all I needed to make my day: one dead dog.

"We oughta check out that neighbor with the parrot," Wil said.

"But I called through the hedge," protested Denise.

"I agree with Wil," I said. "If the parrot cornered poor Hilda again, she might be too scared to bark."

Wil started back toward the street. "So let's go rescue her."

I admired Wil. He had courage. I knew that from when we tangled with those Texas smugglers. And now he sounded braver than I felt. Still, if Hilda was in that yard, I had to save her. I had no choice. Following Wil to the Parrot Man's front gate, I kept repeating, "I'm not scared, I'm not scared."

Wil pushed open the gate, and the three of us stepped inside. As on the day before, all was quiet. I scanned the garden and small shed at the back. Was the Parrot Man hiding, waiting to spring on us? I eyed his cottage. It looked empty, but could we be sure?

"There she *is*!" screamed Denise.

Hilda crept out from under a pile of boards. Wil pounced on the trembling dog. He held her while I slipped the rope under her collar and tied it with a strong knot. Then I nuzzled the little sausage dog.

"Hilda! Why do you keep coming over here?" I stood and gave the rope a tug.

"Come on," I called to Denise. "Let's take Hilda home."

"Wait." Denise was rummaging through a pile of wood scraps. "There might be valuable evidence. After all, the Parrot Man is on our suspect list."

"Even more reason to not get caught," I said. "That

old man could be inside his house, you know."

Suddenly Wil whistled. "Cowboys' bumpers! Get a load of the snakeskin tacked on that old shack—"

He charged toward the shed by the Parrot Man's back fence. Denise threw down the wood scraps and joined him.

"Incredible," she said. "A *diamondback rattler.*"

"Come back!" I shouted, but by now Wil was bounding up the ladder to the roof of the shed. He gave a loud whoop.

"Hey, M.D.K.!" he called. "Here's a telescope."

"Forget it!" I yelled. "Let's go before the Parrot Man catches us."

Ignoring my warning, Wil bent to peer through the eyepiece. "I can see the beach." He swiveled the telescope. "And there's the lifeguard tower."

Denise scrambled up the ladder. Wil backed away to let her look. *"Spectacular!"* she squealed. "You can see our beach house in Malibu."

"You've got a beach house up there? Let me have a look." Wil tried to elbow her aside.

"Wait. I want to see if Floyd's boat is still anchored offshore," she said. "No, it appears he has already gone." She stepped back to give Wil a turn.

"You guys, we're *trespassing*!" I shoved my hands into my jeans pockets and glared at them. "If that man catches us, my whole business is ruined. Nobody'll hire me."

But Wil and Denise weren't even listening. They laughed and chattered as they took turns at the telescope, as if they didn't care about my pet-sitting business at all.

I felt like crying. Instead, I gave Hilda's rope a yank and spun on my heel. "So stay there! But I'm going to finish my rounds."

Then Wil called out. "M.D.K., come back. You're safe."

"What are you talking about?"

"I just saw a wiry little shrimp with a red macaw on his shoulder. Denise says he's the Parrot Man."

"Really?" This I had to see for myself. I rushed back to the shed. Trying to avoid even a glance at the snakeskin, I looped Hilda's rope around the door handle and started up the ladder.

Wil called again. "And M.D.K.—guess who he's talking to? Shirlee Alabama!"

# 7

# The Letter from Brazil

"Is it really Shirlee talking with the Parrot Man?"

Wil nodded. "Cowboy's honor."

Hurrying to look through the telescope, I nearly tripped on those red signal flags I'd seen the Parrot Man using. But there was no time to tell Wil about that now. Squinting into the eyepiece, I saw people milling along Malibu Pier—but no one I recognized.

"Where's Shirlee?" I demanded. "I don't see her . . . or him, either."

"They're there," Wil insisted, and whistling through his teeth, took my place. He swiveled the telescope and abruptly stopped whistling.

"Cowboys' bumpers! They're gone!"

I frowned. "You're sure you two didn't make the whole thing up?"

"We did not. *Honestly!*" Denise said. "They must have gone into Sam's Oyster Bar."

"Why would Shirlee do that? She hates oysters," I said. "Besides, she doesn't even know the Parrot Man."

Wil grinned. "I've a hunch he's that secret admirer."

"You and your hunches. Where would she have met him?" I asked, walking back to the ladder. "All she does is look at TV and go to the Senior Center." I started to climb down. "I think we should get away from here while we can."

"But the ol' guy's up in Malibu. I *saw* him," Wil insisted. He wouldn't leave the telescope. He moved it slowly from side to side, trying to locate the Parrot Man and Shirlee.

I was loosening Hilda's rope from the door handle when Denise called down from the roof. "Wait, M.D.K.—I am coming with you."

"Me too," said Wil, giving up the search.

They climbed down quickly. As we hurried across the Parrot Man's yard, I kept glancing at the rundown cottage.

"*Honestly.* He really is in Malibu," said Denise.

"Ol' Shirlee, too," said Wil. "I'm sure of it."

"I believe you—but I still feel funny staying so long in his yard. What if somebody sees us?"

"We'll say we came to get the pooch," said Wil.

I glanced back at the shed. "I wonder why the Parrot Man has that telescope."

"If I lived this close to the ocean, I'd have one too."

Wil threw back his shoulders. "Good way to check on smugglers," he said, sounding just like his dad. "If law enforcement's your line of work."

"Or to check on law officers," said Denise slyly, "if smuggling is your line of work."

She picked up the splintered board she'd been examining before. She waved it. "Look. It says 'Mexico.' I will bet *anything* that the Parrot Man—"

"Oh, no!" Wil groaned. "Not another suspect."

I studied the board. "It's from an old crate he probably picked up at the dump for firewood."

"On the contrary," said Denise. "It proves the Parrot Man is dealing in contraband."

I snorted. "First it's poor old Mr. Willy-Bones. Then Mr. Parducci down at the market. Now it's the Parrot Man. The next thing, Denise, you'll accuse the three of them of being in this together."

"They could be. However, it is more likely that the Parrot Man operates alone." She rapped the wood. "What better evidence do you need? The Parrot Man could be smuggling birds up from Mexico in packing crates. Perhaps that is how he acquired the red macaw."

"Even if he does bring things across the border, they don't have to be illegal," I said. "Lots of people go to Tijuana to buy stuff. Sometimes my mom travels down to get perfume and those pretty blue hand-blown glasses."

Denise dropped the board to snatch a gray feather from the ground. She waved it triumphantly. "Proof positive! This *has* to be from a baby parrot."

"Let's take Hilda home," I said. I didn't have the heart to tell Denise that the feather came from an ordinary, garbage-dump variety sea gull.

Denise pocketed the feather and picked up a stick.

"Trash often contains valuable evidence," she said, poking the stick through the contents of a dented barrel.

She fished out a paper bag. It was covered with coffee grounds and globs of what looked like chili or tomato sauce.

"Yuck!" I held my nose. "Smelly evidence of what the Parrot Man ate for dinner, that's all."

As Denise dropped the grungy bag into the barrel, I noticed a postcard stuck to it, and also a white envelope pasted with orange-and-green stamps. Thinking of my stamp collection, I grabbed the envelope.

"Let me see that postcard," said Wil. "It might tell us something." But after a glance he flipped the card back in the barrel. "Naw. Just about a get-together in Malibu of some Old-Timer Lifeguard Association."

I stared at the envelope in my hand. "This is addressed to *Jerome Adams*! The person Shirlee talked to last night on the phone was named Jerome."

Wil was looking over my shoulder. Then he whistled. "Those stamps look foreign. . . . My little brother collects stamps. Can I—"

Denise crowded in. "From Brazil," she said. Her eyes widened. "Nearly *half* the baby parrots smuggled into this country come from the Brazilian jungles. There was this article—" She turned to Wil. "It described how the trappers pull the baby birds from their nests and ship them to Mexico, where someone else smuggles them into the States."

Nodding, I wiped the gooey food from the envelope. "This could be important evidence."

"The Parrot Man's contact!" shouted Denise.

Wil studied the return address. "Rúa Misteriosa, thirteen. A suspicious-sounding address if ever I heard one."

Denise was jumping up and down. "I was *positive* the

Parrot Man was the smuggler!" she shouted. "Absolutely *positive!*"

"Too bad there's no letter inside," I said.

Denise began wildly stirring the trash with a stick. "Perhaps I can locate—"

"No!" I stuffed the envelope into my pack. "We've got to take Hilda home, and then show this to Mr. Willy-Bones—right now!"

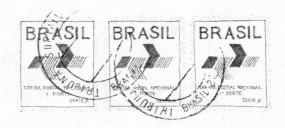

# 8

## On the Trail of Evil Eyes

Racing toward the pet shop, we tried to figure out how the smuggling operation worked.

"The telescope's the key!" Wil's skinny arms flapped every which way. "A boat comes in with smuggled birds. The Parrot Man's at his lookout. He spots it—"

"He signals his contact at Malibu Pier by semaphore," I broke in, remembering the red flags.

"And our evidence is absolutely *incriminating*!" Denise screamed, waving her bedraggled gray feather. "We should inform the authorities right away."

"Mr. Willy-Bones will know who to call," I assured them as we neared the pet shop. And when we burst in, I shouted, "We've *got* to talk to you, Mr. Willy-Bones!"

The shopkeeper turned away from the tall, thin man he was talking to. "Excuse me, Mr. Perry," he said, then added to me, "I'm busy now." His voice had a sharp edge.

I backed away. I didn't like the way this Mr. Perry stared at me, his lips curled in a sneer as he spoke in a high-pitched whine that was almost impossible to understand. I was sure he had mean-looking eyes behind his reflective sunglasses—"evil eyes." I didn't trust him at all. "Wait outside, children," Mr. Willy-Bones said, "I won't be long."

Single file we shuffled back out. What was so secret?

Wil scowled. "Thought you said this Bones dude was friendly."

"He is, most of the time." Slipping my pack from my shoulders, I sank to the curb, in the shade of a parked Thunderbird. "Maybe this Evil Eyes said something to worry him."

Denise fluffed her bangs. "Characters who wear reflective sunglasses are invariably untrustworthy."

"Uh-oh!" Wil grinned and counted on his fingers. "Suspect number—four."

Five, I thought, if you counted Shirlee. Trying to put that idea out of my mind, I spoke quickly. "Denise is right, Wil. Evil Eyes does look creepy. I just hope he's not the one buying Ringo."

Denise settled on the curb beside me. "Impossible, M.D.K. *You* are buying Ringo—with the reward money!" Then, clapping her hands, she jumped up again. "How *spectacular*! If we really *can* catch the smugglers ourselves."

I looked up at Wil. "If the Parrot Man and Jerome

are one and the same—what about Shirlee? She was talking to Jerome last night. Do you think she's involved?"

"Naw! Ol' Shirlee's no smuggler."

If only he was right! I wished he would stay and reassure me further. But already he was strolling around the parked Thunderbird, whistling through his teeth.

"This T-bird's a *classic*! Kinda beat up, though." Wil tried to straighten the bent antenna. "But give it a little polish—"

"When Floyd was into restoring antique cars," Denise said, "he owned a Thunderbird."

The door of the pet shop flew open, and Evil Eyes

came out. He stopped to light a cigarette, then threw down the matchbook. I was sure he was glaring at me from behind those glasses.

"Move it, kid," he ordered, waving me away from the curb.

I jumped to my feet. "Litterbug," I muttered, and scooped up the matchbook.

Stuffing it into my jeans pocket, I gave Evil Eyes a dirty look. He ignored me, climbed into the Thunderbird, and roared off. He ran a red light, turned left onto Sunset Boulevard, and sped north.

"Hope you get a ticket," I yelled after him. But wouldn't you know—Patty, our town's patrolperson, was nowhere in sight.

When we trooped back into the pet shop, Mr. Willy-Bones was hanging up the phone. "That man," I blurted. "He's not buying my parakeet—is he?"

"No," the shopkeeper said. His voice still didn't sound friendly. "He's selling birds, not buying them."

"What kind of birds?" I asked, taking the envelope from my pack. "Parrots?"

Mr. Willy-Bones scowled. "Why do you ask?"

Denise moved closer. "Because if those birds he has to sell are smuggled, we—"

"Children. My business is *my* business. And chasing the smugglers is no concern of yours either."

Wil faced Mr. Willy-Bones. "Seems if that dude broke the law, he should be arrested."

I was glad Wil stood up to Mr. Willy-Bones like that, because Wil was right!

The shopkeeper drew himself up taller. "Selling birds is only illegal if the babies come from a place where their export is prohibited. . . . I keep close contact with the Fish and Wildlife Service. If anything happens, I will notify—"

I broke in. "But Mr. Willy-Bones! We may have found one of the smugglers." I held up the envelope.

"And incriminating evidence!" Denise shouted, waving her feather.

"There's this guy by the cliffs, with a telescope," explained Wil. "He—"

"What we conclude," said Denise, "is that he spots shipments of contraband coming in—"

"A telescope? Many people have telescopes. Maybe 'this guy' likes to look at the ocean," said Mr. Willy-Bones. "I like to look at the ocean too. Does that make me a smuggler?"

Denise gave him a disgusted look, jammed the feather in her pocket, and stomped off.

I thrust the envelope under the shopkeeper's nose. "The man also gets letters from Brazil—where illegal baby parrots come from!"

Mr. Willy-Bones pulled his wire spectacles from his vest pocket. Slowly he wiped each lens with his pocket handkerchief. Then, propping the glasses on his nose, he studied the envelope.

"Foreign stamps mean nothing."

He looked more closely and saw who the envelope was addressed to. He waved it away. "Nonsense. I know Jerome for thirty years. The first time I swim in the Pacific Ocean, he is the lifeguard. Perhaps this friend in Brazil is . . . who knows? . . . A friend from his lifeguarding days."

The Parrot Man—a *lifeguard*? It was hard to imagine *him* saving people's lives. I wondered if he had been as crabby then.

"I assure you," Mr. Willy-Bones said. "Jerome is no smuggler."

Wil sniffed. "Cowboys' bumpers! Something's burning!"

"*Ay!* My coffee! It bubbles over."

Mr. Willy-Bones grabbed the handle of the blue enamel pot, screamed "*Ay!*" again, and dropped it. The pot clattered onto the floor. Coffee splashed everywhere. Waving his arms, the shopkeeper shooed us away. "Out, out!" he yelled, his face flaming. "Out!"

I'd never seen him so mad. We barreled from the shop.

Outside again, Wil's face twisted into a mournful look. "M.D.K.! You forgot to introduce me to Dingo."

That made me laugh. "Let's wait till Mr. Willy-Bones isn't so cross."

Denise rolled her eyes. "I *told* you: That proprietor is a suspicious character."

Wil looked down at her. "So we're back to Suspect Number One?"

"It is obvious," she said. "He and Jerome are collaborators."

"Denise," I said, "how can you accuse dear, sweet Mr. Willy-Bones?"

"His reluctance to accuse Jerome." Denise waved her feather as she listed her reasons. "The way he puts us off when we talk about the smugglers." She looked up at Wil. "When M.D.K. and I came in here earlier, he said that we shouldn't get involved, that it wasn't our concern."

"I can't see why Mr. Willy-Bones would put up that reward poster if *he* is the smuggler," I said.

"A smoke screen," Denise said. "To throw everyone off. And did you know that your 'dear, sweet Mr. Willy-Bones' *also* corresponds with someone in Brazil?"

I was shocked. "Denise! Did you go through his *mail*?"

"Of course not. The letter was on his counter."

I shrugged. "Maybe it was to order something. . . . Brazilian-leather doggy bones . . . or leashes."

Drat! That reminded me. *Again* I forgot to get a leash for Hilda.

Wil hooked his thumbs in his belt loops and stuck out his chest. Except for the cutoffs he looked like his dad. "What I think we oughta do is drop ol' Jerome and Mr. Willy-Nilly for now. And trail that guy with the T-bird— seeing as how he talked about selling birds."

"Perhaps illegally," Denise added, looking solemn.

"But all we know is that he drove north on Sunset," I said. "How can we follow? Run along behind his car?"

"We could go by bus," Denise said. "If we knew his destination."

"Wait—maybe we do." I reached into the pocket of my jeans for the matchbook. "He dropped this."

Before I could read the words on the cover, Denise grabbed it. Her eyes bugged. *"Incredible!* An ad for Sam's Oyster Bar."

Wil whistled. "Isn't that where Jerome and Shirlee were headed—the place on Malibu Pier?"

Denise nodded.

"What're we waiting for?" Wil asked. "Let's go to Malibu."

Denise waved her arms and skipped in circles. "Floyd is gone, so the beach house is empty. It can serve as our lookout. I will run home and get the key."

"Wait, you two!" I shouted. "I still have pets to feed. And what about bus fare? Who has money?"

Denise shook her head.

"I have just enough to get back to Santa Monica tonight," Wil said.

Drat! I chewed my thumbnail, thinking. Then I remembered Mrs. Kenilworth. "Puddy's mom owes me money. I'll collect it when I go up there." I pulled a bunch of carrot tops from my pack. "Can you take these greens to Bun?"

"Sure. Where's he live?"

After I gave Wil instructions, the three of us took off in different directions. We agreed to meet at the bus stop on the corner of Ocean and Sunset.

When I arrived there, twenty minutes later, Wil was waiting alone.

He grinned. "Fed ol' Bun! What'd the kid say about your switching fish on him?"

"Never knew the difference. Not only that, but his

mom liked the new fish so much, she gave me a tip!" I waved two five-dollar bills. "And she says she might start raising tropicals."

Denise raced toward us. "Sustenance!" she yelled, holding high a paper bag. "Muffins and apples for lunch.

"And, M.D.K.," she added when she got closer. "You will never believe who I saw entering the pet shop just now."

"Who?"

"Shirlee Alabama."

"Sure, Denise." I sighed. "Sure you did."

# 9

## Spies on the Pier

I was first onto the crowded bus. Handing the driver one of the fives from Mrs. Kenilworth, I said, "For me and my two friends."

Wouldn't you know? The minute Denise stepped on, she dropped the paper bag. Everything spilled. The muffins were squashed, but we recovered the apples. Wil wiped off his and began chomping on it while working his way to the back. He had to stand all the way to Malibu. Denise and I were luckier. We found empty seats. Mine was next to a woman with a fussy baby who kept pulling my hair. Munching my bruised apple, I puzzled over the connection between Shirlee and Mr. Willy-Bones.

Finally I gave up. Shirlee's friendship with the Parrot Man was mystery enough. For them to meet at Malibu Pier didn't make sense. Why were they there? Did they go into Sam's Oyster Bar to meet Evil Eyes Perry? More questions than answers swam around in my head.

Wil must have done some thinking on the ride too. When we hopped off, he announced, "I bet Shirlee and her birdman sweetie aren't even smugglers. They're after the reward money—same as us."

My jaw dropped. For a minute I was too stunned to answer. Then I asked Wil, "So who *are* the smugglers?"

"It's gotta be that Evil Eyes Perry," he said.

After we crossed the highway to the beach side, Denise was still sputtering. "But . . . but . . . the broken crates from Mexico. The letter. . . . The feather. You mean all our evidence is *inconclusive*?"

"My hunch is ol' Jerome keeps track of Evil Eyes with that telescope," Wil said. "Today he saw something suspicious. So he went up to check. Shirlee came with him."

Usually Wil's hunches proved to be right, but I wasn't sure about this one. "What about the semaphore signals?" I asked.

"Perhaps Jerome and Shirlee have an accomplice," Denise said.

"Only bad guys have accomplices," I told her.

Denise smiled sweetly. "Not necessarily. That is the usual interpretation of 'accomplice.' But it can also be defined as an associate in *any* undertaking."

Quickly I changed the subject. "I'm starved. Let's

start with lunch at Sam's Oyster Bar. My treat—courtesy of Mrs. Kenwilworth."

Wil's forehead wrinkled. "Don't cotton much to oysters."

"It is a varied menu," Denise said. "They serve other foods, such as clam sandwiches. We can have dessert at the beach house. Floyd always keeps *cartons* of orange Popsicles in the freezer."

We headed for Sam's, a wooden shack close to the highway at the entrance of Malibu Pier. Wil sniffed as we stepped onto the pier. "That salt air sure smells good." Then he grinned. "Can't wait to go swimming."

"Swimming?" I said.

"No time for frivolity," Denise added. "We must search out that scofflaw."

"Just kidding." Wil jumped aside to avoid a kid zooming by on a skateboard, then followed us into Sam's. He zeroed in on a redwood picnic table by the window. "How about sitting here? I can watch the surfers while we eat."

We were the only customers. The young man at the oyster bar seemed to be the only waiter. He put down his curved oyster-shucking knife, wiped both hands on his striped apron, and ambled over to take our order.

"Are clam sandwiches on sourdough satisfactory?" Denise looked at Wil and me. He shrugged like he was still unsure, but I nodded.

"Three clam sours," she told the waiter.

"And Tim," she added. "Three glasses of water—with ice."

"You *know* him?" I asked when the waiter was gone. She nodded. "He has worked here for a couple of years."

"So ask him about Evil Eyes," I said.

When he brought our sandwiches, Denise asked, "Tim, do any of your customers drive an old green Thunderbird?"

He scowled. "Jeez, Denny. How should I know what cars people drive?" But when he had settled onto his stool at the oyster bar, he called over. "The waiter who comes on duty at four used to work in the parking lot—he might know."

"So we sit here till *then*?" I asked Denise.

"We can wait at the beach house," she said. "Sam's is visible from our patio. We can eat Popsicles and watch."

After taking one bite, Wil put down his sandwich. He gazed at the menu chalked on a blackboard behind the oyster bar. Then he hooted. "Tex-Mex chili! Cowboys' bumpers, wish I'd known."

Denise nodded. "Sam's cook is *perpetually* experimenting."

"Maybe that's why ol' Shirlee stopped by. For a taste o' home."

"You'd think she'd get enough at my house," I said.

Wil scraped all the clams left in his sandwich onto his plate. Then he stuffed the bread in his mouth and slid from the booth. "Meet y'all out front," he said, heading for the door.

"Where did he disappear to?" Denise asked.

"Bathroom, maybe?"

She shook her head. "The rest rooms are in the other direction."

We quickly finished our food, and I paid the waiter with the other five-dollar bill from Mrs. Kenilworth. Then we went out into the sunshine. Wil hurried to meet us.

"Had a hunch," he said, tugging his earlobe. "Figured maybe that kid on the skateboard might know something. Chased him down. Asked if he'd seen a skinny guy with an old green T-bird." A big smile spread across Wil's freckled face. "The kid knows the guy! Sees him hanging around Sam's all the time."

"So Tim was lying," said Denise.

"Or never noticed," I said.

Wil leaned over the wooden railing to look at cars in the parking lot below. "No classic T-birds there now. We'll have to wait till ol' Evil Eyes turns up."

Denise waved her feather. "Then we follow him—"

"And he leads us to the rest of his gang!" I shouted.

Wil nodded toward the far end of the pier. "While we're waiting, how about we walk clear out on the pier. So I can look down on the *bee-oo-ti-ful* blue Pacific."

He loped ahead. Denise and I followed. From both sides of the pier old people and kids dangled their fishing lines in the water below. Not many caught fish, but

everyone looked happy. We lost sight of Wil when a crowd of laughing, joking people rushed past us, carrying bulging gunnysacks.

"Day-trippers with their day's catch," explained Denise. "They debarked from that fishing boat docked at the end of the pier."

"Those sacks are a good way to sneak baby birds ashore," I remarked.

Denise nodded. "My thoughts precisely."

"Wonder what they'd do," I said, "if we asked to look inside the sacks?"

At the end of the pier, Wil, cheerful as usual, was talking with two leathery-faced men in watch caps who were busy cutting bait. They looked like they were having fun.

Denise tugged my arm. In a loud whisper she said, "Those characters look *highly* suspicious."

I giggled and ran to Wil, but I didn't waste time reporting Denise's latest suspects. "We should head back soon. We don't want to miss—"

One of the grizzled bait-cutters stopped work to listen. I hesitated. Maybe Denise was right. To be safe, I quit talking.

Wil knew what I meant. He nodded. Our feet thumping on the wooden pier, we raced back toward the Coast Highway. After we passed Sam's, Denise pointed south with her feather. "Our beach house is down that road."

She led us along a gravel road between the highway and the back fences of the beach houses. The high fences of wood or stucco blocked our view of the sand, but sometimes, even over the traffic noise of the Coast Highway, we could hear the surf.

Denise stopped at a fence of weathered redwood and unlocked a door. "This is it." We followed her into a two-car garage. Now the only car was Floyd's white Mercedes. Boxes, a bicycle, and stacks of life jackets lined the front wall. Though the bright orange jackets looked new, two were so ripped that the kapok stuffing hung out. I wondered how they had gotten torn. One thing for sure: Wearing one of those wouldn't keep you afloat for two seconds!

We stepped into the small backyard. Wil pointed to four surfboards leaning against a wall. He gave a low whistle. "Cowabunga! Do you do that much surfing?"

Denise made a face. "Not me. Floyd. He and his aging friends have this dream that they are still hotshot surfers."

On the north side, between the beach house and the neighbor's high stone fence, was a gate.

"Where does that go?" I asked.

"Shortcut to the front. But we will go through the house." Denise unlocked the back door. We followed her through the kitchen and dining area and into the living room. The front wall was solid glass, with floor-to-ceiling windows and a sliding glass door.

Wil whistled. "Look at that. Right out there's the ocean." He grinned. "Bet you come here a lot."

Denise shook her head. "This is where Floyd always meets with his cronies—and he hates having me around."

"Meets about what?" Wil asked. "Surfing?"

"Who knows? Ever since *Kiddie Brigade* went into reruns, Floyd has been trying to make a TV comeback. He is *perpetually* concocting some new scheme to make money."

That surprised me. I had this notion that TV stars— even has-beens like Floyd—had more money than they knew what to do with.

"From the patio we can see Sam's." Denise unlocked the sliding glass door. "Go on out. I will bring the Popsicles."

"None for me," Wil said, pointing to kids skimming the surf on Styrofoam kickboards. "Y'all watch for ol' Evil Eyes. I'll be back." With a wild Texas "Yahoo!" he was gone.

He was already splashing in the surf by the time I threw down my pack and settled into a yellow-canvas director's chair on the patio.

Denise came out, a frown on her face. "For some weird reason, not a *single* Popsicle in the freezer." She handed me a plastic tumbler. "Have some water."

After one sip, I set the tumbler on the glass-topped table. Yuck! The water was lukewarm.

Denise handed me a copy of *Animals in the Wild*. "Here is the magazine I was telling you about. Floyd must have brought it up yesterday. The article on smuggling is on page twenty-three."

She leaned over my shoulder and pointed. "Here it describes how the poachers reach the parrots' nests."

I squirmed away. "Denise! Just 'cause I don't get

straight A's in reading like you doesn't mean I don't know how."

"Sorry! But can you *believe*? They chop down an entire tree." She still hovered over me. "They destroy the parrots' nesting place *forever*—merely because it makes collecting the birds simpler." She waved an arm. "Here it shows—"

"*Denise!*" I shouted.

Too late! Her elbow bumped the tumbler. Water splashed my hand, and I dropped the magazine.

"Sorry!" she cried.

I picked up the soggy magazine. "It's soaked."

"Never mind. Just leave it on the table to dry."

"Hey, you two!" Wil charged through the sand toward us. "Guess what that Old Geezer was doing?"

"Geezer?" I stared at him.

"That bait cutter. The one I talked to, on the pier. He has semaphore flags, like Jerome's . . . and he was sending signals."

I gasped. "Who to? The smugglers?"

Denise danced around, kicking up sand and clapping her hands. "I *knew* it. . . . I *told* you that bait cutter looked suspicious. This proves it."

I pulled my sketchbook and a colored pencil from my pack to write down important clues.

"Where was he signaling?" I asked Wil.

He pointed south. "That way—toward Pacific Cliffs."

"The Parrot Man!" I drew in my breath.

"Can you decipher semaphore?" Denise asked Wil.

"What was the message?"

"I can read it—sort of. But it doesn't matter, anyhow. By the time I figured what was happening, the Geezer'd stopped. But my hunch is that he's Jerome's lookout."

"So *he* is the accomplice of Jerome and Shirlee," Denise said. "Which means he is also in pursuit of the lawbreakers."

Wil frowned. "Unless . . ."

I studied his wrinkled forehead. Was he having second thoughts about Shirlee and the Parrot Man too? Then the creases vanished and Wil grinned. "*Naw!* No way could ol' Shirlee be a smuggler's moll."

Denise fiddled with her feather. "One thing is obvious. The pier is their headquarters."

Wil looked up from tying his sneakers. "Or maybe Sam's Oyster Bar."

"I'm calling Mr. Willy-Bones," I announced. "He'll be mad about what we're doing—but I don't care. He might know who this Old Geezer is. And I think it's time for him to call the Fish and Wildlife Service."

"Can you trust him?" Denise asked.

"We have to. What else can we do?" I looked back toward the oyster bar. "This is dumb. We were supposed to be watching for Evil Eyes. By now he could have come—and gone again."

"Let us check the parking lot by Sam's," said Denise.

We went inside, and she locked the sliding glass door at the front. We left the beach house the way we entered.

"Shouldn't we sweep up?" I asked. Our gritty trail of sand stretched clear through the house.

Denise shrugged. "Let Floyd. It will be even messier when he returns from his fishing trip and unloads all his gear."

As we walked back to Sam's, Denise apologized about the mix-up with the Popsicles. "But there is a snow-cone stand on the pier," she said.

I shook my head. "It must be nearly five, and I've got to be home by six."

Denise stopped twirling her feather long enough to consult her Swatch watch. "Four fifty-four, to be precise."

"In that case forget the snow cones *and* Evil Eyes."

"Come on, M.D.K.," Wil protested. "Just a quick look into parking lot."

We did. Denise hurried across the wooden pier ahead us and let out a squeal. She pointed with her feather at the parking lot below. Two men stood next to the green Thunderbird. I had never seen the lunky one with the bumpy complexion before. But I recognized the tall, thin man in the flowered Hawaiian shirt. It was Evil Eyes.

"Get down," Wil ordered in a low voice. "And keep quiet." After dropping onto our stomachs, we inched toward the edge of the wooden pier until we could peek over. It was the perfect place to spy. From below, the words of the two men drifted up.

"Message just came ... ship-to-shore radio," Evil

Eyes said. "The boat's due on Friday . . . about twelve."

"How many birds?" the lunky man asked.

"Dunno. . . . Transmission was garbled—"

*"Oops!"* Denise shrieked as her feather floated down toward the men. Evil Eyes spun around.

*"Who's up there?"* he demanded, shaking his fist.

# 10

# The Promise

We flattened ourselves on the rough wooden pier. Nobody breathed. Nobody moved. We had drawn back from the edge the instant Denise had let out that shriek. Evil Eyes hadn't seen us—I was almost sure. I found a crack between two boards wide enough to peek down at the two men. Evil Eyes was looking all around. He seemed puzzled by Denise's yelp.

"Forget it," his friend with the lumpy face said. "Just some wiseacre kids."

Still Evil Eyes glowered up at the underside of the pier.

"C'mon, Ernie," Lump Face urged. "Let's go have a beer."

The two men finally moved off. We scrambled to our feet as soon as they hurried up the incline and disappeared inside Sam's.

Denise peered down at the parking lot. "I must retrieve my feather. It could be vital evidence."

"You'd never find it," Wil said.

"And anyway," I shouted, sprinting toward the Coast Highway, "here comes our bus."

Reluctantly Denise raced after Wil and me. We reached the stop at the same instant the southbound bus did. This time we found three seats together at the back. Wil sat in the middle.

"I'm still in shock," I said. "They really *are* smuggling birds!"

"*Undoubtedly,*" Denise said, her eyes round as beach

balls. "That Ernie 'Evil Eyes' Perry is *sinister*!"

"And so is his friend Lump Face," I said.

Wil nodded. "Had a hunch those guys'd come by boat."

"So all we have to do," I said, "is be there when they dock at twelve—"

"At night!" Denise interrupted. "Obviously such underworld types operate after dark. Less danger of detection."

"If it's midnight, forget it," I said. "Shirlee will never let me go up there that late."

"Unless she is there herself," Denise said.

"Could be that's what the Old Geezer was signaling to Jerome." Wil shifted in his seat. "I wonder how much those two old guys and Shirlee do know. Maybe we should join forces."

"And let them claim the reward?" Denise snorted. "Forget *that*. M.D.K. needs enough money to buy her parakeet."

"Doesn't matter," I said. "We can't worry about Ringo now. All I want is to nab those smugglers." I stared out the window as the bus rumbled down the Coast Highway. I couldn't believe I'd just said that. But once the words tumbled out, I realized that that was how I felt. More important than the reward was stopping those evil men before they harmed any more poor birds.

Wil smiled at me. "Don't worry, M.D.K.—you'll get ol' Bingo."

"Maybe," I said. Then quickly I added, "But Friday's the day after tomorrow. If that's when their smuggled birds get here, we haven't much time." I reached into my pack, on the floor at my feet, and brought out my sketchbook. "We'd better start planning."

"Right, Detective Kincaid." Wil gave me a salute. "So first we figure *when* and *where* the smugglers are due to arrive—"

"And where they go afterward," said Denise. "Undoubtedly they will try to foist their illegal birds on several pet shops."

"Which reminds me," Wil said. "M.D.K., you were going to give your old friend Mr. W.B. a call."

Drat! I knocked my fist on my forehead. "I meant to phone Mr. Willy-Bones from the beach house. And I forgot."

"By the time we get back, he will be closed," Denise said.

I nodded. "I'll go and see him first thing in the morning."

"Do it by phone," Wil said. "You should stick with Shirlee tomorrow. Like *glue*. We need to know what she's up to."

"Now," he said, sitting straighter in the seat. "For our plan of action." Sometimes Wil acted goofy, but he was better than me at getting organized. "Notebook ready, Detective Kincaid?"

"Ready." I waved a red drawing pencil.

"Better hurry," Denise said as the bus turned to begin its climb toward Pacific Cliffs. "We are practically home."

"Right," Wil said. He scratched his head. "Denise, can you trail the Parrot Man tomorrow?"

"I can only keep him under surveillance until ten," she said. "Then I have an optometrist's appointment."

"It'll have to do." Wil wrinkled his freckled nose. "And I'll chase after the Geezer and Evil Eyes. And this new dude, Lump Face."

"If I have to stay home all day," I said, "who's going to take care of the rabbit and the tortoise and—"

"Maybe Wil can stop off on his way to Malibu," Denise said.

Wil nodded. "Sure. Stuffing lettuce in a cage is no big deal."

"Before my appointment, I will have time to care for Hilda and Conrad," Denise said.

"Can you take care of the canaries, too?" I asked her.

"Do I have to?"

"If I stay with Shirlee all day, I don't see how—"

Wil broke in. "Never mind. Let me do it. I like birds."

Good old Wil. Always the peacemaker.

"It is not a matter of *like* or *dislike*," Denise said. "I absolutely *abhor* seeing wild birds caged."

"Canaries aren't wild birds," I said. "And they're better off in cages than out where a dumb cat can eat them."

Denise scowled. "Cats are not dumb."

I scowled back. "They can't talk, can they?"

"Neither can birds," Denise said. "Mimicking is not the same as actually talking."

My whole body tensed up. I stared from the bus window, counting to ten. Sometimes Denise really teed me off. Why did she have to rub it in about Ringo and caged birds?

"You *guys*!" Wil yelled. "This is your stop."

I stuffed my notebook into my pack. With Denise at my heels I raced for the door. "Call you tonight," I shouted to Wil as we hopped off. I could give him instructions for the pets then.

As soon as the bus pulled away, I turned to Denise. I smiled. She had been a big help. Her feelings about caged birds were no reason to fight. "Thanks for all the help pet-sitting," I said.

"Sure." She smiled too. "And just remember, when you ferret information from your sitter, be casual. The operative words are nonchalant, noncommital, and disinterested."

"I'll try."

"By the way," Denise said. "Do you recall that tabby that was by my house the other day? She returned. I have been feeding her."

"What about Floyd's allergy?"

She grinned. "I will let him worry about that when he gets back."

We parted at the corner with a wave. All the way to the top of my hill I practiced being casual, nonchalant, noncommital, and disinterested. Not easy, considering

I was excited, curious, and highly suspicious—of Shirlee Alabama.

"Hi, I'm home!" I shouted, bounding into the house. The usual smell of chili greeted me. After a week I was used to it.

"Lordy, Miss Margaret!" Shirlee marched from the kitchen, strings flapping on her checkered apron. "It's nearly seven. I been worried sick. . . . If your mama only knew—"

"Sorry I'm late." I gave her a smile I hoped was casual. "We were in Malibu, and the bus—"

"*Malibu?*" she screeched. Her red eyebrows formed an angry V. "Why on earth were you up there?"

"Denise invited us . . . to her beach house." Drat! This whole thing was going backward. *I* was supposed to be the one asking questions. Before Shirlee could ask anything more, I gave her a nonchalant smile. "Any phone messages? Did my folks call?"

"Mail's on the hall table," she snapped, and stormed back to the kitchen.

I dropped my pack. First I read Mom's postcard, mailed from Redding, a town in Northern California. She was fine. She had another week and a half of flying her politician around the state, and then she'd be home. She would try to call me on Friday.

*Friday!* That reminded me of my assignment to "ferret information," as Denise put it. Shoving the letter from Dad into my pocket to read later, I hurried into the kitchen. I tried a noncommital smile. Shirlee was too busy at the stove to catch it.

"So how was your day?" That seemed disinterested enough.

She swiped a bony hand across her forehead. "Not bad, considerin' I was over a hot stove since the crack o' dawn."

"But isn't Wednesday your day at the Senior Center?" I tried to pretend it was a casual question and that I really couldn't care less.

Shirlee's cheeks turned redder under the rouge spots. "Well, I did run over to the Center for a half hour or so. Then I had to get back to fix your supper."

I stared at the chili bubbling in that pot. Why cook more? Already dozens of jars of the stuff jammed the fridge. What I *ought* to ask Shirlee was: Why so much Tex-Mex?

"Didn't count on your gettin' back this late." She clucked and stirred. "Not safe . . . a young girl like you . . . out at all hours."

I gave up trying to quiz her and pulled out Dad's letter to read. He was fine, same as Mom. He had a week or more of business to finish up and he might not get home until Labor Day.

"Supper's ready," Shirlee squawked.

Stuffing Dad's letter into my pocket, I started to sit down. Then I remembered my dirty hands. After I washed them at the sink, I slipped into my chair at the kitchen table, gave Shirlee another noncommital smile, and began to eat.

When the phone rang, we both leaped up. We nearly collided. Shirlee got to it first. All she said was "Yes,"

"No," and "Mebbe" between long silences. Finally I gave up listening and went back to eating. Suddenly she cackled.

"Yer dern-tootin' I'll be ready. Just see that you have that van here on time," she said, and hung up.

When she came back to the table, I shrugged my shoulders. Nonchalantly.

"Good news?"

Shirlee didn't answer. She only jammed a loose hairpin firmly into her topknot and cleared the table. Soon she set before me a huge slice of gingerbread. It was still warm from the oven and smelled heavenly. I was suspicious. Except for occasional baked apples Shirlee *never* gave me dessert. Now two nights in a row she had plied me with goodies.

"Baked it myself!" she crowed, smiling proudly.

"Yummy," I said, diving in. It looked an awful lot like Sara Lee, but how could I be sure? Between bites, I searched for telltale bits of plastic wrap, but couldn't find any.

Shirlee looked down her thin nose at me. "So what did you do in Malibu, Miss Margaret?"

Her question was so unexpected, I nearly choked.

"Goofed around." I stared at my plate. "Showed Wil the beach."

"You didn't talk to any strangers?" she demanded.

"Never do!" I knew better than that.

Leaning an elbow on the table, she waved a bony finger. "See that you don't. . . . There's unsavory types about . . . purse snatchers, bird smugglers—"

My head jerked up. "Bird smugglers?"

"So I hear. At the Center my friend was sayin'—"
She suddenly returned to the stove and began stirring
the pot on it. "Never mind. But I don't want you gallivantin' after smugglers, like you did down in Texas."

I didn't say anything. I didn't know what to say.

" 'Cause I won't have it, you hear?" She waved her
wooden spoon at me. "Don't want you mixed up with
people like *that* . . . so don't get it in your head to go
lookin' for 'em—"

"I . . . won't." I felt my cheeks burning.

"Do you promise, Miss Margaret?"

"I . . . I promise," I said.

# 11

## The Message in the Margin

**E**ven with my hand under the table and my fingers crossed, I felt bad about lying to Shirlee. But Denise and Wil and I were in this too deep. We'd found the smugglers—some of them anyway. We knew their plans. If we stopped now, they might get away with their evil deed.

Shirlee returned to her pot of chili. I got up and went into the living room.

"Where's the *TV Guide*?" I shouted. "It's not on the set, where it's s'posed to be."

"Mighta left it in the den," Shirlee called.

She didn't say "don't go in," so I figured she wouldn't mind. Being there felt strange. It was the first time I'd gone into the den since Shirlee had taken it over as her room. Pink hair curlers and wads of Kleenex cluttered the top of Dad's oak desk. Her pink chenille robe was draped across the back of Mom's antique rocking chair.

The program guide lay under a jar of cold cream on the desk. Flipping through the guide, I saw a note in the margin in Shirlee's handwriting: *Del. B.P. Friday, 12:00.* But what did it mean?

The day and the time grabbed my attention. Twelve on Friday was when Evil Eyes expected that big delivery. Did this note mean Shirlee was a part of the smuggling ring after all?

After ripping off the corner of the page with her writing, I rushed from the den. Wil should know about this *right now*! So should Denise. But when I got to the kitchen, Shirlee was still fussing at the counter. With her there I couldn't call anybody. She was sifting flour. From the smell of spices I could tell she was about to bake more gingerbread. Chili beans boiled on the stove. What was she planning—a welcome-home party for the smugglers?

I went to my room and noted this latest clue in my sketchbook. Afterward I tried reading a mystery, but every few minutes I got up to check if it was safe to call my friends. At last I heard the TV set blaring. Good! Shirlee was finally out of the kitchen.

Sneaking to the phone, I tried to reach Denise, but there was no answer. I held my breath and dialed another number. "Hello?" Wil answered on the first ring. Breathlessly I told him about the note in the *TV Guide.*

"Aha! Detective Kincaid uncovers the Mysterious Message in the Margin."

"Be serious, Wil. This could be important." I kept my

voice low. "The 'Del' must mean 'delivery' . . . but I can't figure out 'B.P.' "

"Beats me," Wil said. "The initials of a friend, maybe?"

"Jerome, the Parrot Man, is her only friend that I know about," I said. "But she did talk to somebody on the phone during dinner about a van. What can that mean?"

"Maybe 'B.P.' stands for 'ball park'. Could be that a van is hauling Shirlee and her Senior Center buddies to a doubleheader!"

"There's no ball game around here on Friday, Wil."

If only Denise were home. She'd figure it out right away.

Then Wil laughed. "What about 'big pizza'? Maybe she's having one delivered for your lunch on Friday."

"Don't I wish!" But this was no time to clown. Why couldn't Wil be serious?

"Wait," Wil said. "I have it! Remember that beauty shop a few doors down from Billy-Boy's pet shop? It's spelled like *D e l* . . . something."

"Delia's?" I gasped. Sometimes that goofy Wil really surprised me. "Wil, you're a genius. That's *it*! Delia's Beauty Parlor!—'Del. B.P.' I'll bet Shirlee made an appointment to get her hair dyed." I giggled. "It's about time. The gray roots are starting to show."

The explanation made sense. And although the van was still a mystery, I was relieved. It didn't look like Shirlee was part of the smuggling ring after all.

"Another thing, Wil. Shirlee says there's talk at the

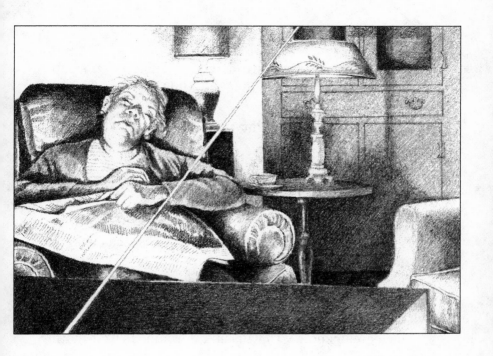

Center about smugglers in the area. She made me promise not to get involved."

"You mean you want to back out?"

"We can't back out now, Wil. But I can't let Shirlee find out. She'd *kill* me."

"You can count on me, M.D.K. I'll never squeal."

After giving Wil directions for feeding Bun and the tortoise, I hung up. When I passed the living room, Shirlee was asleep in the E-Z lounger. Her snoring was louder than the blaring TV set. I tiptoed to my room, slipped on my nightie, and popped into bed.

When the phone jangled, I bolted upright, instantly awake. Had something happened to Mom or Dad? I jumped from bed, not sure how long I had been sleeping. It felt like the middle of the night. I groped down the hall.

In the kitchen the light was on. Hearing Shirlee's voice, I stopped to listen.

"Why, Jerome. I was just a-fixin' to call you. . . ."

So it wasn't Mom or Dad in trouble. *That* was a relief! I remained in the shadows, listening. The clock struck twelve. Why a call from the Parrot Man at this hour?

". . . So is it all set for Friday?" Shirlee was asking. "And you can borrow the van?"

The van again! So the phone call earlier must have been from Jerome too. But what did the van have to do with her appointment at the beauty parlor?

Shirlee clucked. "Stop fussin', Jerome. It'll go without a hitch. . . ."

*What* would? Her appointment at Delia's? For gosh sakes! Dying hair wasn't *that* risky. And what was Jerome—her chauffeur?

Or maybe his bad-tempered parrot was having its feathers dyed. I almost giggled out loud.

"The only thing worryin' me," Shirlee said, "is four deliveries in one day. Besides the two in Malibu, we've got the one here in town . . . and Santa Monica besides. Think we oughta leave Santa Monica till Saturday?"

She said nothing more except "Good night" before setting down the receiver. I tore back down the hall to my room.

Lying in the dark, I puzzled over Shirlee's conversation. "Del. B.P." did *not* stand for Delia's Beauty Parlor, of that I was certain. Now I was sure that "Del" stood for delivery, just like I'd thought at first. And whatever Shirlee planned to do Friday at twelve, Jerome and his van were involved in it too. Maybe the Old Geezer, as well.

So what was "B.P." Bean Pot? Bad Penny? The clock chimed one. Still I couldn't figure out what the initials meant. Was it Baked Potato? Blue Pencil? Not being able to solve what could be the key to this whole mystery was a *Big Pain*! What kind of detective was I, anyway?

I thought about trying one more time to call Denise. But what if Shirlee heard me? So instead I got up, switched on my bed lamp, and opened my dictionary. I would unscramble that message if I had to go through every page of *B*s and every page of *P*s.

On the first page of the *B*s I broke the code. *Baby!* What a dumbo! I should have guessed right away. And the second word *had* to be *Parrots*. This proved Shirlee and Jerome knew about the smuggling operation. But did that mean they were part of it? Was all that chili for feeding the rest of her gang?

Sharing my house with a smuggler scared me. It was spooky. But it was too late to make any more calls. Nothing could be done until morning.

Nothing, that is, except barricade my room.

I shoved a sturdy toy chest against my door. It was one Dad had built of thick mahogany planks when I was a mini-kid. I loaded the chest with every heavy object I owned—books, shoes, a lamp, my paint box, my stamp collection, even my flute in its leather case. For good measure I tossed my beanbag chair on top.

If Shirlee tried to push past all that, I would have loads of time to escape through the window.

# 12

# A Crisis!

I dreamed of baby parrots. Poachers snatched them from their jungle nests, stuffed them into nylon panty hose, crammed them under car seats and in spare tires. The poor birds were smuggled across borders—their tiny beaks taped so they couldn't make a sound. It was horrible. I kept waking up, only to fall asleep and dream again of helpless baby parrots and evil smugglers.

In the morning I leaped from my bed to phone Wil. Then I came up against that barricade. Drat! Removing enough junk to budge the toy chest took so long that when I finally got free and raced for the kitchen, Shirlee was already up and cooking breakfast. So much for calling Wil.

"French toast this morning, sweetie?" Shirlee gave me a wide smile showing all of her gold fillings.

"No, thanks." Any other time my mouth would have

watered at the good smell of butter sizzling in the skillet. But how could I eat food cooked by a smuggler's moll?

I poured myself a bowl of Cheerios and studied Shirlee's wrinkled cheeks, still pale before her daily coating of rouge. How had this old lady from Texas gotten mixed up with smugglers? Jerome's doing, probably. She had met him—it didn't matter where—and he had lured her into joining his smuggling ring. She'd needed the money, so why not? She'd make more than she did selling Tex-Mex at her little café in Riverbank.

No wonder she didn't tell Wil and his dad why she might stay in California.

"Sure you won't try even an itty-bitty piece of French toast?" Shirlee asked, interrupting my thoughts.

Shaking my head, I swallowed another spoonful of Cheerios. They didn't make me feel cheery at all. Shirlee took the skillet to the sink. Mincing across the linoleum in her tight jeans and boots, she just didn't look or act like a criminal. She was hard to get along with sometimes—"Feisty," Mom had called her—but how could Shirlee be *that* bad?

"Aren't you s'posed to be doin' your rounds?" she asked.

"What? Oh . . . well, I—" Her question had caught me off guard. I felt my face turning red. "My friends want to do them alone for a change." It was more white lie than real fib. "So I decided to lounge around the house all day."

I had better watch my step or she might discover what we were up to. Now I knew why she'd made me promise not to go after the smugglers. It was not to keep me from getting hurt. It was to keep *her* and the others from getting caught.

I slipped my empty cereal bowl and spoon into the sudsy water in the sink and glanced up at the kitchen clock. After nine! Too late now to phone Wil. He would already be on the bus, coming up from Santa Monica to feed my pets. And Denise had that doctor's appointment. But I *could* phone Mr. Willy-Bones if Shirlee ever left the kitchen.

Although we had an electric dishwasher, Shirlee preferred to wash dishes by hand. I picked up a dish towel and started to dry the ones that were draining. Anything to speed things up.

Then the phone rang. I raced for it, but Shirlee had already grabbed it.

"And good morning to you, sweetheart," she said. "You're up bright and early. Any word from your daddy?" Shirlee practically purred. "Did he catch any fish down there in Baja?"

So it was Denise! Simpering, Shirlee handed over the receiver. "It's your little friend." In a loud whisper she added, "The one whose daddy does that TV show."

"Stepdad," I muttered, grabbing the phone.

Shirlee went back to the sink, but washed the dishes so quietly, I knew she must be listening.

"M.D.K. !" Denise shrieked. "You will never *believe*!

This morning when Izzy and I went over to feed Hilda—"

"Izzy?"

"I have named that adorable tabby Isadora."

"What about Mrs. Eastley's dachshund? What happened?"

"Nothing. She is fine. But parked in front of Jerome's gate is an old van. And in addition to *that*, I saw him sending a *semaphore message*—"

Shirlee stopped washing dishes altogether.

"Not so loud," I told Denise. "You're killing my eardrums."

"I get it. You are not *alone* . . . right?" Denise lowered her voice to a husky whisper.

"Right."

"To continue. . . . I wrote down which directions the flags pointed . . . for Wil to translate." Denise's voice grew so soft, I barely understood her. But that was all right. Shirlee wouldn't be able to either.

"But I must leave *immediately* for my optometrist appointment," Denise went on. "Can you deliver this paper to Wil for me? The message could be of the *utmost* significance."

I guess she meant "important." It probably was. But how could I spy on Shirlee and get the paper to Wil, too?

"In present circumstances . . . impossible . . . to vacate premises." I hoped Denise understood my code.

"You mean you have to stay there and snoop?"

"Affirmative. Unexpected developments. . . ." This

was fun. For a change, I was the one using the big words. But with Shirlee listening, I didn't dare say more. "I'll explain later."

"I must dash anyway. My mother is sitting on the car horn," said Denise. "I will leave the paper on the porch, beneath a brick—"

"Denise, I can't—"

But she had hung up. Whatever that important message was, I knew there was no way I could collect that paper.

Replacing the receiver, I noticed strange marks on the notepad by the phone. There were zigzag lines and arrows, and also letters—*MALXX, WBX, SMX*. I realized they were Shirlee's scribblings from that midnight conversation with Jerome. But the marks didn't make sense. I ripped off the sheet anyway and stuck it into my pocket. It could be an important clue. A map, maybe. Or a kind of code.

For the rest of the morning I trailed Shirlee. It was a waste of time, though. She went through her morning routine. She sorted laundry, washed a couple of windows, vacuumed the hall. I even followed her into the backyard when she buried the garbage.

"But we've got a disposal in the kitchen," I said.

"A friend at the Senior Center tells me it makes flowers bloom better."

I scratched my head. Our garden was mostly weeds, except for Mom's geraniums. And they seemed to be doing fine on their own.

Around lunchtime Shirlee disappeared into the bathroom. I dropped the peanut-butter sandwich I was making as soon as the shower started. I raced to the phone book. There it was, the number of the pet shop. I dialed it.

Mr. Willy-Bones didn't answer. I let the phone ring three times. Then I heard his voice. Only it wasn't him. It was a recording: ". . . unable to come to the phone. . . . Leave a message . . . sound of the beep." Ugh! I *hated* answering machines. I was still trying to figure what to say when the bathroom door opened. Shirlee dashed out in her pink robe, a towel wrapped around her head. She swished by me and into the den.

I put down the receiver. I couldn't leave that message now. Not with Shirlee listening. And anyway, what I had to say was too important to trust to a dumb tape recorder. I needed to talk to Mr. Willy-Bones. Time was running out.

By early afternoon Shirlee had settled in the E-Z lounger to do her nails and watch the soaps. With her hair in curlers and her feet propped up, she looked as if she wasn't going anyplace for ages.

But I was! I had wasted far too much time already.

On a card by the phone Mom and Dad kept important numbers, such as the police, the fire department, our doctor, and the Pacific Cliffs Taxi Service. What fun to dial 911, but I didn't dare. Instead I called for a taxi.

"No, this isn't a joke," I told the man who answered. "It's an emergency. I'll be waiting at the corner of Chautauqua and Ellis streets—and I have money to pay."

I had never ridden in a taxi before, but I knew they were expensive. I rushed to my room and dumped out all the bills and coins from Sinclair, my dinosaur bank. This time I wouldn't bother with my pack. Instead I stuffed my entire savings into my jeans pocket. Whatever the cab ride cost, that should cover it.

I slipped from the house and raced to the corner. A black-and-red taxi approached and stopped. I jumped in.

"First take me to Edgecliff Estates," I told the driver. "Then to Malibu. And hurry! This is a *crisis*."

# 13

# Caught in the Act

I ran to the end of the pier. Wil wasn't there. I'd already checked the beach, and Sam's. Where *was* he? Then I looked toward Denise's beach house. There was Wil, lounging in a canvas chair on the front patio. He wasn't acting like there was a crisis.

I raced over. "How'd you get in without a key?" I demanded.

He laughed. "Don't need one for the patio." Then he squinted. "Thought you were sticking with Shirlee."

After I caught my breath, I spread the three pieces of paper on the glass-topped table.

"Evidence," I said. "Had to show you. Right away."

Wil grinned. "So let's have a look at your Mysterious Markings in the Margin." He studied the scrap of paper from the *TV Guide*. "Yup. 'BP' has to be 'Baby Parrots' all right. Ties in with the meeting Friday at twelve."

"And 'Del'? It's 'Deliveries,' right?"

Wil nodded again.

Then I handed him my next piece of evidence—the scribbling from the telephone notepad.

"Now look at this crazy map—or whatever it is," I said. " 'WBX.' 'MALXX.' 'SMX.' And arrows and lines and a big question mark in a circle. What do you think?"

Wil shook his head. "I'm plumb buffaloed."

" 'MALXX' starts out like 'Malibu,' " I said, chewing my thumbnail. "And without the *X*, 'SM' *could* stand for 'Santa Monica.' "

"So what are all the *X*s—"

"Deliveries!" I cried. "That *has* to be it."

"Deliveries of what?"

"Birds, of course."

"So 'XX,' " I went on, "would be the two deliveries to Malibu that Shirlee talked about—"

"And 'SMX'—that could be the one to Santa Monica," he said.

"Right! Prob'ly Shirlee wrote the question mark because they weren't sure if they should make the Santa Monica delivery Friday or wait until Saturday!"

Wil grinned. "Now we're getting somewhere. But what about 'WBX'?"

I ran my fingers over the paper. "A map, I think. Malibu at the top. Santa Monica at the bottom. And 'WB' in between."

"You mean 'WB' stands for some town?" asked Wil.

I began chewing my thumbnail again. "It should. Except that the only town between Malibu and Santa Monica is Pacific Cliffs."

"Initials P.C.," he said.

"I'm stumped, Wil."

Next I took out the paper from Denise with the semaphore message. "What about this? Can you decode it?"

Wil frowned. "When my little brother was a Cub Scout, we used to practice signal flags. But it's been a while." He turned the paper around and smiled. "Can't tell which way's up. Too bad you didn't copy the signals, M.D.K. You're an artist. You could draw the flags better."

He studied the paper some more. Finally he nodded. "I think I remember some of the letters. Got a pencil to write them down?"

"Darn! I *knew* I should've brought my pack. It's full of pencils. But tell me the letters." I got to my knees. "I'll scratch them in the sand."

Wil began, "*T*, blank, blank. . . . Cowboys' bumpers! I can't remember half of those letters any more." He scratched his head, then went on. "*Z*, blank, *R*, *O* . . . blank, *O*, blank, *R*. . . ." By the time he had finished the message, there were quite a few blanks. He gave me a sheepish grin. "Forgot more than I thought."

I studied the scrapings in the sand: T_ _ Z_RO _O_R N_ARS AR_ _O_ R_AD_

OLD B_DD_. "At least we know it has to do with something old." I tried to sound grateful. Wil *had* done his best.

"Think that last word might be 'bird'?" he asked. "It has a *B* and a *D*."

"No. One too many *D*s, and it's in the wrong place," I said. "I wish Denise were here. She may be a klutz, but she's smart." As I scrambled to my feet, I noticed that something was missing.

"Wil! That tumbler that Denise knocked over yesterday—it's gone. And so's the magazine we left out to dry."

"Somebody prob'ly walked off with them," Wil said. "Anyone could come onto this patio from the beach." He grinned. "Like me."

He stuck Denise's notes in his pocket. "I'll keep this. In case I remember more of the letters."

I brushed the sand from my knees.

"The library might have a book on semaphore," I said. "I'll check on my way home this afternoon."

"Even without this, you've got plenty of high-powered evidence," said Wil. "Things don't look as good for ol' Shirlee and her birdman sweetie as they did. What does your Willy-Nilly man think?"

"Oh, darn!" I rapped my forehead with my knuckles. "I meant to call Mr. Willy-Bones after I talked to you. We've got to find a phone."

Wil glanced toward the sliding glass door of the beach

house. "Sure would be handy to call from here. Too bad we can't get in." Then he moved closer to the door. "Did Denise close those curtains when she locked up yesterday?"

"Never noticed," I said. I came closer too, and gave the glass door a slight tug. It slid open!

Wil and I stared at each other.

"Guess Denise didn't lock up after all," I said.

"Maybe she didn't turn the key all the way." Will shrugged. "Or maybe her stepdad got back early."

"*Hope* not," I said.

Wil stepped inside and gestured for me to follow.

"I feel funny going in without Denise," I said.

"Don't reckon she'd mind our making a quick call," Will drawled.

I found the telephone on a stand in the dining area, but no phone book.

"Can't remember Mr. Willy-Bones's number," I said. "I'll have to call information."

There were pencils in a jar next to the phone. I tossed one to Wil. "Use this to write the semaphore letters you figured out."

He took the paper from his pocket, sat down at the dining table, and started writing. An information operator finally gave me the pet shop's number. I jotted it on a scratch pad, then dialed. There was no answer.

"He can't *still* be out buying his lunch," I said, hanging up before the recorded message had a chance to come on. "He must be getting doughnuts for his afternoon snack."

Wil leaped to his feet. "Speaking of chow, how about we amble over to Sam's?"

"Didn't you have lunch yet?"

He nodded. "But that was two hours ago. And I'd like to sample their Tex-Mex—compare it with Shirlee Alabama's."

I tore the top sheet from the scratch pad. "I'll take this number along and try later from a pay phone."

"So do we exit this place by front gate or back?"

"The front door," I said. "The way we came." I was anxious to leave. The house felt strange, different. Was a chair out of place? Something about the curtains?

We stepped onto the sandy patio.

"Shouldn't we lock up?" Will asked.

"We can't without a key."

On the way over to the oyster bar I asked Wil how he had made out with feeding my pets.

He grinned. "A snap!"

Outside Sam's Oyster Bar, Wil grabbed my arm. "The green T-bird—it's heading into the parking lot."

We rushed across the sand. By the time we reached the asphalt parking lot under the pier, Evil Eyes was already gone.

"Let's check out his car," said Wil.

"But what if he sees us?"

"Then you keep watch," said Wil. "I'll check it out alone."

I stood guard a few yards away while Wil walked around the car, looking in the windows and trying the doors.

"Hurry up, Wil." I looked around, feeling more and more scared. "If he catches us—"

A hand clamped my shoulder and yanked me around. "Wiseacre kid! What're you up to *this* time?"

I stared up at my own reflection—on the shiny black surface of Evil Eyes's sunglasses.

# 14

# A Secret Visitor

Lump Face hunched beside Evil Eyes. Up close he looked even lumpier.

"Wil!" I screamed.

Wil raced over. Evil Eyes let go of my shoulder and turned to scowl at him.

"Whatya doing, messing around my car?" he demanded.

Wil gulped. "Just looking. It's a . . . a real classic."

"I don't like nosy kids messing around my car."

"And we don't like 'em spying on us," Lump Face added with a snarl.

"But we weren't—"

"Shut up, brat." Evil Eyes shook his fist at me, then at Wil. "Clear out—both of you—before I call the cops."

The two men lunged into the green T-bird.

"Wish they *would* call the police," I said as the car roared out of the parking lot. "Or maybe *we* should."

Wil shrugged. "But we don't know if they broke the law."

"Not yet," I said. "But they're planning to."

He shook his head. "According to the law, that's not sufficient evidence."

"Why? We know they're waiting for a delivery of birds," I said.

"They didn't say they were being smuggled—"

"For gosh sakes, Wil! They wouldn't come right out and *say* it. We have to assume—"

"The law won't let you assume. You need proof."

"So what do we do? Trail them, to catch them in the act? We can't do that, Wil. It's too dangerous."

He tugged at his ear. "Wish Dad was here. He'd know what to do."

"Wil, I'm scared."

"It'll be okay." He gave me a comforting smile and started walking. "That ol' guy at the pet shop might have some ideas," he said. "Come on. From Sam's you can phone him."

Following Wil into the Oyster Bar, I felt awful. We were almost positive those two guys were smugglers— and we couldn't do anything about it.

At Sam's we sat at the same table we had eaten at before. Tim took our order. Wil gave him a toothy grin and pointed to the menu.

"A bowl of that Tex-Mex!"

"Sorry," Tim said. "New item. We won't be offering it till this weekend."

Wil looked disappointed. He rubbed his chin. "Then how about . . . a glass of milk? And a hunk of that sourdough bread with butter? But *no* clams."

"Just apple juice for me," I told Tim. "And . . . is there a telephone here?"

"By the door." He pointed. "But it's out of order."

I jumped up. "Forget the apple juice. I'll meet you later, Wil. I'm going back to the beach house to make that call."

Outside I noticed a green car starting down the gravel driveway between the row of beach houses and the highway. The car disappeared before I got a good look at it, but the turquoise green was definitely the shade of Evil Eyes's T-bird. But how could I trail him on foot? I continued along the beach to the patio of the beach house.

Before going in, I shook my sneakers. No sense tracking more sand into the house.

Then it hit me! Today the tile floor was shiny. That's what was different. Yesterday's sandy tracks were gone! And the secret visitor who had swept the floor

must have taken away the tumbler and the wildlife magazine, too. But who was it?

Were there more clues inside? As I reached for the door to slide it open, I heard a noise. My hand dropped.

Was someone in the beach house?

• • •

# 15

# Where Is WB?

I raced back toward Sam's. Then I saw Wil running in my direction, waving his arms.

"M.D.K. !" he shouted. "Guess what?"

"The floor of the house," I cried. "It's *clean*—"

"Tim told me—"

"And I heard—"

"—he knows Evil Eyes—"

"—a noise inside!"

"And he says—"

Face to face by now, we stopped yelling and began to laugh. Then Wil pointed to me. "You first, M.D.K."

When I told him that someone had taken a broom to the tile floor, Wil only shrugged.

"The maid, prob'ly, or a cleaning service. That's who left the door unlocked, I s'pose."

"But I heard a sound, from inside the house."

"Maybe Denise's stepdad really is back."

"She didn't mention it this morning on the phone," I said.

"Wait'll you hear *my* news," Wil said enthusiastically. "I got to talking with our waiter. On a hunch I described Evil Eyes Perry—and Tim knows him!"

"But he told Denise he *didn't*."

Wil shook his head. "Didn't know what car the guy drove, that's all. Tim says Perry and his lump-faced friend come to the oyster bar all the time." Wil clamped a hand on my shoulder. "And get this, M.D.K.! They're friends with Denise's stepdad *and* a bunch of old ex-surfers who hang around the pier."

"Like the Old Geezer?" I asked.

"And maybe the Parrot Man, too."

I started up the incline from the beach. "We've got to find a phone. I must tell Mr. Willy-Bones about Evil Eyes."

"Tim says the nearest pay phone is across the highway."

We hurried to the crosswalk, and as soon as the light turned green, we dashed across Pacific Coast Highway to the phone. Between us we dug up enough dimes to call Pacific Cliffs.

"Read me the number while I dial," I said as I handed Wil the paper I'd torn from the notepad at the beach house.

He frowned. "Why'd you write it twice?"

"But I *didn't*." I stared at the two numbers—the second in someone else's handwriting. "It must have been there already. I never noticed."

"Who else would want to call the pet shop?" Wil asked.

"Not Denise. Until I introduced them, she didn't even know Mr. Willy-Bones. And she told me Floyd didn't know him either."

Then I gasped. "Only one person up here knows Mr. Willy-Bones. Evil Eyes Perry! Remember? He even said he'd phone the pet shop when he had some birds to sell."

Wil scowled. "What would ol' Evil Eyes be doing in the beach house?"

"He knows Floyd. Tim said so. That means he knows that Floyd's gone . . . and the beach house is empty," I said. "What better place for Evil Eyes to run his smuggling operation?"

Wil shook his head. "Pretty far-out theory, M.D.K."

"There's something else I forgot to tell you. After leaving Sam's, I saw a green car on the road behind Denise's beach house. I'm almost positive it was—"

"Hey, girlie?" A gum-chewing surfer leaning against his upright board glared at me. "You gonna make a phone call or what?"

Flustered, I dropped in the coins and dialed while Wil read me the number.

Again no answer, and after three rings the answering machine. This time I had to take a chance. I waited for the beep and began babbling—about Evil Eyes and deliveries and the Fish and Wildlife people. In the middle of it all a second beep sounded. My time was up.

We left the phone to the sullen surfer and crossed the highway.

"I'm not even sure what I said," I told Wil. "Or if it made sense. Or if I told all I meant to. I *hate* talking to answering machines."

Wil grinned. "Never talked to one."

By now the sun was low over the ocean. Cars were pulling out of the parking lots, and the beach crowd was thinning. Only a handful of determined fishermen still dangled their lines off Malibu Pier.

"Must be after five," I said. "I've got to be getting home."

Wil nodded. "Tomorrow's Friday—the big day," he said. "We should meet early, in case the boat Evil Eyes is meeting arrives at noon."

"And if it doesn't?"

"We'll just have to camp out till midnight."

"I don't care if Shirlee *does* object," I said. "I'll be there!"

While waiting for the bus, Wil handed me the semaphore notes. "You'll need them to look up the signals at the library."

On the ride back to Pacific Cliffs, I puzzled over Shirlee's doodling. "If the *X*s stand for deliveries of baby parrots . . . then that 'WBX' must mean one delivery at 'WB'—"

"Whatever town that is."

I drew in my breath. "Oh, Wil—'WB' is not a *town*."

"What is it?" He started to grin. "Whale Barnacles?"

"No," I said. "It's Mr. Willy-Bones, otherwise known as Wilhelm Bjornson!"

# 16

# The Zero Hour

I stepped through the front doorway and sniffed. Fried chicken! That was a switch! Why? I wondered. What happened to all those jars of chili?

Shirlee got up from the E-Z lounger and switched off the television. "Thought you were goin' to stay home all day today, Miss Margaret."

"Changed my mind," I said.

She looked down her thin nose at me. "So where have you been?"

"Out."

Shirlee eyed me suspiciously. "Not gallivantin' after lawbreakers, tryin' to be a hero, are you?"

"Me? Why would I do a silly thing like that?"

"Hmph," she snorted. "Not silly—dangerous!'

She stomped into the kitchen. I followed, trying to

convince myself she was no criminal, but only my well-meaning, nosy sitter.

During dinner I had no chance to ask what *she* had done all day. She began asking more questions as soon as we sat down. It was like being on trial.

"Did you go up to Malibu again?" Shirlee demanded.

Did she know? I stared at her, then nodded. "For a little while. . . . Wil wanted to . . . go surfing."

So it was stretching the truth. But Wil *might* have gone surfing, if we hadn't been trailing our suspects.

Her eyes narrowed. "You didn't talk to strangers?"

"Of course not."

"You're sure?"

The way she said that so quickly, I could tell—she *did* know! I drew back. "Well, I . . . talked to the bus driver . . . and to people fishing on the pier." That was true, anyway.

After I finished eating, I jumped up from the table.

"Why don't you go watch TV?" I said. "I'll do the dishes tonight."

Her red eyebrows arched, then she smiled. "Why, thank you, Miss Margaret. I *am* tired—it's been a busy week."

I'll bet!

But instead of settling in front of the TV, Shirlee headed for the den.

"Going to bed this early?" I asked.

She gave me a tight-lipped smile. "A busy day to-morrow."

Her door closed. I had no chance to ask, "Doing what?"

It didn't matter. I already knew. She and Jerome had those two deliveries to make in Malibu, and the one delivery here in town to 'WB'—Wilhelm Bjornson. But deliveries of what, I didn't want to know.

While loading the dishwasher, I thought about Mr. Willy-Bones. Even though he seemed to know Shirlee, I still couldn't believe he was plotting and planning with the smugglers.

Maybe I should try one more time to call him.

But before I got the chance, the phone rang.

I grabbed it on the first ring. It was Denise. Since Shirlee didn't come running, she must be asleep already.

"Did you get the semaphore message to Wil?" Denise asked. "Was it important?"

"We figured out part of it and hoped you could unravel the rest. But how can you by phone?"

"I will copy it and have a try," Denise said. "Should be a cinch, if you have watched as many episodes of *Wheel of Fortune* as I have."

Pulling out the paper, I read the letters and the blanks to her.

"Simple!" she said. "You start with vowels." There was a pause. "I'm not sure about the first word. But obviously the next one, *Z*, blank, *R*, *O*, is 'zero.'" Another pause. "*N*, blank, *A*, *R*, *S*, is 'nears,' of course. And the last word—"

"Wil suggested 'bird,'" I said, trying to be helpful.

"Ridiculous. 'Bird' has only one *D*. Undoubtedly it ends in a *Y*. But I don't know what the vowel is after *B*. So the word is either 'baddy' or 'beddy' or 'biddy'—"

I rubbed my forehead as I tried to think. "Shirlee is Jerome's girlfriend, so he wouldn't call her an old biddy."

"I have it!" shouted Denise. "It is 'buddy.' He called the Geezer 'old buddy.' "

Knowing the signs for *E*, *U*, and *Y* made it easy for us to figure out more words. As Denise and I worked together, I scribbled in the letters. Then I read from my scribbling.

"Listen to this," I said. " 'The zero' . . . something . . . 'nears. Are you ready, old buddy?' "

"Obviously 'zero *hour*,' " Denise cried. "The hour at which a previously planned operation takes place."

"Meaning the arrival tomorrow at twelve of the smuggled birds," I announced triumphantly.

Now for sure it seemed that the Parrot Man and the Old Geezer were on the side of Evil Eyes and his fellow smugglers. But what about Shirlee?

"Incidentally, after my optometrist's appointment I checked Jerome's mailbox," Denise said. "Thought there might be another letter from Brazil."

"Denise! Tampering with the U.S. mail is a federal offense."

"I didn't tamper. I looked," she said. "But the box merely contained another reminder about that Old-Timer Lifeguards' beach party on Friday at Malibu.

'Food, fun, frolic with friends.' Sounds ghastly."

"Just so they don't get in our way when we track down the smugglers," I said.

"What is tomorrow's schedule?" she asked.

"We meet Wil on the bus that gets here at nine," I said. "So we have to take care of the pets really early."

"Would it help if I assist with the birds after I tend Hilda and Conrad?"

"It would!" I said. "Oh, and I almost forgot—I discovered when I took your notes up to Wil in Malibu that someone broke into your beach house last night."

"Was a window smashed?"

"No! No broken locks, either. It was really mysterious."

"You are positive someone broke in?"

I recounted the clues: the swept floor, the pet shop's telephone number on the notepad, and the unlocked door.

"Oh my gosh," said Denise. "Floyd will have a *fit*."

"When will he be back?"

"This weekend sometime."

"He's in for a surprise," I said. "My theory is that Evil Eyes uses your place as a headquarters for his smuggling operation."

"M.D.K., that is absurd!"

"I know," I said. "But what other explanation is there?"

Suddenly I heard Shirlee's door open. As she padded into the kitchen, I slammed down the phone.

"Couldn't sleep," Shirlee said. "Too much on my

mind. Think I'll make myself a cup of cocoa. Want me to make some for you, too, sweetie?"

"No, thanks."

I went to my room and flopped onto the bed.

But before switching off my light, I opened my sketchbook and flipped past the lists of clues and evidence. On a blank page, I printed in huge purple letters: AT LAST, THE ZERO HOUR!

# 17

# Lookout for Smugglers

It was still dark when my alarm went off. I dragged myself out of bed. The sound of muffled voices came from the kitchen. Was it burglars? I panicked. Should I stay in my room, or make a run for the front door? Then Shirlee's familiar cackle calmed me. There was nothing to fear.

Or was there? I kept forgetting that I was sharing the house with a smuggler's moll capable of almost anything! And for Shirlee to be up this early was highly suspicious.

Quickly I put on my purple T-shirt and white shorts—fresh from the dryer. Yuck! Shirlee had even *ironed* the shorts. Oh well—I guess she was only trying to be nice. But . . . would a member of a smuggler's gang do that?

Maybe we were wrong about her. Or was this a trick of Shirlee's to throw me off?

I pulled on my sneakers, grabbed my pack, and rushed into the hall. On hearing a man's voice, I skidded to a stop.

"Mrs. Alabama, does this go too?" I recognized the voice. The Parrot Man!

"You bet!" said Shirlee. "Put it in that box over there."

Put *what* in a box? Were they stealing Mom's silverware? I ran back to my room. Now what? Those two mustn't see me leave. Luckily Mom had left the screen off my window, for quick escape in case of emergency. And this was an emergency!

I tossed my pack, then jumped. Was I glad we didn't have a two-story house. But as I dashed across the front yard, Shirlee and Jerome came out of the house, carrying two big cardboard cartons. I ducked behind a thick eugenia bush. They mustn't find out I was on my way to Malibu.

Parked at the curb was a battered blue van. Why was it here? What were they up to?

I watched them load the boxes into the van. At least they weren't stealing Mom's silver. She didn't own that much. They brought out two more boxes. What was in them? As soon as Shirlee and Jerome again disappeared into the house, I rushed to the van and peered in.

"*Away!*" squawked the red parrot from inside the van. "*Go away!*"

Jerome came running. I fled down the street without looking back. Had he seen me or not? Long after the sound of Casper's screeching had died, I kept running. My heart still pounded when I got to Bun's yard. But by the time I fed him and left, I had calmed down.

On the way to feed the tortoise, I met Denise. She was carrying a blanket and a big beach bag.

"Rising at dawn is *so invigorating.*" She fluffed her hair. "I even had time to play with Izzy. I decided to keep her—no matter what Floyd says."

While scattering lettuce for the tortoise, I told Denise about the van and the cartons Shirlee and Jerome were loading.

"Possibly containers for transporting smuggled birds."

"But if the boxes were empty, why carry them so carefully?"

Denise rolled her eyes, gazing upward as if in a trance. "In time the answer will reveal itself." Then she grinned. "How ironic. A week ago I never *dreamed* we would be friends and I would be assisting in the apprehension of underworld malefactors."

"I guess," I said, not sure what she meant. "But how strange—it was all because of that red macaw. When he ruined Hilda's leash, I needed money quick and went looking for clients in Edgecliff Estates. . . . You saw me . . . we became partners . . . you saw that reward notice—"

"Rather like that old saying: 'For want of a nail

the shoe was lost, for want of a shoe the horse was lost—' "

"Never mind." I couldn't see what horses had to do with parrots. "Your bag looks heavy. What's in it?"

"Books, Floyd's binoculars . . . and sufficient sustenance to last until midnight—if necessary."

"Let's hope it isn't."

We fed the canaries and rushed for the bus, getting to the stop as the bus eased to the curb. Wil sat up front. I flopped beside him and rested my pack on my knees. Denise settled into the seat behind us.

We were quiet once I'd filled Wil in on the strange activities of Shirlee and Jerome. Halfway to Malibu I suddenly thought: What if the smugglers never showed up? I turned to Wil. "This *could* turn out to be a wild goose chase."

"Wild parrot chase, you mean." He grinned.

"What if Mr. Willy-Bones never got my message? What if he never called the Fish and Wildlife agents?"

"Don't worry," Wil said. "I'll bet the pier is already swarming with undercover agents."

"How do we recognize them?"

"Prob'ly won't," drawled Wil. "Otherwise they wouldn't be undercover, would they?"

As soon as we got off the bus, we hurried across the Coast Highway.

"Let's set up our command post close enough to the pier so we can spot the boat when it arrives," Wil said.

"Sorry I cannot let you use the beach house," Denise

said. "But my mother forbade me to go near it. She is coming up this afternoon to discuss the break-in with the authorities."

After some searching, we found a deserted stretch of beach south of the pier, halfway between the beach house and the water's edge.

"Perfect," said Wil. "And we've also got a good view of Sam's and the parking lot."

"And of the beach house, too—in case it's the hideout of Evil Eyes." When I said that, they both gave me weird looks.

We dubbed our location Station One. Denise spread the blanket on the sand and brought out potato chips and lemonade.

"Two of us at a time can go on patrol," Wil said between gulps of lemonade. "Whoever's at Station One can survey the whole area."

"What if there's an emergency?" I asked.

"The person at Station One can wave a blanket," Denise said. "And since we patrol in pairs, one of the two can run back."

"Right." I crunched a potato chip. If things got desperate, would I still remember all those rules?

Wil looked thoughtful. "Prob'ly the smugglers will dock at the end of the pier in one of those fishing boats."

He and Denise took the first patrol. As they started off, Wil pointed. A boat plowed toward the pier, a flock of hungry gulls circling overhead.

"This could be it," he yelled to Denise, and off they went.

Soon they were back.

"False alarm," Wil told me. "Denise and I'll check Sam's and the parking lot. Keep your eyes peeled for smugglers."

I scanned the beach crowd. It was like when I fly with Mom and we scan the skies for traffic. Only this time I was looking for Evil Eyes and his gang. I didn't see them anywhere.

By noon we'd raced to the pier a dozen times to check out fishing boats. All were just that: fishing boats. By then we had finished all the lemonade and chips and most of the apples and muffins Denise had brought. I dug into my pack.

"Time out for emergency-supply trail mix," I said.

After that Wil and I went on patrol. That's when we saw the blue van. It was in the parking lot, and unloading cartons from it were Jerome and the Old Geezer.

"The Loathsome Twosome!" shouted Wil.

I peered through the binoculars Denise had lent me. "Should we close in?"

"First let's see what they're up to. . . . Maybe they'll make contact with Evil Eyes."

I scanned the crowd with Floyd's heavy binoculars. A bag lady in a striped stocking cap pulled in a fish, but there was no sign of Evil Eyes.

Next I checked the ocean. Beyond a string of small sailboats with brilliant spinnakers, two power boats zoomed toward shore. Gulls circled above one of them, which probably meant it was a fishing boat with a good catch.

Suddenly Wil shouted. "Jerome is heading for the beach. The Geezer, too. I'll trail them."

"Wait!" I shouted. "I may have spotted—" But already Wil was loping across the sand.

# 18

# Trapped!

I couldn't follow Wil. My legs weren't nearly as long as his. I'd never catch up. Should I alert Denise? No. I'd stay here to find where those power boats were headed.

Near shore they separated. One nosed toward the pier. The other turned south.

Clutching the binoculars, I ran up the incline next to Sam's Oyster Bar. That fishing boat would dock soon. Were the smugglers aboard? I had to warn the Fish and Wildlife agents.

Sneakers thumping, I raced along the wooden pier. Visible through cracks in the boards, the surf roared onto the sandy shore, then surged back again. Farther out, beyond the breakers, the blue-green ocean lay beneath me. It was a long way down. I grew dizzy.

At the end of the pier, past the sightseers and people fishing, I stopped. What now? Who in that mob were undercover agents? I couldn't very well call out, "Hey, agents!"

Feeling like a real dork, I turned around and ran back along the creaky pier to Sam's. I scooted down the sandy incline onto the crowded beach. Glancing toward the parking lot, I spotted Evil Eyes. He was climbing into his car. Then the green Thunderbird roared from the lot, pulled onto Pacific Coast Highway, and headed south.

He was taking a load of smuggled birds to the pet shop in Pacific Cliffs—that *had* to be it! We were too late. The smugglers had slipped past us.

Now it was Mr. Willy-Bones I had to warn. I raced to the beach house to phone him. Even if it was Evil Eyes's hangout, he was gone. It was safe now.

I pushed the sliding door at the front. It wouldn't budge. Had Evil Eyes locked it? But that was impossible. He'd need a key.

I crept around through the shortcut at the side of the house to check the back door. It was unlocked. What luck! I slipped inside and tiptoed through the kitchen and into the dining area. Then I stopped. In the living room people were talking.

But who? Evil Eyes was on his way to Pacific Cliffs. I crouched behind the counter to listen.

". . . so first thing tomorrow we'll come by." The man spoke with a deep, husky voice. There was a pause.

Then he said, "Right. . . . With the birds. . . . See you then. . . ."

It wasn't two people. It was one man, talking on the telephone. I recognized the rumbly voice. It was Lump Face!

I backed into the kitchen, darted out the back door, and raced for the garage. That was the quickest way out.

Before my hand touched the doorknob, it began to turn.

Someone was coming in through the garage.

I ran to the side yard and pulled the gate closed behind me. Then I stood motionless.

The door to the garage squeaked open, then slammed shut. All was quiet. Then feet thumped on a step. Paper rustled—a grocery bag, maybe? A door opened and closed.

Whoever it was had gone in the back door. He—or she—was now in the beach house. Trying to escape through the front patio was risky. The garage was still the way to go.

But when I tried the door, it was locked.

I dashed to the side yard again, then crept through the shortcut to the front. Before pushing open the gate, I had to make sure no one was in the patio.

The gate was a foot higher than the top of my head. I looked around for something to stand on. I spotted a small corrugated-cardboard box. That might work. After dumping out the weeds, I turned the box over and stepped on it gingerly. Then I peeked over the top of the gate.

Horrors! Lump Face and Evil Eyes were sitting in the patio.

I was trapped!

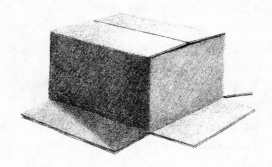

# 19

## A Prisoner

I hopped off the box and huddled on the brick path, hugging my knees. What now? I was right about Evil Eyes. He *had* taken over the beach house for his hangout. But being right didn't solve my problem. How was I going to get away from here?

The garage was locked. The fences around the beach house were much too high to climb. As for leaving through the front patio, forget it! Those two were *smugglers*! If they found I was spying, they'd be furious. No telling what they'd do to me.

What I needed was my pack. It contained things I could use right now, like a bandanna to wave for a signal to Wil and Denise, or paper to fold into an airplane so I could sail an SOS message over the neighbor's fence. My Swiss Army knife would be the most useful of all right now. I could pick the lock in the garage door.

I could even make a run for it. With my knife I could defend myself as I raced past those two.

Was there anything useful in the trash from that box? As I sifted through the weeds in it, I found a yellow-green feather. But this downy-soft feather was not from a gull! It must have come from a baby parrot!

This was my proof that there *was* a smuggling operation. And this beach house was its headquarters.

But being right didn't help much this time either. I was still a prisoner.

"Hey, Ernie?" It was Lump Face's gravelly voice.

Were they about to make plans? I jumped back on my box to eavesdrop. The two men wouldn't notice. They had their backs to me.

"I told you to get grape," Lump Face grumbled. "Didn't the 7-Eleven have any grape?"

"Yeah, they had grape."

"Then how come you didn't get any?"

"Eat your orange Popsicle and stop complaining. . . ."

They weren't making plans. Evil Eyes hadn't delivered smuggled birds to Mr. Willy-Bones. He had gone to the 7-Eleven for Popsicles!

Was I wrong about the feather?

"But I don't *like* orange. . . ." Lump Face was still grousing.

I licked my dry lips. A cold, sweet, sticky, juicy Popsicle—any flavor—would taste so good that I tried not to think about it. I was so hot and thirsty, I was ready to faint.

"How come you didn't get grape, Ernie?"

" 'Cause Floyd only likes orange. So knock it off, willya?"

Floyd? Then it wasn't a break-in. Floyd knew they were there. But if he was back from his fishing trip, where was he?

"All I'm sayin' is *next* time—"

"*Shut up!* I'm trying to concentrate on what I'm doin'."

Evil Eyes had finished his Popsicle. He was scanning the beach with binoculars.

"Whatya see?" Lump Face asked.

Evil Eyes mumbled something I didn't hear.

Whatever he was looking at, I wanted to see it too. I lifted the binoculars hanging from my neck and rested them on the top of the gate.

I scanned the beach. The Parrot Man waved semaphore flags. At first I thought he was signaling the two men at the beach house. But Evil Eyes paid no attention. I looked more to the left. On a bluff the Old Geezer stood, waving his flags.

"So whatya see?" Lump Face asked again.

"Boat's at anchor . . . the dinghy's heading for shore."

What boat? The smugglers'? Ignoring the Parrot Man, I scanned farther out. I couldn't locate the boat they talked about. But I saw the dinghy, bobbing and tipping in the surf. Three men were trying to drag it onto the beach.

"Floyd's havin' a little trouble," said Evil Eyes.

Floyd? Was he one of the *smugglers*? How awful! How would I ever tell Denise?

"The dinghy's tipping!" cried Evil Eyes.

"Lemme see!" Lump Face snatched the binoculars.

Elbowing him away, Evil Eyes grabbed them back.

While they fought over the binoculars, I watched the little boat. A huge wave scooped it up and flipped it over. Around it the surf was dotted with orange blobs. What were they?

Waist-deep in water, the men floundered, grabbing for the blobs.

"The jackets! They got dumped out!" yelled Evil Eyes.

"Think we oughta go help 'em?"

Why all the excitement? Those men wouldn't drown. They were *already* wearing life vests. Why did they need more?

Suddenly my cardboard box began to sag. With both hands, I grabbed the gate top.

"*Yikes!*" I cried as the gate swung out, taking me with it.

I dropped onto the sandy patio floor. Before I could scramble to my feet, Evil Eyes grabbed my shoulder.

"It's the wiseacre kid!" Evil Eyes snarled. "What're you doin' here?"

"Nothing. Let me *go*!" I tried to break free. "I didn't do anything. . . ."

"You been spyin' on me." Gritting his ugly yellow teeth, Evil Eyes leaned over until his face was close to mine. "Whatya think, I'm stupid or something? I saw you and your little friends up on the pier."

"But we *weren't* spying." I began to cry.

"Gimme the binoculars, Ernie. I want to see how Floyd's doing."

Evil Eyes didn't give them up. "No. You take care of our wiseacre friend," he said, running from the patio. "I'm going down to help."

Lump Face locked pudgy hands on both my shoulders and called after him. "Whatya want me to do with her?"

"Lock her in the closet," Evil Eyes shouted, "—for now."

# 20

# Contraband

"**G**et moving."

When Lump Face ordered me into the house, I dug my heels into the sand. He struggled to drag me in.

Suddenly I screamed. "Behind you! *Look out!*"

The oldest trick in the book—but the lunk fell for it. He turned around. His grip loosened. I squirmed free and ran across the patio. Then I whirled to face him.

"You want binoculars? *Here! Take these!*"

Yanking Floyd's heavy binoculars from my neck, I swung them by the strap and let go. They struck his shoulder. Lump Face reeled back, and I sprinted.

The Old Geezer was just ahead. I wasn't sure I could trust him. But I had no choice.

"Help!" I shouted, pointing back at Lump Face, who was chasing me. "He's a smuggler. And those guys . . ."

I waved toward the beach. ". . . in life vests . . . smugglers too . . . baby parrots . . ."

The Geezer flipped his two flags for a couple of seconds. Then he charged at Lump Face. For an old guy, he was fast—and strong. He planted a fist in the lunk's doughy stomach. Lump Face went down, and when he scrambled to his feet, the Geezer came at him again. He raced for the beach house, the Geezer on his heels.

I headed for the men from the dinghy. Evil Eyes was with them now. They staggered up the sloping beach. Their wet pants and shirts stuck to them. Each man wore a life jacket and clutched two or more. What was in those jackets?

"*M.D.K.!*"

I turned. Wil ploughed toward me through the soft sand.

"Where you been?" he called. "We searched *everywhere!*"

"Long story . . . come on." I broke into a run.

Wil jogged beside me. "But Denise is looking for you. . . . We should tell her—"

"No time. . . . Those guys . . . with the orange vests. They're smugglers."

"You're sure?"

"Positive. . . . No time to explain. . . . Trust me." In the dry sand my feet sank. It was like running through molasses.

"Cowboys' bumpers! Ol' Floyd's with them."

"He's part of the gang. . . . So is Evil Eyes."

When we got closer to the men, I began to shout.

"We know what you are!"

They walked faster.

"Everybody knows!" I yelled. "We've caught you—"

"Get lost," one of them yelled. All the men began to run. They split up.

"We'd better split up too," said Wil. He zoomed off.

"*Yahoo!*" The loud Texas shout echoed down the beach. Wil leaped over a kid's sand castle and tackled Evil Eyes.

I chased a short, fat man—the slowest of the group. He zigzagged around the kids playing ball. Closing in, I snatched at one of the vests the man carried.

"Get lost, punk!" he shouted.

"No way!" I yelled at him. "We'll tell the FBI . . . the lifeguards . . . the police."

He glowered down at me. "I said beat it, kid."

People glanced up from their sunbathing and card playing.

I screamed even louder. "We've called the Fish and Wildlife people. . . . They're here. . . . You're smugglers, and *we've caught you!*"

Now sunbathers and card players leaped up and formed a semicircle around the man and me. He tried to slink away, but I snatched at one of the life jackets he was carrying.

He snarled and backed off. "Brat! Leave that alone."

I grabbed again. The man twisted away, dropping the orange vest on the sand.

I reached for it.

"Give that *back!*" he shouted.

I took off, but my feet sank deep into the dry sand. I tried to go faster as the man started after me. But I couldn't. Then two surfers lunged at him, knocked him to the ground, and sat on him. A lifeguard raced over, blowing his whistle.

Jerome ran past, the squawking parrot perched on his shoulder and three lifeguards running beside him.

"The guys . . . with the life jackets!" I yelled. "They're bird smugglers."

The guards and Jerome ran on. But I couldn't go another step. Panting, I flopped onto the beach with the orange vest.

"M.D.K. !" Denise stood over me. "Where have you *been*? We thought you were *kidnapped*."

I sat up. "Almost was—by the smugglers."

She looked back toward the pier. "But we were watching—"

"The smugglers landed on the beach."

A lifeguard truck sped by on the hard, wet sand at the water's edge. Another followed close behind. From the other direction rolled another official-looking car. Its siren wailed.

"Come on, M.D.K.!" Denise yelled. "We have to help."

"Hold it," I shouted. She stopped, then dragged back. "They only had two left to catch." I didn't add that Floyd was one of them. "By now they must have them all."

Denise stood drooping on the sand. "Apprehended already. And I missed it all."

"Maybe not *all*." I pointed to the life vest in her hands.

"Feels lumpy," Denise said, patting it.

Then she gasped. "Listen! Hear that?" From under the jacket's orange nylon cover came a faint bleating sound like a baby lamb.

"Denise," I said. "There's a *bird* in there."

# 21

# Two Mysteries Solved

We had no trouble finding a Fish and Wildlife agent to give the orange life jacket to. By now uniformed officers seemed to be everywhere.

Afterward Denise and I sat for a long time, talking. I told her what had happened at the beach house, and about the feather, and as much as I knew about Floyd. She cried when she found out.

"I'm really sorry, Denise. Even if he was a crim— I mean, even if he broke the law, he *was* your—"

She broke in. "That's okay. It was just a shock. . . . That is all." She got to her feet. "I think I had better phone my mother." She managed a half smile. "M.D.K., if I go up to Oregon to stay with my dad for a while . . . would you look after Isadora for me?"

I nodded. "Sure. What's one more pet?"

Denise's mother was already at the beach house when

159

we got there. As I left them, to head down the beach to look for Wil, I turned to wave to Denise. "See you soon, partner."

She grinned and waved back. "You bet!"

By now sunbathers had returned to sunbathing, card players to card playing. Kids were again building sand castles. Music from transistor radios and the sweet smell of coconut suntan oil filled the air. Frisbee games started up again.

I met a Fish and Wildlife agent carrying one of the orange life jackets.

"Will the baby birds be okay?" I asked.

She smiled. "Those I've seen so far are just fine. They're luckier than most. As far as we can tell, they're just scared—and terribly dehydrated. They'll be all right, I think. We'll get them to an animal hospital right away."

"Then what happens to them?"

"Those that survive both the stress of their illegal entry *and* the rigors of quarantine will be sold at auction. Run by the U.S.D.A."

I looked up, puzzled.

"U.S. Department of Agriculture," she explained.

"I hope someone nice buys them," I told her.

"Maybe you will—with your reward money."

I gasped. I'd forgotten the reward. The five hundred dollars was ours. Wow!

Then I shook my head. "I almost bought a parakeet. But I've been thinking about birds and cages. I want my parakeet to live in a bird zoo."

She nodded. "In a cage so big he won't know it's there, right?"

I grinned. "Right!"

Wil stood at the water's edge, watching surfers help lifeguards beach Floyd's blue-rubber dinghy.

"That was a surprise about ol' Floyd," Wil said.

"I was just thinking about all those life jackets in his garage," I said. "I wondered why those brand-new ones were ripped up. Now it makes sense."

Wil nodded. "And when Tim told me about Floyd and Evil Eyes being buddies, I had a hunch there was more to his trips to Mexico than catching fish."

I smiled at Wil. "Should've followed through on that hunch."

We walked behind three Fish and Wildlife agents who were moving up the beach toward the pier. I pointed to a grungy character joking with them.

"See that bag lady in the striped stocking cap?" I whispered to Wil. "I saw her earlier, fishing from the pier."

"Undercover agent, prob'ly," Wil said.

"So I finally found out what they look like."

Wil stopped and sniffed. "With all that's happened, I must be getting delirious," he said. " 'Cause I swear— I smell chili."

I pointed ahead to where a cluster of old people surrounded Shirlee Alabama. "I'll bet what she's heating over my dad's camp stove is her world-famous Tex-Mex."

"Why would she do that?"

"Because I *think* this is the Old-Timer Lifeguard Association get-together," I said, grinning at Wil. "Remember that postcard in Jerome's trash?"

Wil slapped his thigh. "Detective Kincaid, you did it again."

"Hey!" he added. "That must be what the semaphore message was about. Maybe the Geezer's an ex-lifeguard too."

"And that's why Shirlee made all the chili, I'll bet. Then she and Jerome hauled it to the beach party in those cardboard cartons—" Suddenly I shrieked. "*Beach party!* That's it, Wil. That's the 'BP' in the note!"

Shirlee looked up. She gave a cackly laugh when she saw us.

"What're you-all doin' here at the beach?"

Wil grinned. "We thought we might do a little surfing." He winked at me.

"Long as you're here," Shirlee said, "get in line. . . . Join the party. Did you catch the excitement down the way?"

We nodded and tried to look nonchalant.

Dad's little propane camp stove couldn't begin to keep that huge pot of Tex-Mex hot. But I was so hungry, and Shirlee's chili was so hot with spices, that even stone cold it tasted good.

"What's the occasion, ma'am?" Wil asked after we gobbled down the chili and were returning the bowls.

Shirlee pressed her thin lips in a smile. "Get-together of all the old lifeguards who worked this beach. My friend Jerome used to be a lifeguard, you know."

I looked at her. "Why didn't you tell me why you were cooking so much chili?"

"You never asked," she said.

"That's a lot of work, ma'am," said Wil. "To feed a mob this size."

"It's my new business," Shirlee told him, her pointy chin jutting out proudly. "A caterin' service. . . . Didn't want to tell your daddy till I was sure how it'd work out. But it's doin' just fine." She looked around and beamed. "Why, I've lined up customers from Santa Monica to Malibu—"

I broke in. "Like maybe Mr. Willy-Bones?"

"That nice Swedish fella?" Shirlee nodded. "Him too. Why *ever'body* seems to like my Tex-Mex. Including my new partner." She fluttered her lashes at Jerome, standing nearby. "So I guess I'm in California to stay."

From the pocket of her jeans she took two business cards and handed them to Wil and me. The cards had red-checkered borders and said SHIRLEE'S TEX-MEX. SURELY THE BEST IN THE WEST.

# Shirlee's famous Tex-Mex recipe

1/8 lb. finely chopped suet *

3 lbs. Round Steak, cut up

6 Tbsp. Chili powder

1 Tbsp. ground oregano

1 Tbsp. crushed cumin seed

1 Tbsp. salt

1/2 to 1 Tbsp. Cayenne pepper

2 large garlic cloves, chopped

1 Tbsp. hot pepper sauce - "if
          you dare!"

1 1/2 quarts water

1/2 cup white corn meal or
      3 Tbsp. masa harina

      Fry suet until crisp - add meat &
brown. Add seasonings, water & boil.
Simmer 1 1/2 hrs. Cool & skim fat. Stir
in cornmeal. Simmer 30 minutes.
      Serve with

                        corn bread and
                    gallons of iced tea!

* 3-4 Tbsp. of Crisco or cooking
    oil may be used instead

# THE
# FORESHADOWING

*Marcus Sedgwick*

WENDY
LAMB
BOOKS

Published by Wendy Lamb Books
an imprint of Random House Children's Books
a division of Random House, Inc.
New York

WENDY LAMB BOOKS and colophon are trademarks of Random House, Inc.

www.randomhouse.com/teens

Educators and librarians, for a variety of teaching tools, visit us at
www.randomhouse.com/teachers

Library of Congress Cataloging-in-Publication Data

Sedgwick, Marcus.
The Foreshadowing / Marcus Sedgwick.
p. cm.
Summary: Having always been able to know when someone is going to die,
Alexandra poses as a nurse to go to France during World War I to locate her brother
and to try to save him from the fate she has foreseen for him.
ISBN 0-385-74646-6 (alk. paper)
[1. Extrasensory perception–Fiction. 2. World War, 1914–1918–France–Fiction.
3. World War, 1914–1918–England–Fiction. 4. Nurses–Fiction. 5. Great Britain–
History–George V, 1910–1936–Fiction.] I. Title.
PZ7.S4484For 2006
[Fic]–dc22
2006005135

Printed in the United States of America

10  9  8  7  6  5  4  3  2  1
First Edition

Lines on page 97 from "Song of Cassandra," © 1999 John Gilbert

*For Fiona Kennedy,*
*my superb editor*

ACKNOWLEDGMENTS

I would like to thank the following for their assistance with the research for this book: Helen Pugh and the staff of the Red Cross Museum and Archives Department, the helpful members of staff at the Imperial War Museum, Martin Nimmo and Sue Rubenstein of mybrightonandhove.com, and Elizabeth Garrett, for her invaluable research into Clifton Terrace, and Brighton in general, in 1916.

I have found many books invaluable for capturing the spirit of the time, including Vera Brittain's *Testament of Youth* and *Chronicle of Youth,* Enid Bagnold's *A Diary Without Dates,* Robert Graves' *Goodbye to All That* and Captain Dunn's *The War the Infantry Knew. A Brief Jolly Change,* the diaries of Henry Peerless, edited by Edward Fenton, was not only informative, but delightful to me, since it features members of my own family.

*So, believe me, or not,*
*What does it matter now?*
*Fate works its way,*
*And soon you will stand and say,*
*my words were true.*

AESCHYLUS, *Agamemnon*

# PART ONE

# 101

I was five when I first saw the future. Now I am seventeen.

I can't remember much about it. Or maybe I should say I
*couldn't* remember much about it, until now.

For years all I could recall was laughter, nervous laughter,
and later, silence, then later still, anger. I felt ashamed, guilty,
hurt when I thought about it, but I had quite forgotten what
*it* was. Or rather, I had made myself forget.

Memories, half hidden for twelve years, have started to
surface, in bits and pieces, until I see a picture of that day
long ago, when I was just a little girl.

We weren't living in Clifton Terrace then, with my wonderful view of the sea, but I don't know where we did live. There
was a big garden, bigger than the one we have here. I was
playing in this garden with another girl about my own age.

Edgar and Tom were young then too, and even played with us sometimes when they weren't trying to fall out of the big cooking-apple tree.

It was summer, and the girl and I were best friends. Her name was Clare, and she was the daughter of friends of my parents. It was a long and happy afternoon, but eventually it was time for Clare to go home.

And this is the part I had pushed away and hidden in the depths of my memory for so many years.

I was standing in the hall, giggling with Clare while grown-up chat buzzed above our heads.

Then I said something. I said something that stopped the grown-ups talking and started the silence.

"Why does Clare have to die?" I asked.

Because no one said anything, I thought they hadn't heard me, so I tried again.

"I don't want Clare to die tomorrow."

Then they did start talking, and I knew they had heard, because Mother was scolding me, and Clare started crying and her mother took her away.

I was wrong. Clare didn't die next day. But I was only five, and, I suppose, didn't understand that *tomorrow* meant something more specific than *soon*.

Soon, however, I *was* right. Clare died of tuberculosis. It came quickly and there was nothing the doctors could do to save her. I can remember very clearly now wishing I could have helped her. Stopped her dying.

Then the silence started.

Not long after, we moved house, here to Clifton Terrace, and gradually I forgot all about that day when I was five.

Until now.

# 100

I have seen the future again, and it is death. I can no longer pretend it is my imagination.

I wasn't sure. That I had dreamt about something that came to be might just have been a coincidence. It was a month ago that I dreamt George had been killed. The morning after my dream Father was reading the *Times* at breakfast.

"George Yates," he said, without looking up. "That's Edgar's friend, isn't it?"

Mother nodded.

Father read from the paper, still without looking up.

" 'Captain George Yates died of wounds, Vermelles, September 26, 1915.' "

I was too shocked to know what to think.

"Poor George," said Tom.

"Poor Edgar," Mother said, thinking of her other son. Her elder son, away somewhere in France.

Clumsily she began stacking the plates from breakfast. Tom, my other brother, rose to help her.

"Edgar is fine," Father said. "He's a strong young man."

Now he looked up from his paper for the first time, to fix his eyes on Tom.

"And where's that blasted girl?" he went on, meaning Molly, our maid. "Don't we pay her enough to do that?"

Tom ignored him and carried the plates out to the kitchen.

"No harm will come to the strong," Father said. "The brave."

He started to read the casualty lists again. I don't know why he has to do it. He spends all day with the sick and the dying in the hospital.

"Where is Molly?" Father snapped.

"Cook's away and Molly's busy," said Mother.

"Alexandra," Father sighed. "Help your brother."

I jumped up and tried to lend a hand, but I could only think about George. He had been at the front; he had been killed. That was not unusual, not anymore. But I had dreamt that it had happened, the night *before* news of it had reached us.

Was that possible?

Over the following days I tried not to dwell on it.

I continued my studies during the day with Miss Garrett and in the evenings I sat with Mother. She's always busy organizing her circle of friends, as well as running the house, and Cook, and Molly, who's sweet, but scatterbrained.

I tried again to persuade Father to let me help around the wards, but still he refused. He says it's not fitting for a girl like me, and once his mind is made up, it usually stays that way.

6

Although I tried to forget George, I couldn't. Images of his death came to me; I don't know where from. One morning I was sitting at my mirror, brushing my hair and thinking how long it was getting, when into my head came a picture of George's mother reading the telegram that gave her the news. I saw George caught on the wire, the barbed wire of the no-man's-land between our trenches and the enemy's. But that may have been my imagination. I don't know how he died.

I was frightened, but the days passed and I told myself it was a coincidence. Thousands of men are being killed in France each week, and the fact that I dreamt about the death of one of them could be nothing more than chance. I even wondered whether I might have already heard about George's death and not taken it in. Maybe it had already been posted in the lists and Father had missed it. It seemed unlikely, but I clung to this explanation until time allowed me to put it to one corner of my mind, if not to forget about it entirely.

But after what happened yesterday, I can no longer pretend it is my imagination.

Mother and I were walking down Middle Street. We passed the Hippodrome, where I used to love to go to see the circus when I was little. I dawdled outside, remembering a silly act we'd seen there once featuring Dinky, the high-diving dog. Mother pulled my hand.

"Come on, Sasha," she said. Sometimes she still uses my pet name, as though I'm her little Russian princess.

The sea was in front of us. It's late October, and there was a grim gray sky above us. Waves were being whipped against the seawall by fierce winds. As so often, the town was full of soldiers; a mass of khaki uniforms.

We would have walked up to the hospital to see Father, but it looked as if it might start to rain any moment. People scurried past us; a horse and empty cart hurried for home, its driver glancing nervously at the sky.

"We'll take the tram," Mother said, so we turned and cut through to the Old Steine, to the stop outside Marlborough House.

There was a long queue. Everything was perfectly ordinary as we waited for the tram. When it arrived the ladies jostled a little to be first on, but in a good-tempered way.

Mother looked at the gathering clouds.

"Come on," she said, taking my hand.

"No," I said.

She glanced round at me, surprised.

"Don't play games, Alexandra, I'm cold and it's about to rain."

"I'm not," I said.

I didn't know what was wrong.

I just knew I didn't want to be on the tram. That I *mustn't* be on it.

A soldier waiting behind us was impatient.

"Come on, darling," he said, "get a move on."

But I didn't move.

I could see Mother was embarrassed. The soldier pushed past, bumping into me as he got onto the tram. He spun round on the step. I stared straight into his eyes.

"Sorry, gorgeous, can't hang about," he said. There was a cheeky smile on his lips, but as he looked at me, the smile lost its life, and died on his face.

I *knew* he was going to die. I don't know what else I can say. I saw it. Not in France, not in the war, but soon. Here.

"Are you feeling all right?" Mother said, not cross now, thinking I was unwell.

"I don't want to go on the tram."

"Sasha . . . ," Mother began, and then stopped. She sighed.

People pushed onto the tram, but the soldier stood on the step, still looking at me. Mother saw him, and I think it was that, and no other reason, that made her let me have my way. I knew what she thought about "rough" men.

"We'll walk," she said, and the tram moved off.

As it went, the soldier was still staring at me.

I watched it go. Mother tugged at my arm, impatiently, but I couldn't move. It was as though I was rooted to the spot. It all happened very slowly then. But somehow very quickly too. The tram got up to speed and rumbled away toward Grand Parade.

The rain began to lash down then, very suddenly.

A wheel lifted from the tracks somehow, on a point, maybe. The tram came off the rails and lay down on one side with a tremendous crash. It hit a wall and there was a shower of sparks and rubble.

I was aware of noise all around us. The noise of the tram hitting the wall seemed to take the longest time to reach us, and to be the quietest sound. The sound of screaming was the loudest.

Mother finally dragged me away. Last night, before I went to bed, I asked her why we had left, and she told me that there was nothing we could have done. That lots of people, too

9

many, perhaps, had immediately swarmed around the tram to help others off. The police had arrived, and ambulance cars took the injured to the Royal Sussex, where Father used to work until he was put in charge of the Dyke Road hospital. I still feel I should have done something. I should have helped.

This morning I read in the paper that most people in the accident had not been too badly hurt, but that one man had been killed.

A soldier.

Thinking back to yesterday, I remember feeling one emotion from my mother. Fear. But not fear of the accident.

Although she doesn't know that I have remembered, I know what she's thinking about. She's thinking about a day long ago, when I was five.

War. That's all there seems to be.

It's all around us. Nothing is unaffected by it, no one is immune. Everyone has suffered, everyone has lost someone, or at least knows someone who has. There seems to be little else in the newspapers, little that anyone talks about.

It is over a year now since the war began, but it seems no time at all since I sat listening to my brothers arguing about it, and with Father, too. I was sixteen then, and not supposed to have an opinion. But I sat and listened, in the corner of the room, while they talked. It may have been the actual day we declared war on Germany.

Edgar and Father were very excited, Tom was quiet.

"You don't want to enlist in the ranks," Father said to Edgar. "You can take a commission. With your OTC experience you'll be snapped up."

"It would have been better if I was a regular already," Edgar said. "It'll all be over before I get there. By the time I get a commission and hang around on a parade ground for months, it'll all be over."

"Then better you don't delay. Move quickly and you'll get your share of the glory."

I was listening to Father, but I was watching Tom. Edgar and Father stood by the dining room table, poring over the morning's *Times*.

Tom was gazing out at the sea lapping way beyond the West Pier, his thin frame silhouetted by a bright summer's sun outside. It made me think as I often did that it was hard to imagine my two brothers were related. Edgar's so much bigger, and stronger. He never seems to worry about things, he just does them, whereas Tom worries about everything and everyone. I'm told that once, when I was little, I was crying about a dead bird in the garden, and he put his arm round me and told me that animals go to heaven too. I don't suppose that's true, but he wanted to make me happy. That's how much he worries about people.

Father turned to him.

"Never mind, Tom," he said. He meant because Tom was still only seventeen, and too young to enlist for almost another year. "You can still go to Officer Training Corps and then you'll be ready. Maybe the war will still be on."

"Father!" Edgar exclaimed. "Don't talk nonsense. That's the sort of rot the pacifists spout."

Father didn't like being spoken to like that, not even by Edgar.

"Edgar," he said, tersely. "I am simply trying to keep

Tom's chin up. It's a shame for him to miss out when you'll be away fighting."

Edgar glanced at Tom.

"He wouldn't go anyway," he snarled. "He's only too glad he's too young."

"What do you mean?" Father said.

"Just what I say."

"That's an unkind—" Father began, but Tom interrupted him.

"It's true," he said.

That stopped us all for a moment. It was the first time he'd spoken.

"What?" Father spluttered. "You're not falling for all this Socialist nonsense, are you? I won't have a pacifist in my house!"

"No, Father," Tom said. I could see he was scared of Father. "No," he said. "I'm not a pacifist. But I don't want to fight."

Father tried to interrupt, but Tom was brave enough to keep talking.

"I want to train to be a doctor," he said. "Like you."

What could Father say to that? He calmed down a bit.

"That's a good thing, Thomas," he said. "A good thing. But there's a war on now. If the occasion arises for you to do your bit, then you must! You will go and fight."

He seemed to think that was an end to the matter, but I, for some unknown reason, decided to speak.

"Why should he go and fight," I said, "if he doesn't want to?"

Edgar turned on me.

"Stupid girl! You don't understand anything about it. Don't interfere."

I wasn't surprised. Edgar says things like that to me. If he says anything to me at all, that is, these days.

I could feel my face flushing red.

"I only let you stay here because I expect you not to speak," Father said. "You don't understand these matters. That's all there is to it."

He sent me to my room. Tom forced a smile as I went, but I could hear their row go on as I went upstairs.

I shut myself away, and stared out to sea. I suppose I should have been hurt by Edgar, and Father, but I'm used to their ways. That's just how Father is, with everyone in the house. Not just me. Mother, too. I wonder sometimes what she was like when they got married, but I can't picture her. I only know her as she is now, at Father's beck and call. But I know he loves us, really. I know he does. And Edgar, well, it's simply that it's not that long since we were children, and we had fun sometimes. It's just sad it's not like that anymore. We've all crossed a line; it has to happen sooner or later. Even Tom and me. I know I'll never be as close to him as when we were children, however much I try.

I could half see my reflection on the glass, and half the world outside. Across the waves, not so very far, I could imagine France. Everyone I knew was excited about the war, everyone in town, and we heard later there had been mass celebrations in London, in Trafalgar Square.

I looked across the water to France, and felt like the only person in the world who thought the war was a bad thing. That only bad things would come of it.

14

# 98

As I came down to breakfast this morning I heard my parents talking. I was late. Mother had let me sleep in after the business with the accident.

Something made me wait awhile on the darkness of the stairs. I gripped the mahogany banister tightly, feeling its familiar smooth, dark surface under my touch. I remember sitting there as a child, watching Cook and the previous maid going about their business. I'm far too tall to sit on the stairs anymore, though somehow I'd still like to.

Then I heard Mother say something about the tram.

"Nonsense!" Father said, loud enough for me to hear clearly.

Quickly I moved down to the bottom of the stairs. My hand hovered by the dining room door handle. I knew if I went in they would stop talking.

"But Henry," she said, "what if we *had* got on? We might have been desperately injured. Even killed."

I didn't hear Father's reply.

"Well, you explain it, then," Mother said.

"I don't need to because it's ridiculous."

Suddenly I heard Father walking to the door. It sprang open.

"Alexandra!" he snapped. "Always watching, always prying!"

He plucked his coat and hat from the stand and went off to work.

"Father, wait!"

He had left his armband behind.

As soon as the war started he had been sworn in as a special constable of the Brighton Borough Police. He goes patrolling the streets two or three nights a week. What for, I don't know, but he has to wear an armband to show his status.

He looked at me and took the armband.

"See if your mother needs help," he said as he left.

"With what?" I asked. The door was already shut.

What with being a special constable and his work at the hospital, he is hardly at home these days. The New Grammar School was only open for a year before the war turned it into the Dyke Road hospital, which Father now runs. It's not the only school that's become a hospital.

In the evening, while Father was still patrolling, I tried to talk to Mother while she sat doing needlework.

"Mother," I said, "are you all right now?"

She stopped and looked at me.

"What do you mean, Sasha?" she asked, smiling.

"After the accident," I said. "I thought—"

Her smile disappeared. "We weren't hurt, were we? Whatever do you mean?"

"I know, but it was such a shock!"

She looked away.

"Yes," she said, "we had a lucky escape. If you hadn't . . ." She paused.

"What?"

She didn't answer, so I tried again.

"What? If I hadn't told you I didn't want to get on the tram? Is that what you mean?"

"I'm busy, Alexandra. Don't pester me."

The moment was lost. I wasn't Sasha anymore, I was Alexandra. But I wouldn't let it drop.

"That's it, isn't it?" I said. "That's what's bothering you. How did I know we shouldn't get on the tram?"

"That's enough!" she said. "You didn't *know* we shouldn't get on. I decided not to. We had a lucky escape. That's all."

"But I knew!" I insisted. "I knew."

"Don't be ridiculous," she shouted, with sudden anger. "Now go to bed before your father gets home."

I was so amazed that she'd shouted at me that momentarily I stood motionless; then I ran upstairs.

My room, like the sitting room, has a clear view of the sea, even from the bed. It's the most wonderful thing I have, my view. I can see across the little gardens that belong to the whole street, then away over town to the sea itself. When we moved into Clifton Terrace I begged to have the room in the attic so I could see the sea, and though Edgar and Tom protested, I got my wish. I think it was the only time I ever made a fuss as a child.

17

I sat on my bed, and wondered. I wondered about the war, and what it was doing to people. But can I really blame the war for the arguments between Father and Edgar, and Tom? Or for Mother's shouting at me? Or are those things there anyway, but just not seen until now?

Night waves washed along the summer shore, like a gentle thunder in some show of pretending. I gazed across the sea to the real night horizon, and felt the storms over the water. I knew the thunder rolling across the fields of France was no pretense.

# 97

It was a bright and bone-chilling day today, a sign that winter is not so far away.

I went out for the first time since the accident. A piercing wind sailed in off the sea and up Ship Street as I went down to the seafront. It cut right through me even though Mother had made me put on my warmest overcoat.

It was on another sunny day, though a warm August one, that Edgar went away to join the army. He decided to put his training to become a lawyer on hold, and didn't go back to Oxford that autumn. Instead, Father made some 'phone calls, and just as he said, Edgar got a commission. He had been on OTC camp; he had been to a good school. The army was eager to have him. He spent a couple of months at the regimental depot, learning to drill and be drilled, and whatever else officers need to know.

For a while he wrote to us, complaining that the war

19

would be done before he had even started, but he need not have worried. The news from France was bad. There was a miserable article in the *Sunday Times* about heavy British losses, and the general invincibility of the German army. Even though the war had really only just begun, it had become a dreadful stalemate, and wounded were arriving in Folkestone and Harwich every day.

They had said it would all be over by Christmas, but Christmas came and went, and the war stayed. In the new year Edgar got the posting he had been waiting for, and went to France. Since then most of another year has come and gone, and still there is nothing but the war.

# 96

On many occasions I've asked Father if I might help in the hospital, but he says nursing is no occupation for a girl from a respectable family. If the truth be told, he thinks I shouldn't have any occupation at all, but just wait for someone of the right sort to marry me. The right sort means rich, and from a good family. But I want to do something. I think I really do want to be a nurse. It goes way back to when I was tiny; I always wanted to be useful, but when you're a little girl no one takes you seriously. You're not allowed to help people.

People like Clare.

I was only trying to help, but somehow that day put a wall between me and my family, a wall of guilt and fear.

I've grown up now, and I still want to nurse. Edgar is mean to me about it. Ever since I was little he teased me, saying I would be scared, and that I would faint as soon as I saw

21

blood. Then Tom would tell him to shut up and they'd start to fight instead, until I would cry and that stopped them both.

But I think things may have changed, because I heard Mother and Father talking this evening after they'd gone to bed. I can often hear them from my room. I don't think they realize how thin the ceiling and floor is between their bedroom and mine.

I stopped brushing my hair and bent down to the floor, pressing my ear against the boards.

"She's quite a young woman now," I heard Mother say. "She's pretty, but she's even more intelligent. And she's seventeen. You know she wants to do something."

"It's still not the sort of thing she should be engaged in," Father replied. "You don't know what they're like, Dorothy. They're a rough bunch of girls."

He meant the nurses in his hospital.

"Perhaps," Mother said, "but they do the job that needs doing. And the war is changing things."

"Don't preach to me about my own profession," Father said, curtly. "If Alexandra becomes a nurse, you know the sort of people she'll have to deal with."

"She could join the Women's Emergency Corps. That's only for decent women. The uniform alone costs two pounds."

Father snorted.

"If by 'decent women' you mean suffragettes . . ."

"Well, she'll have to do something. Sending her to Miss Garrett's for private tuition is all very well for now, but what then? You know what she's like. All that sitting, watching. She should have something to occupy her."

"Are you talking about Alexandra now? Or do you mean to bring up your own complaints again?"

"No, Henry, no," Mother said, quickly. "You know I'm content. Really. But Alexandra . . ."

"Maybe," Father said. "We'll see."

"And she's always wanted to be a nurse."

"And you know why!" Father said, suddenly raising his voice. "You know when it started!"

Mother hushed him and their voices fell quiet, so that I couldn't hear any more.

So there was hope after all! I couldn't sleep for a long time, but when I did I dreamt of playing with Clare in that summer garden, where she was alive once again.

# 95

Last Easter, about six months ago, Edgar came home on leave. We sat around the dining table at Sunday lunch, just as we always had, but something was not the same.

Although he'd been away for just a few months, Mother stared at him as if she'd never seen him before. He looked very smart in his captain's uniform, it was true.

"Well, my boy," Father said, beaming. "Tell us about the army."

Tom pulled a face, which only I saw.

"Actually, it's been a pretty dull show," Edgar said. He couldn't hide his disappointment. "We've been in reserve mostly. And the other officers . . . I get a hard time because I'm a special reserve captain."

"Never mind," Mother said, smiling. "You're doing your best."

Father nodded. "Your chance will come."

"Yes, you're right," Edgar said. "And you'll get your chance too, Tom, after all. You'll be eighteen in July."

We all looked at Tom.

"Well, Thomas?" Father said. "Edgar's right."

"I want to be a doctor," he said, slowly.

That afternoon, we went out for a stroll along the seafront, past the West Pier, and along to Brunswick Lawns. What a fine, proud family we must have looked. Mother and Father arm in arm. Father was well known, and respected, and men nodded to him as he walked, with his children behind, me in the middle, Tom on the right and Edgar on the left, in his uniform.

The lawns were very busy, though before the war they would have been packed on a fine afternoon, and the ladies' clothes much more flamboyant. We passed a family we knew, with their invalid son in a chair. Father had treated the boy for many years, though without much success. His father smiled as we passed.

"What a fine daughter you have, now, Mrs. Fox!" he said, and Mother smiled, but I thought about their son. I looked away.

The sun shone and gulls cried overhead when suddenly, I saw a flash of color at our side. I looked round to see a young woman in a dark blue dress approaching us. She had two friends with her, girls a little older than me, also in expensive dresses. Before we even knew what was happening, the girl was talking to Tom.

She was very pretty, and at first Tom smiled as she pressed something into his hand.

Tom looked down at what she'd given him and his face fell. It was a white feather.

The girl muttered something and hurried off to rejoin her friends.

"But I'm not even eighteen yet," Tom protested as she went.

We went home straightaway, and no one said a word.

# 94

When we got in there was an awful row.

Edgar didn't even have to say anything. The look on his face was enough to tell Tom what he was thinking.

"The disgrace!" Father snorted. The white feather meant the girls thought Tom was a coward, shirking his duty in the war.

"But I'm not even eighteen," Tom said, again and again. "Why didn't any of you tell them that?"

"But it's true!" Edgar said. "You don't want to go to war. It doesn't matter what age you are or aren't. There's a name for people like you!"

"Edgar!" Mother cried. "Stop it."

Without realizing it, I held her hand.

"It'll only get worse," Father said, "the older you get. When people know. You have to do your bit."

"Is that all you can ever say?" Tom shouted at Father. I

27

shuddered. None of us has ever raised our voice to him, but strangely, Father let it pass.

"That's all that counts," he said.

"What?" asked Tom. "Going to war? Killing?"

"Not killing," Edgar said. "Doing your bit. That's all. Fighting for what's right."

"You haven't even done any fighting," Tom spat at Edgar.

That really upset him. He stormed over to Tom, and for a moment they looked like they did when they were young boys, Tom trying to stand up to Edgar, even though he is five years younger, and so much weaker.

"That's not my fault," Edgar shouted. "And when I get the chance, I'll fight. I'm no coward!"

"Is that what you think I am?" Tom said angrily.

Maybe Edgar hadn't meant that. I don't think he did, but now the word was spoken, it seemed impossible he could take it back.

"Yes. Coward."

Tom stood rigid, his face drained, his teeth clenched. He took a deep breath.

"All I want to do," he said finally, "is to go to medical school. I'd rather save men here than kill them over there."

He stepped past Edgar, and, avoiding Father's eyes, made his way upstairs as calmly as he could.

# 93

When we were children, we fought about little things, and sometimes Tom and Edgar would fight because Edgar had been mean to me. It seemed deadly at the time, but we all grew up, and the years between Edgar and Tom and me began to tell. The two of them bickered instead of punched, and while Tom and I were still close as we got older, Edgar grew distant, and paid me no attention.

The argument over the white feather reminded me of all that. Except now we were fighting about something truly deadly.

That was six months ago, the Easter of 1915. Edgar went back to the war, and got his wish. He wrote to us that his battalion was being called up from reserve and would soon see real action. Mother is very worried, but tries not to show it. Father is proud.

Tom has gone, though not to the war but to Manchester to study medicine.

I miss him. My brother who is almost a twin to me, although there is a year between us.

But something good has happened. I don't know why, but Father has finally agreed to let me spend some time on the wards at the Dyke Road hospital, to see if I want to go into nursing properly.

At last! This is my chance to show everyone that I can be useful, that I can help people.

Tomorrow, I will see what the future has in store for me.

# 92

"Sister Cave will take you round," Father said. "Stick next to her. Don't say anything unless she asks you a question, do everything she tells you to. And don't get in anyone's way."

He walked away down the dimly lit corridor. Sister's about my mother's age, I suppose, and quite friendly, but I felt nervous. If anything were to go wrong Father would never let me come back.

We pushed through the half-glass doors and were in the ward.

"Wait here while I get the trolley," Sister said.

Ahead of me I could see the beds, but it was nothing like a normal hospital ward. The building had been built as the new boys' school only two years ago, but as soon as the war had started it had been commandeered as a military hospital. In this makeshift arrangement, the beds are crushed in tight together.

It was all very quiet. I don't know what I'd been expecting but I was surprised that there wasn't more noise. I took a couple of steps forward, and noticed another room opposite the one Sister had gone into.

The door was open. Something made me take another step and I saw a man in pajamas sitting on a wooden chair. He was young, but had thinning hair.

He gazed intently ahead, but when I came closer, I saw nothing but a blank white wall.

I jumped as I heard a clatter behind me, and turned to see Sister wheeling the trolley toward me.

"Right, Alexandra. Or should I be calling you Nurse now?"

I smiled and looked back at the man in the white room, a question on my lips.

Sister came over. "Him? Mental case."

She said it loud enough for him to hear, but he showed no sign of having done so.

"Nothing we can do for him."

She emphasized the word *we*.

"Doesn't he do anything?" I asked. "Say anything?"

"Occasionally," she said. "But it's all nonsense."

"What's his name?"

She looked at a chart by the door.

"Evans," she said. "David. Welsh. Heaven knows how he ended up here."

She moved off with the trolley, and I followed.

We went from bed to bed, and Sister dispensed medication. She gave morphia to those in pain, but for many there was nothing to do.

Then came a moment I had been dreading.

"We need to change this dressing," Sister said.

I looked down at the man in the bed. He was at least twice my age, and I felt my lip tremble. He was only half awake, but as Sister pulled back his sheets, he hissed in pain and his eyes shot open.

"We'll be as fast as we can," Sister told him, and he nodded. His face showed no expression at all.

The wound was in his thigh, and Sister deftly cut off the old dressing and dropped it into a metal bin underneath the trolley.

"Good," she said. "No need to inflict iodine on you today."

She smiled at the man, then turned to me.

"Pass me that one," she said.

I handed her the clean dressing, and she bandaged his thigh again. She moved so rapidly I barely had time to realize how disgusting the wound was, how there was no muscle where there should have been.

Everything was going well, and I felt proud of myself, though still nervous.

Then we came to the last bed.

The man who lay there was younger than all the others. Sister smiled.

"Not much to do here either," she said. "He's nearly better. Gas case. His eyes and lungs were damaged, but he's on the mend. Be back in France before he knows it."

"Where's Nurse Gallagher today, then, Sister?" the man asked.

"You've got me today. And this is Alexandra. She's a special visitor, I'm showing her the ropes. You can be my guinea pig.

"Lungs," Sister said. "And look. Take a close look at his eyes. Can you see the inflammation of the tear ducts?"

I leaned right up to the man and peered into his eyes.

"Of course, it was much worse, nearly better now."

That was the last thing I heard Sister saying.

I looked into the man's eyes, but I didn't see inflamed tear ducts. I saw an empty bed. I saw death.

I think I began to shake, and then I heard the man speak.

"My God," he said. "My God. Her eyes!"

He tried to back away from me, squirming in the bed.

"Her eyes!" he shouted again, and other people began to call out from their beds.

Then he began to cough and choke.

"What does he mean?" I asked. "What's wrong with—"

"There's nothing wrong with you," Sister said quickly, "but you'd better go home. I'll tell your father."

"No!" I cried.

"Don't worry, it's not your fault. Go on."

She turned to soothe the man, who still lay hacking and coughing in bed.

As I went I took a last look, and saw him staring back at me. I was too far away to hear him, but I could read his lips.

"Her eyes!"

It's late now and I'm in bed.

I didn't have long to wait until Father arrived home. He came up to my room.

"I heard there was some trouble," he said, standing in the doorway.

"It wasn't anything to do with me," I began, but he held up his hand.

"I didn't say it was. The hospital is full of damaged men, Alexandra. Sometimes it's not their bodies that are damaged."

34

I nodded.

"Is he all right?" I asked.

"Physically, yes. He'll be home in a week."

I said nothing. Nothing of what I've been thinking.

Father took a step into the room.

"You did well today," he said.

"That man, you're sure he's going to be all right?"

"Absolutely," Father said. "But you must understand. If you want to be a nurse, you'll see plenty more men who won't be."

I've tried to sleep, but I can't.

Father says the man is all right, Sister said so too, but I know that he's about to die.

I know it.

And there's something else: what he said about my eyes. I have spent all evening looking at myself in my mirror. I can see my long dark hair, the white skin of my face, and the redness of my lips, but in my dark eyes I see nothing.

Nothing.

# 91

Something is happening to me.

I knew immediately that that man is going to die. I didn't see anything specific, just a bed emptied of its body, a body emptied of its life.

I've waited all day for Father to get home. I need to ask him, yet I dread it, because I already know the answer. But I forgot that he was patrolling this evening, so he won't be home for another few hours yet.

Something is happening to me that I don't understand. And yet it's becoming clearer.

Clare.

When I saw what was going to happen to Clare, I was only five. What form do a five-year-old's thoughts take? I spoke then without hesitation, without self-awareness. I said what was in my head.

With George, Edgar's friend, well, that was just a dream. With the soldier on the tram, it was a sensation, but I didn't really know what I was feeling. But in the ward yesterday, I started to see something, a vision of death, and the knowledge of exactly what it meant.

And if I saw something, then so had he. He saw something in my eyes that terrified him.

If I can see the future, then what does that mean? It would be like knowing the end of a story right from the start, almost as if you were reading it backward.

And who wants to know how their own story ends?

# 90

Three days have passed since Father came home and told me he was dead.

His name was John Simpson. Each day I would ask how he was and Father told me he was fine.

"Are you trying to be a diligent nurse?" he asked, taking off his coat and hanging it in the hall. "Is that it?"

I shrugged, but next day when I asked, he was angry, and told me I was not a nurse in his hospital, not yet, and that I ought to spend more time supporting Mother, whatever that means. She's not allowed to do anything.

On the third day, the first thing he saw was me, waiting in the hallway.

He had a very grim look, and I was scared, but not really of his anger.

He made to walk past me to the drawing room, but I stood in front of him.

"How is he?"

Father glared at me.

I followed him into the drawing room.

"Simpson," I said. "How is he?"

"Alexandra, leave it be!" Father shouted. "You are obsessed!"

"He's dead, isn't he?"

The words tumbled from my mouth.

I had my answer. Later I learned that a pneumonic infection had set in suddenly.

"Why are you cross with me?" I asked Father. "It's not my fault!"

"Of course it isn't," he shouted as Mother came running into the room.

"But why do you think I kept asking about him?" I turned to Mother. "You know I kept asking about him!"

She looked from me to Father, then went and held his arm to calm him down.

"But I knew it was going to happen," I said. "I knew."

"You knew nothing," Father said. I could see he was tired as well as angry. "You are a silly girl who is too sensitive to be a nurse. A man has died, Alexandra! Show some respect. Please—go to your room."

I was only halfway up the stairs when I realized I'd been foolish to say anything. They don't want to talk about it, and now Father will probably stop me from visiting the hospital again.

I was stupid to say anything, but I couldn't help it.

I'm scared.

I have seen the future four times, and each time the future has been death.

# 89

It is November 1915.

The war continues, with no sign that it will end before this or any other Christmas. It's like an avalanche started by a single gunshot, but which roars down the mountain more loudly than a thousand cannons. Every day there are new complications, new engagements, new political battles.

Even so, there's some better news. Edgar wrote a few days ago and thinks he'll be getting leave soon. It will be good to see him and will put Mother's mind at rest too. To have one brother home for a few days might make things seem more normal. The house is much too quiet. Tom writes almost every other day from Manchester. I'm so proud of him for doing what he thinks is right, but I know it's been hard.

He says he's been white-feathered again in the street. When Father read that part of the letter he grunted and wouldn't read the rest, though Mother and I did later.

I only hope he gets to finish his training. There's been talk in the newspapers that the government might introduce conscription, and then that would be that. Tom would have to join the army whether he wanted to or not. But maybe he could join the medical corps, so he could at least keep on being a doctor.

I've been studying as usual, visiting Miss Garrett's house with the three other girls who attend her private lessons. And I've been trying to persuade Father to take me back to the hospital. So far he refuses to discuss it, though he himself said I did well on my first day there.

I know what he's afraid of.

# 88

Edgar doesn't write much. The last time was to tell us about his leave, but he did say that his battalion had seen action at last.

Father read the letter out loud at breakfast. Edgar is a captain. He is twenty-four. These two things seem not to belong together, but they're true. He has a company of men to command.

"I'll write to Thomas," Mother said.

"What for?" Father asked, looking up from the letter.

"To see if he can come home. When Edgar does."

"What for?" Father asked again.

"It will be nice for us all to be together."

Father put down the letter and took up the paper.

"The boys will want to see each other," Mother continued. "We ought to try to be together as a family when we can."

Father snorted.

"We won't know when he's coming," he said. "We may not get any warning at all, so you won't be able to tell Thomas."

"Well," said Mother, "we'll see. Maybe Edgar will be able to let us know."

"He won't," Father said.

Mother put down her teacup with a rattle in its saucer.

"And maybe he will," she blurted out. I looked up at Father, who had dropped the paper and stared at Mother. He got up and left the room without another word.

Mother stood up too without even calling Molly to clear the things away. I heard her open the back door and go into the garden. I stared at the tablecloth, a blue gingham. I noticed all the tiny crumbs from my toast lying on it, and then I noticed fat tears dropping onto them from my eyes.

I knew why Mother was upset, and I felt it too.

I sat by myself at the table.

# 87

There is no one I can talk to about what I feel, what I have felt each time it has happened. That it's just as real to me as any other emotion.

Mother won't listen to me, because she loves me too much. To her I'll always be Sasha, her little princess.

Maybe I could talk to Thomas. He's got a scientific mind, that's why he'll be a good doctor, but he's open-minded, too. I know he'd listen to me at least, but he's not here. I wouldn't even try to talk to Edgar.

Maybe I could talk to Miss Garrett about it. I'm not sure it's wise. I certainly wouldn't talk to the other girls in her class. They're so silly, and just spend their time gossiping and giggling. And odd things have been happening to me there, as well.

Small things, chance occurrences, coincidences.

I've been studying *The Iliad*, the story of Troy. Of Helen

44

and Paris, of Agamemnon and Clytemnestra. Today Miss Garrett broke off from her discussion of the death of Achilles and began to tell us about something else. She was very animated and engaging as she spoke of the recurrent symbols of myth.

Miss Garrett is amazing. She's not that young, and despite the fact that she's quite beautiful, she hasn't married yet. She went to university and has been teaching privately ever since. She has such energy in what she does. I want to do the same with nursing.

She was talking about specific symbolic meanings, and as she did, I knew just what she was about to say before she had said it. And as I felt this, I remembered a dream from last night, a vivid dream, which I had quite forgotten.

"I mention this," Miss Garrett was saying, "because we have been looking at the battles before the walls of Troy. Such dramatic events as these in human history of course give rise to many striking thoughts and images."

It was a strange feeling, and not a nice one, to hear her say exactly what I knew she was going to say, just a moment or so before the words actually left her lips.

"One such symbol that occurs in many mythologies, including the Greek, the Celtic and the Norse, is that of the raven. It has become a symbol of the battlefield, a harbinger of ill omen and death. Why? Because the raven is a carrion bird, and would have flocked to feed on the corpses of the Greek and Trojan warriors."

The raven.

That was my dream.

I saw a raven swooping down toward my face, all black beak and claws and feathers. The bird clawed at my face, and

I felt its feathers brush my hair, smelt their mustiness. It came back to me so strongly as I sat there that I was unaware of anything else, and even Miss Garrett's words came to me as if over a great distance. I felt as unreal as if I was a figure in a photograph, in black and white, not a person at all.

Though there were four other people in the room, I felt utterly alone.

# 86

As I was leaving Miss Garrett's yesterday, I asked her if I could borrow a copy of *The Iliad*.

She looked a bit surprised.

"I didn't think you were interested," she said coldly. "You appeared rather distracted in class."

"Miss?" I said, not knowing what to say. "Could you lend me a copy, please? I would like to do some more reading."

I don't think she believed me entirely, but after the other girls had gone she led me into a different room, one I have never seen before. Every inch of wall was lined with bookshelves. Only the windows and the fireplace were not devoted to books. She pulled the curtains to let in some more light and began scanning the shelves.

"The primers we use in class are a little dry. They miss out on so much," Miss Garrett was saying.

She stood on a small stool and pulled a book from a high shelf.

"Here we are," she said. "This was my copy when I was your age. You can borrow it."

She handed me the book.

"There's not just *The Iliad* in there. There're many other stories from the Greek myths too. I hope you will enjoy it."

I nodded.

"I'll take good care of it," I said, and she smiled.

I got home a little while ago.

I thought about the dozens—in fact, hundreds—of books on her shelves, and felt proud that she was happy for me to take the little leather-bound edition that belonged to her.

I've been reading it in bed. I thought I was looking for something, but I realize now I just wanted to read a good story, to escape from everything that's been happening in my head. The stories are full of deaths, awful deaths, and battles and tragedy, but somehow it's comforting. It reminds me that what's going on, what Edgar's been seeing, is not so unusual. And that reminds me that one day, things will be normal again. Things will be all right, if we all try hard enough to make them that way.

# 85

Edgar came home yesterday. The first we knew was when he sent a telegram from Folkestone to say he was about to catch a train to Brighton. Even if we got in touch with Tom now, by the time he gets here Edgar may have gone again.

As much as Mother wants her family to be together again, a part of me thinks that maybe it's for the best, really.

It was very late when Edgar arrived. Mother said I couldn't wait up any longer and sent me to bed, but of course I couldn't sleep. I heard him arrive sometime after the clock in the hall had struck twelve. I heard Mother's voice, high with excitement but not loud, and then Edgar's and Father's voices, deep and quiet.

He went to bed after just a few words—I heard him come up the stairs. He went along the landing on the floor below me to the bathroom.

Something felt different.

I wanted to see him, but I hesitated and listened as he came out of the bathroom and back to his old room again. I knew Mother would be cross, but I crept out of my room and looked down the stairs to the landing.

"Edgar!" I whispered, waving a hand.

He jumped and turned at his door in the dark hallway. I heard him breathing, softly.

"Oh, Alexandra," he said, looking up the stairs. "It's you. Go back to bed."

His voice was flat, and his eyes wouldn't fix on me.

"I'll see you in the morning," I said, trying to sound cheerful, but his door was already shut.

I lay awake, listening to the noises of the house. Boards creaking and the November wind rustling the empty branches of the magnolia beneath my window, brushing fallen leaves along the high pavement of Clifton Terrace. I could sense my parents and Edgar asleep in their rooms, lost in their own dreams, and though Thomas was missing, it felt almost normal.

# 84

I didn't see Edgar this morning. I woke with my head full of dark clouds, struggling to rouse myself. I think it was quite early when I finally dropped off. By the time I got downstairs Edgar had gone out.

"I hardly saw him myself," Mother said.

"Where's he gone?" I asked.

"He's gone for a walk," she said, as if it were a crime.

"He probably just wants to have a look at the town, you know. To make himself feel at home again."

"On a day like this?" Mother looked out the window at rain slanting across the houses and the sea in great gray swathes.

Lunchtime came and went. It's Sunday, and Mother asked Cook to make a proper Sunday lunch. We've had to skimp recently on those kind of things, and today she wanted it done properly, but Edgar still hadn't returned.

Father, Mother and I ate lunch without him, in the end, though much of it was cold.

"That was lovely," Father said, without smiling. "Thank you, dear."

It was suppertime before Edgar came back.

Not a word was said about where he'd been, or that he'd missed lunch. We all pretended nothing had happened, and sat down for some bread, cheese and cold meat. Father opened a bottle of beer for Edgar and one for himself. I watched as the beautiful dark brown liquid frothed into the glasses, making such a lovely, comforting sound. The clock on the wall ticked, very slowly.

"So," said Father, "tell us what you've been up to."

Edgar was staring at his plate, and methodically pushing food into his mouth. It was clear to me he didn't want to talk about anything.

But Father was quite unaware.

"What's been happening in your section? Much action? I expect you've shown the enemy a thing or two."

"There's not much to tell," Edgar said, and took another slice of bread. "We're doing our bit, you know."

"But you must have seen a sight or two," Father went on. "Tell us something."

"Yes," Edgar said, "we've seen a sight or two. Now, if you'll excuse me, I think I ought to go to bed."

He got up. Father frowned.

"But—"

"Henry," Mother cut in, "he's tired. Let him sleep."

I was surprised at Mother's boldness, but Father just

52

sighed and went off to the drawing room to read by the fire.

I stayed with Mother while Molly flapped around us, clearing away. When it was done we sat together for a while.

"Why?" I asked Mother, quietly.

"Why what, Sasha?"

I could hear the sick weariness in her voice, but I couldn't stop myself.

"Why won't you believe me? Why won't anyone believe me?"

I wished I hadn't said it.

Mother came round the table and put her arms around me.

"Please don't, Sasha," she said. "Please stop saying it. Please."

She put her face in my hair and began to shake and then I realized she was crying.

I stood up and held her.

"I'm sorry," I said. "I'm sorry. I don't want to upset you."

She said nothing for a while, but then stood back from me, wiping her eyes.

She was about to speak when we were interrupted.

"Will there be anything else tonight, ma'am?" Molly asked from the doorway.

Mother shook her head.

"No, thank you, Molly. Alexandra is just going to bed. We shall follow shortly."

I tried to hold Mother's eyes, but she wouldn't return my gaze. I went upstairs.

It's always the same. I'm their dutiful daughter. That's who they want me to be. And if I show the slightest sign of

53

being difficult or strange, they simply won't accept it. How I long to do something! If I don't, then it would be better to have been Clare; for my life to have finished before I did anything to upset anyone.

I got to sleep quite quickly for once, but I woke suddenly. I heard talking from Edgar's room. Then I realized it was just one voice. Edgar's. He was calling out in his sleep. Crying out.

Some of it sounded like people's names.

Then he began to whimper, like a beaten dog. It went on and on, then stopped. It started again, not so loud, and stopped again.

I think he's sleeping more peacefully now, but I'm wide awake.

What sights has Edgar seen to make noises like that?

# 83

Edgar has gone back to France, sadly before Thomas even knew he was in the country. It's a shame because Christmas is coming and at Christmas a family ought to be together.

He left a day early, too. He said in his telegram that he had six days, but he was gone by Wednesday morning. If I'm honest, though, it was a bit difficult anyway. Mother would be furious with me for saying something like that, but it's true. Edgar spent much of the time out of the house, who knows where, as if he was an animal that didn't like being locked up. When he was at home he was silent for the most part. Mother kept on smiling and having Cook put food in front of him. Father did all the talking, and spoke about the war and the army, while Edgar sat staring into the fire clutching a glass of beer with his big hands.

I sat and watched, pretending to read Miss Garrett's *Greek*

*Myths,* while inside I felt a sadness so strong it seemed to paralyze me.

It was strange that Edgar left early, as if he thought he would be more comfortable in France than he was here. What could make him feel like that?

When the time came for him to leave, Father said he would walk with him to the station, but he forbade Mother and me to go. He said we would only get upset. I have walked past the station a hundred times and seen women saying good-bye to their men, some calm, but many with tears streaming down their faces. Father is probably right, but I don't see what would be wrong with getting upset.

So the moment came for Edgar to say goodbye, and it was a moment I had been fearing, in case . . .

In case I should feel something.

He gave Mother a kiss, and she smiled at him, but there were tears in her eyes.

He took a step toward me. I froze. Then he put his arms around me and kissed me. It has been years since he has done that, since I was a child. I could feel him, strong and wiry under his smart uniform, and it was a surprise to me. And though he was home for five days and had a bath almost every day, I could smell the war on him still.

I could smell earth and things that I don't know the names of. A faint but clear aroma of something chemical that pricked the back of my nose, a smoky smell.

I could sense it all, but as my heart began to calm itself, I realized I could sense nothing of death.

I pulled away from Edgar, relieved, smiling.

"Have a good Christmas," I said, and almost for the first time since he had returned, he laughed.

"Bless you, Alexandra," he said, and then he went.

# 82

At last I have been able to get back into the hospital. Father called me to see him a few days ago. It was quite late and he was obviously tired, but he seemed to want to talk there and then.

"You're still serious about this nursing business?" he said.

I was taken aback, but this was no time to appear vague or uncertain.

"Yes, Father," I said. "Yes. I really want to do it."

"Very well, then. You may begin your training as a VAD nurse. You know what that is?"

I said I did. I'm seventeen, so it means I can work part-time in one of the hospitals, though I will live at home.

"You'll be among the youngest. There are Voluntary Aid Detachment nurses at my hospital. I've got you a place there, starting next week. But you'll have to fit this in around your studies, you understand that?"

"Yes, I do," I said. "Thank you!"

I smiled from sheer happiness.

"Don't let me down, Alexandra, will you?"

There was no smile on his face.

"No," I said, "I promise."

"Off you go, then," he said, as if I were ten years younger.

I turned, but then stopped. I had to know something.

I wondered if he had forgotten, or decided to ignore, the business with Simpson. Whatever else, I am pleased that nothing has happened since those three recent occasions when I saw the future. I hardly dare to think it, but maybe it has stopped. Things come in threes, after all.

"Father?"

"What?"

"What made you change your mind? About me working in the hospital?"

"That's none of your concern."

"Isn't it?" I said. I was taking a big risk questioning him, but I thought it too odd to drop the subject.

He looked at me, but I could read nothing from his face; as if he were a stranger.

"It was your brother," he said, eventually.

"Thomas?"

"No, Edgar."

"Edgar?" I spluttered.

"When I walked him to the station, he said you ought to have your chance. He convinced me. So I'm giving you your chance."

I smiled, my hand lingering on the brass doorknob.

"It's a good thing, Father," I said. "I believe I should have work to do."

"He also said he didn't think you were up to it."

He looked away out the window.

The smile left my face and I left the room. As I closed the door behind me, I heard Father say one more thing.

"Prove him wrong."

# 81

I spoke to Thomas on the telephone this evening, and Mother let me have almost the whole three minutes myself. Father didn't talk to him at all.

When I told Thomas about Edgar's visit and what he had done for me, he said, "That's wonderful," but you wouldn't have thought so from the sound of his voice.

It's hard to tell what someone is really thinking on the 'phone. I could only feel the distance between us.

It's such a long way to Manchester. In fact, it's a funny thing that Tom is farther away from us in Manchester than Edgar is in France. But Edgar's not just in a different place, he's in a different world now too.

# 80

It was my first day as a VAD nurse today. I am only allowed to work part-time, but it's a big step forward from my few days' trial earlier in the autumn.

I walked to Seven Dials and carried on up Dyke Road. At the corner of the Old Shoreham Road the hospital stood waiting for me. It's a massive building, of red brick, with an elaborate sculpture on the portico above the entrance, and on top, a small cupola with a copper dolphin weathervane.

I stood for a moment, feeling scared, but then two girls brushed past me, laughing.

"You lost?" one of them asked.

"No," I said. "Well, a little. It's my first day."

"Well, you don't look like a patient, that's for sure! You need to report to reception."

Before half an hour had passed I was standing in my uniform outside Sister's office, waiting to be called in. The uniform felt strange, and itchy, but I was happy to be wearing it. It's a long gray dress, with full sleeves. Over the top I wear a white apron with a bold red cross.

Sister Maddox is not nice. She's a small, thin woman, maybe in her fifties, but I'm not sure, because I have tried not to look at her directly. She seemed hostile before I had even opened my mouth.

"Fox," she said, "you may only be a Voluntary Aid Detachment nurse, and a part-timer at that, but in my hospital you will behave correctly. You will refer to me as Sister, and my nurses as Nurse such-and-such. You will not refer to VAD nurses by anything other than their surname, nor will you expect to be addressed in any other way yourself. Clear?"

I nodded. I didn't want to speak in case my voice sounded as scared as I felt.

"VADs are here to relieve the workload on my nurses, those who have proper medical training. And you are only here because of who your father is. Now report to Staff-nurse Goodall."

That was my introduction to the world of nursing, but I am determined not to let one horrible sister spoil it. Later in the day, talking to other VAD nurses, I discovered that Sister Maddox hates all VADs because we haven't had full medical training and yet are in demand. The soldiers call everyone Sister, out of friendliness, or politeness, or maybe just ignorance, when really they shouldn't, and that annoys her even more.

"So don't take it personally," one girl said.

"But it is personal, with me," I said.

"Oh, yes. Your father," she said. "But don't worry, most people around here like him. And they respect him because he has hard work to do. He works on the neurasthenia patients."

"The what?" I asked.

"Neurasthenia. The ones with shell-shock."

I noticed that the corner of her mouth twisted slightly as she said the word. She got on with her work, and I with mine.

It was a hard day, and by the time I got home this evening, I was ready to cry. Fortunately Father was working late. Mother seemed to realize I'd had a difficult time. She didn't question me, just asked Molly to bring my supper. Then she sat and talked to me.

"My first day, too," she said, but I didn't understand. I felt guilty because although I could see Mother wanted to talk, I needed silence.

"What do you mean?" I asked, forcing myself to talk.

"My first day alone. Father at work. Edgar and Tom gone. And now you."

"Mother, I—"

"It's all right, Sasha. I'm just saying. That's all."

"You had Cook, and Molly."

Mother dropped her voice.

"That's hardly the same," she said, pulling a face.

In spite of myself, I laughed. I knew what she meant.

"I'll get Molly to bring in your favorite supper. I've had her make an omelette for you."

Any other day I would have been delighted. But I was just too tired.

I made an excuse and left Mother by herself in the dining room.

I came upstairs to bed, where I am now. I know it's selfish, but I don't want to think about anyone at the moment, not even Tom.

# 79

After half a dozen shifts at the hospital I'm no longer nervous each time I close those great front doors behind me. And I feel proud walking up the Dyke Road in my uniform.

As I pass women in the street, they smile, and some even say a word or two. Perhaps they have sons fighting in the war and I'm doing something to help. That means a lot.

This morning a postman standing in the doorway of a café whistled at me. Mother would have been appalled, but it made me smile. He meant no harm, and I marched into the hospital ready to face Maddox, or whatever else came my way. In my few days I have already seen some awful sights.

The worst are wounds to the face. A missing leg or arm is bad, that's true. It's terrible to think how that must feel, but at least you can still see that the patient is a person. But some facial wounds stop a man from looking human. There's a poor man in one bed who has a hole where his nose and mouth should be. He's covered in bandages, of course, but even that is wrong. There's no bump where his nose should be. His face is just a flat round ball of bandages, with a tube to feed him through. It's impossible not to wonder what will be there when the bandages come off. And somewhere he must have family, a wife or a brother. Certainly a mother and father, though no one has ever come to see him.

Despite these horrors, I'm enjoying it at last. I know I have a more privileged background than many of the nurses here, but I'm trying hard to be one of them. The work is hard and constant and we're all in it together. The main difference is something on the inside. The other nurses see the war differently, they see the soldiers differently.

"What brave men!" they'll say.

"Poor things."

"We'll soon get them right, then they can go and sort them out!"

The Germans, they mean.

And they crow about our brave men. It's not that I don't think they're brave, it's simply that when I look at a broken body, all I feel is sadness. Not pride, or pity, or horror, or hatred. To me those are false feelings, emotions that we put on top of our sadness, because of the war, because of our country or because we don't want to feel afraid.

I just wish it didn't have to be like this.

As I went to bed last night I saw the *Greek Myths* Miss Garrett loaned me. I've barely picked it up since then; I've been too tired in the evening to think about reading.

Maybe there's another reason too.

At first I read the stories greedily each night. They're so full of wonderful characters; heroes and heroines. Such awful things happen to them, it's easy to sympathize. I wondered who I would be, if I was in the myths. And after a few nights I found my answer.

I read a few lines, just a very few lines, about a young girl from Troy called Cassandra. A prophetess who sees the future, and whom no one believes.

Suddenly I found I didn't want to read anymore, not these stories of people killing and loving and dying. There's too much of that going on as it is. I don't want these stories now, even though they were comforting before.

Thomas wrote to me today, which was wonderful.

I put his letter in my pocket because I knew it would irritate Father if I read it at the breakfast table.

"Are you going to be at the hospital this afternoon?" Father said to me. "I would like you to have tea with me. Four o'clock?"

"Yes," I said, surprised.

So after I got back from Miss Garrett's I changed into my uniform and made my way up to the hospital.

I could tell Sister Maddox was not happy when I said I was to meet my father as soon as I reported for duty, but there wasn't much she could do about it. He's the doctor, after all, and she's a sister. That's how things work.

When we got to Father's office on the second floor, he wasn't there.

"Well, I suppose you'd better wait," she said. "Since you're his daughter I'm sure that will be fine."

I looked around. I wondered why I had never visited him here before, but then, there's a lot I don't know about my father. He doesn't talk much about his work at home.

I soon got bored with waiting, and went over to the window with its view across town and down to the sea. It was as if I could feel something tugging at me again. From France, across the waves. It was stronger this time, and I was scared. I didn't want Father to see me like this.

I sat down at his desk and flicked through the papers on his desk, then realized what I was doing and stopped.

There was a book lying facedown on his desk. *The Duality of the Mind* by Arthur Wigan. It looked very old. It was next to a sheaf of papers, the top one of which was much more recent, dated 1908, and called "Memory of the Present and False Recognition," by someone called Bergson. I had a struggle to understand what the title meant, but it took my mind away from the window.

"Alexandra."

Father was at the door.

I jumped up.

"I'm sorry I'm late. Sometimes it's hard to leave."

He seemed distracted, but came and sat in the chair I had vacated.

"I've sent for some tea. . . ."

"Were you doing rounds?" I asked.

"No," he said. "I don't do that kind of work here. I see . . . special cases."

I nodded, and smiled, trying to show I knew what he meant.

He didn't elaborate.

"Where's that confounded woman?" he said, looking out through the door. There was no sign of the tea.

"What exactly do you do here?" I asked. He must have seen me looking at the papers on his desk.

"I'm doing tests," he said. "I'm involved with a group of doctors here. A lot of men are getting hurt in this war, badly hurt. But some of them aren't hurt in their bodies at all. Do you see?"

"I think so. Is that what they call shell-shock?"

"Shell-shock. Shell-shock," he said, spitting the words out. "Yes, that's what people call it. The group I work with here, we're doing tests to find out more about it. My colleagues are of the opinion that these men are as badly wounded as the fellows in the ward you work in."

"But you don't agree?" I asked.

"No, I do not."

He paused.

"I have no doubt that there are some cases who have severe mental illness, but the vast majority do not. Those who are ill were probably prone to it before they went to war. And the country needs every fit man to do his duty. To fight. We cannot bear the weight of malingerers.

"Where's that tea?" he said again, then turned to me. "Well, look at you. My daughter is a nurse!"

I smiled.

"How is it? Are you sure it's what you want to do?"

"Yes," I said. "I'm sure. But I had better be going. Sister Maddox . . ."

He laughed, but without amusement.

"Yes, I see. Off you go, then. I'm sorry about the tea, but if Maddox gives you one word of trouble you let me know."

"Yes, Father," I said, and went back down to the wards.

## 77

I've been working. I've been happy. It was almost as if I'd dreamt about what the future held, rather than it having happened. And the memory of a nightmare is much less frightening than the nightmare itself.

Then, yesterday, the nightmare came back.

I was on the ward, making a bed. Without warning, everything seemed unreal. I felt detached, like that time in Miss Garrett's lesson. My body felt like an empty shell.

Slowly, I turned my head, straightening up as I did so. It seemed to take forever to make that simple movement.

I realized that I had deliberately turned to look at a patient on the other side of the ward. He was talking to a nurse. I knew him. Shrapnel in the back of his head and shoulders.

"You'll be out of here soon," the nurse was saying. "You can get back to your friends."

"Couldn't you keep me here a little longer?" he said,

joking with her. "The food's so nice and the nurses so pretty!"

She smiled.

"Couldn't do it if I wanted to!" she said. "Need your bed for someone else, won't we?"

Then everything slowed right down. He was speaking at a normal speed, but to me his words came out of his mouth so very, very slowly.

"Fair enough," he said. "I'll be a good boy. Let you have the bed back!"

I heard those words, but I heard others, too.

Somehow I heard him say unspoken words.

"And I'll be dead in the morning anyway."

They came to me clearly, from across the ward. The nurse kept on teasing him, he joked back, and everything else was perfectly ordinary.

I panicked.

"I'll be dead in the morning anyway."

I ran from the ward.

I don't think anyone saw me go, but as I got to the doors, I saw Sister turning into the corridor, coming my way.

Without thinking, I ducked into the nearest door. Shutting it behind me, I found myself in the darkness of a linen room. There was one at the end of each ward, full of clean sheets and other bedding.

I crouched in the darkness, wondering if Maddox had seen me, but though footsteps passed outside, the door did not open.

My head was spinning. The feeling of detachment had gone, I was back in my body. I knew that from the way my heart was pounding inside my chest. For a long time, I leaned against a stack of blankets and shivered, trying to blot out the words the man *hadn't* spoken.

It was no good. They ran round and round in my mind, though I boxed my ears with my fists and shook my head from side to side.

Then I thought I heard something.

Something in the linen room with me.

I stood up, and, fumbling for the light switch, turned on the small lamp in the ceiling.

"Turn it off," said a voice.

It came from behind the shelves of sheets in the center of the room.

I froze, too scared to do anything.

"Turn it off," said the voice, plaintively. "It hurts my eyes."

I turned if off. Then I realized how rash I was to turn the light off in a small storeroom with an unknown man in there with me.

For I could tell it was a man's voice, though it was small and feeble.

"Who's there?" I asked.

There was no answer.

"I'm not afraid," I said. That seems a stupid thing to say, but it was all I could manage.

"Who are you?" I said. "I'm not afraid."

"I am," said the man. "I am."

# 76

Unwittingly, I had said perhaps the one thing that got him to talk.

"What are you afraid of?" I asked.

"Everything," he said, and there was such feeling behind that single word it made me shiver.

I wondered what I should do. I felt like running out of the room, but I had always wanted to be a nurse, and if I ran from this chance to help someone, I would have failed.

"Are you sure you wouldn't like the light on?" I asked.

"No!" he said. "It hurts my eyes. It's better in the dark."

It was obvious he was a patient.

"Why does it hurt your eyes?" I asked.

No response. I thought about what to say. There was something obvious, at least.

"What's your name?"

He answered so quietly I couldn't hear what he said.

"Sorry?"

"Evans," he said. He paused. "David Evans."

I knew he was a soldier then, from the way he gave his surname first. The name was familiar, but I couldn't place it.

"What are you doing in here, David?"

"I come here," he said. "Get away from the light, the people. That man."

Now I recognized his Welsh accent.

"No one knows," he continued. "Too busy to care, even if they notice. As long as I'm back before bedtime."

"Why don't you like the light?" I asked again. I was going round in circles, but I couldn't think what else to say.

"It hurts. My eyes hurt. Flashes in the dark, all the time. It hurt my eyes. And now I'm here, and they still want to shine lights into my eyes, see? It hurts, so I come here."

"Who shines lights into your eyes?" I asked.

"That man," he said. "That doctor. Says he wants to look into my eyes, but it hurts, it hurts."

With a lurching feeling I realized he might be talking about Father. Then I knew why his name was familiar.

Evans. He was the shell-shocked patient I'd seen on that very first day with Sister Cave. He was one of the soldiers my father had been doing his tests on.

"They shine it in my eyes," he said. "And they stick things to my head."

"What things?"

"Wires," he said, in a small voice. "They stick wires to my head and put electrics through it."

That was what he said. Electrics.

"Why?" I said, though I knew I was asking the wrong person.

75

"To make me better, they say, but it hurts, and everything goes weird."

"Weird? What do you mean?"

I heard noises in the corridor outside. Voices calling, and footsteps. Running footsteps. But they went past the door to the linen room.

"What do you mean?" I asked again.

There was silence for a while. I decided to move closer to Evans, even though I couldn't see him. My legs were starting to cramp, anyway. I stretched, and eased my way round the side of the stacks of blankets.

"What are you doing?" came Evans' voice.

"Just coming closer," I said. "I can't hear you properly. Tell me about what happens. When they put the wires on your head."

"It hurts," he said, "and it makes something strange happen. I feel like it's all happened before."

"What? What's happened before?"

"Everything. The room, them, the wires, the pain. Like I'm going through it all over again. Living it again. Do you know what I mean?"

"Yes," I said, "I think I do."

There was more commotion outside, coming from the ward.

I felt torn, but I was supposed to be on duty. I had to see what was going on.

"Stay here, David. Don't go anywhere."

I opened the door and edged out. A couple of young doctors rushed past me into the ward and ran to one of the beds.

With a shock I realized that it was the bed of the man with the shrapnel wounds.

Of course it was him. I was disgusted with myself for even wondering who might be in trouble. I ought to have known better than to doubt myself. He said he'd be dead by the morning.

Nurses crowded round, but as the doctors pushed through, I saw that there was a pool of blood collecting on the floor, dripping from the bed.

He was already gone.

"There you are!" said a voice.

I spun round, but the voice was not directed at me.

Evans stood in the open doorway of the linen room. An orderly had spotted him.

"Come on, then," he said, leading Evans away. I could see now that he was a tall, strong young man, at least in body. He looked back at me imploringly, as if I were to blame for his capture.

"Complete case, that one," said a nurse next to me. "Shell-shock. Hasn't spoken a word of sensible English since he got here."

I must have looked puzzled.

"Honestly," she said. "Only talks in gibberish. Not a word anyone can understand."

But that can't be right. Evans was a frightened, hurt and timid man, yet I had understood every word he said.

# 75

In the confusion, no one spotted that I wasn't on the ward when I should have been. I couldn't have done anything to help. Just because I knew it was going to happen doesn't mean I could have stopped it.

I didn't know when he would die, or how.

I feel betrayed now, betrayed by my own emotions.

There's a word for what I have been feeling.

Premonitions. Each one has been more clear, more categorical than the last, and they refuse to be ignored.

Although I hadn't foreseen anyone's death for a long time, there had been no deaths on the ward since I joined. Until yesterday.

It's not that surprising.

Most men leave the hospital alive, but that's not always much to do with us. Of course, it's a good hospital, and we do our best to see the patients get the help they need, but

78

that's not what I mean. A doctor told me that if a soldier gets hurt at the front, and if he manages to survive being pulled off the battlefield, and the journey back to the base hospital, and the ship home, then he's probably going to survive anyway. If he's badly hurt, he'll be dead before he gets six miles from the front.

So we don't actually see many deaths, and I am glad of that. But it allows you to think that maybe things aren't as bad as they must really be.

Then yesterday came my clearest premonition. I heard a man tell me he was going to die, and minutes later, he was dead.

Were it not for the fact that it is happening to me, I would not believe it. Why do I only see deaths, and not good things? Why do I not see everyone's deaths? As I walk past people in the street, why am I not witnessing all their endings?

A thought strikes me. What if I see something about someone I love, someone in my family? What if I see something about myself?

And if I really can see the future, then what does it mean? Is there any sense in our lives if everything is already out there, just waiting to happen?

For if that were so, then life would be a horrible monster indeed, with no chance of escape from fate, from destiny.

It would be like reading a book you know very well, but reading it backward, from the final chapter down to chapter one, so that the end is already known to you.

# 74

Tom's letter.

I forgot all about it till last night as I sat in bed thinking about everything that had happened. I had been late getting home, and Mother fussed over me.

"How are you getting on?" she asked. "At the hospital?"

I forced a smile.

"Fine."

Father wasn't home yet, so she can't have known what had happened on the ward. But he wouldn't mention it anyway. Why should he mention a patient's dying? It was only to me that it had a terrible significance.

"Just fine?" she said. "Sasha?"

I wanted to shout at her, shake her with words if not with force, and tell her she had to *believe* what was happening to me. It would be the only way she could help me. I stared into the fire, struggling to think what was best to say. But I knew.

"Yes, Mother," I said. "Everything's fine."

I even smiled as I left the room to go up to bed, and she smiled back.

"All right, dear. Sleep well."

She knows things aren't right with me, but I won't talk to her about it again. She didn't believe me when I tried to before. When did she lose the desire to have a life? I know she cares. I know she loves me. But not enough to cross Father. Not enough to be on my side when it really matters.

I will never let myself become like that, let my spirit be crushed as I see has happened to her.

And yet I long for her to make everything all right again, as if I am still her little girl. I long to be a child again, and not to know the things I do.

Then I saw Tom's letter poking out of the pocket of my dress.

It's a long letter, about life as a medical student. He says the feeling that we are at war is no different in Manchester, people there are just the same. He stays in a lot, in his digs, when he isn't studying, because he's got into too many arguments about not going to fight.

He thinks the chances of completing his training are small, and says that everyone around the college thinks conscription is on its way. He's already had to comply with compulsory registration.

*Now there's this new scheme going on. Have you read about it? They're trying to get all men to say they'll fight if called upon, but they've said they won't ask a married man to fight until the supply of single ones has run out. So there's plenty of married men signing up, looking as though they're doing their bit, but thinking they won't ever have to. And then, of course, when they are needed, they'll get no support from the friends and family of the poor single men who are already dying in France. It's a clever ruse by the government, but quite dishonest.*

Tom sounds very political, and I don't understand it all. If Father saw what he'd written, I don't think he'd ever let him back in the house.

How can all the people I love so much have such different views on things? But then, there are so many contradictions. I love Father, but the way he runs our house is old-fashioned and cruel. And the way he treats Mother. If he had his way, I'd be married to some rich idiot, and never do what I want to do. But I still love him, and so does Mother, I suppose. And Tom and Father may have different views, but they both want to help people. So do I.

In fact, there's someone I badly want to help right now, and who can maybe help me too.

# 73

It wasn't hard to find Evans, even though the one place he never seems to be is in his bed. I'm glad of that in a way, because the ward for patients like him is not a pleasant place. It's on the top floor of the hospital, and even on the floor below you can hear the cries and shouts of the men.

You can dress a wound, put iodine on it, give morphia for the pain, amputate a gangrenous limb. But what can you do for the mind, when it is damaged? I don't quite know what Father is doing with his colleagues, but I admire them for even trying to help. I wouldn't know where to begin.

But I did know where I would find Evans. He has the run of the hospital, it seems. He's less trouble than many of the patients on his ward—some are violent and noisy, or need their sheets changed often, or need hand-feeding. Evans is docile, so they don't always bother trying to find him. He comes back when the ward is dark anyway.

I didn't know which linen room he'd be in, but it wasn't the one he'd been in before. I took the chance when everything was quiet to hunt through the other wards. If anyone stopped me, I would just say I was fetching more blankets.

As soon as I put my head round the door of the fourth storeroom, I knew he was there. I went inside and closed the door.

"I won't turn the light on," I said.

"Who is it?" came his voice.

"Alexandra, we spoke the other day. Do you remember?"

There was no reply.

"Yes," he said, eventually, his voice dull.

"There's nothing to be—"

"What happened to him?" he asked, interrupting me. "Did he die?"

"Yes," I said, trying to sound as calm as possible. "A wound they didn't know about. Ruptured his lungs."

We were silent for a while. I wondered how long I could be away without being missed.

"May I come closer?" I asked.

I was apprehensive. I was scared, and not because I was afraid of him. He wouldn't harm me, I knew that. No, I was afraid of myself, of what I might feel about him, for I feel sorry for Evans, I want him to be all right.

I moved close to him in the dark, feeling my way around the room.

"May I ask you something?" I said. I felt my knee touch him, and drew back. "It's about what you told me, about when they put electricity into you."

"Oh," he said, in a voice of such unhappiness that I wanted to cry.

"What does it do to you? Would you tell me again?"

There was silence.

"No," he said.

Then the door opened, and the light came on.

Evans tried to scramble away, knocking over a pile of blankets as he did so.

"Who's there?"

A nurse stepped into view and jumped when she saw us.

"What on earth—"

It was the girl who'd shown me around on my first day.

"I was just looking for Evans . . . ," I said. "I was trying—"

"I don't want to know what you were doing in here. With him," she said. Evans tried to make for the door, but she stood in his way. He stopped and waited, squinting against the light.

"No," I said, "I was just trying to find him."

The nurse put her head on one side.

"Is that what you call it? Well, you've found him now. For heaven's sake."

She turned to Evans.

"You go back to your ward and stay there for once."

Without a word, he slunk out the door.

"And you . . . ," she said, turning back to me. "If Sister found you in here with a man, you'd be out of here and never let back. What were you thinking of?"

"Please," I said. "Please believe me. I wanted to talk to him, that's all. About what they're doing to him."

She sighed.

"Any other girl in this hospital I might not believe. But you. I don't think you even know why what you've done is so wrong."

"I only want to know what they're doing to him. He says it hurts."

She looked surprised now.

"He doesn't say anything that isn't nonsense."

"He makes sense to me," I said. "He says when they put the wires to his head, he sees things as if they've already happened."

"He says what?"

Her voice had softened.

"Yes," I said, encouraged. "Why do you think that is? What are they trying to do?"

"They're trying to make him better," she said.

"But it hurts him. Why are they doing it?"

"He's your father, why don't you ask him?"

"Please," I said. "You don't understand. I need to know. Things have been happening to me that I . . ."

"What things?"

I hesitated, but couldn't help myself.

"I see things," I said. "I see things before they happen."

She took a step backward, and flicked off the light.

"I think you'd better get back to work," she said, her voice sharp and thin. "Don't you?"

# 72

When I got home there was pandemonium in the house. I could hear Mother in the kitchen, almost wailing at Father.

They stopped talking the moment I came in.

"What's wrong?" I asked.

Mother hurried past me, her hand to her mouth.

I saw a letter on the table.

"What is it?"

Father put up his hand.

"Edgar's been wounded. Don't worry," he added. "He's fine."

"Father?"

"Yes, he's fine. He couldn't write that if he wasn't, could he?"

"What happened?"

"Not sure," he said, shaking his head. "But it's just a scratch. He spent a few days in hospital in Boulogne, in the middle of November. He's back with his battalion now. Fighting fit!"

"But what happened?"

"That's enough, Alexandra! Do you not realize you upset your mother with all your questions?"

That seemed unfair. Mother was already upset before I got home, and had already left the room. But I knew not to say anything more while Father was in that kind of mood.

I looked at the letter. Edgar's letter from France, lying on the kitchen table. I wanted to read it, but Father picked it up and left the room.

I followed him, and as he went into his study I made my way upstairs, pausing just long enough to see him put the letter in the drawer of his writing desk. Then I found Molly and asked her to bring me something to eat in my room. I went up to bed.

# 71

Molly brought me soup and some bread. I ate it slowly, thoughtfully, thinking things through.

My eyes fell on Miss Garrett's book. I hadn't looked at it for ages. I picked it up and flicked through it. Cassandra. Her name leapt out at me from page after page. Daughter of King Priam of Troy. She was given the gift of prophecy by Apollo, but because she refused to sleep with him in return, he cursed her gift, making sure that no one would ever believe her. She ended her life telling of the doom of Troy, but still no one believed her. It didn't matter in the end, because everything she saw happened anyway, including her own death. Taken captive by Agamemnon, spirited away from Troy to Argos, she was slain by Agamemnon's jealous wife.

Perhaps she went crazy waiting for someone to believe her at last, to take notice of her, to let her help.

And did she gaze out on a view of the sea like I do?

Maybe she did, dreading the conflict that was to come across the water. Did she feel alone, as I do? Maybe she looked at her reflection, trying to see what was different about her, trying to understand her gift.

A gift, or a curse? I knew which I thought it was. The book trembled in my hand. I shut it before my tears ruined something which I'd promised to take good care of.

After Mother and Father had gone to bed I went back down to the study. On Father's desk is a green-shaded reading lamp. I put the lamp on and began to open the small drawers in the back of the desk.

Edgar's letter was easy to find. I could smell it almost before I saw it. It smelled of cold air, of damp, of earth, of smoke. It was only a few weeks old and yet looked as though it had seen more history than most of us will see in our whole lives.

I have the letter in front of me now.

At the top, in Edgar's handwriting, it says: *No. 14 Stationary Hospital, Boulogne. 13th November.*

It's taken over three weeks for the letter to get here. It's very short. He must have been exhausted while he was in hospital, and unable to write much.

> *Dear Family,*
> *I am well, but I must tell you I have received a small injury which has put me in hospital. Don't worry, though, it is nothing serious. A shell exploded near our dugout, and I took a small piece in my chest. I will be back in action soon.*
> *I send you my best wishes,*
>
> *Your Edgar*

I thought I might feel something from the letter, that I might see something while holding it, but nothing happened. And I had had no inkling of Edgar's injury, though it happened weeks ago. I had not suspected a thing. So this curse I have cannot even be relied upon to be consistent. To actually be of some use.

But I wonder why the letter smells of the battlefield, when it was written from hospital. Maybe I can sense something of Edgar from it, after all.

# 70

It is Monday evening.

The weekend was a miserable affair. Mother was quiet almost all of the time, worrying about Edgar, and the one time she did speak it was of him.

"I wonder where Edgar will be for Christmas," she said.

Not such a bad thing to say, but Father raised his voice, and told her to stop fretting about Edgar all the time. Then he went out.

That was Saturday morning, and as soon as he had gone, I took the chance to replace Edgar's letter in Father's desk before it was missed. That would only cause more trouble.

I tried to comfort Mother not by talking but by doing. I took her out shopping, but she stared at things in a listless way, and would barely speak to the shop assistants.

In Needham's, Mother stopped by the glove counter.

Hoping to catch her interest, I asked her if she wanted new gloves for the winter.

She stared at the counter.

"Mother? Did you want something?"

Still she gazed down, saying nothing. I could see an assistant dithering, wondering whether to come over or not.

"Mother?"

"I wonder if Edgar's hands are warm."

I looked at the assistant and smiled, but shook my head to keep her away.

"I'm sure he's fine," I said.

"But it must be cold, and wet."

"I'm sure the army kits them out well. Remember how smart he looked in his uniform? He'll have everything he needs."

"Do you think so, Sasha?"

Now at least she stopped looking at the gloves and looked at me, but the weight of the pain in her eyes was enough to break my heart.

"Yes," I whispered. "I'm sure of it. Come away now. Let's go to Hannington's, see if they have your material."

I nearly had to pull her out of the shop, but at last we were outside. It was raining by then, and we gave up. To be honest, I was relieved to go home.

I got changed to go to the hospital for a late-afternoon shift.

It was bitter, inhospitable weather as I made my way up to Seven Dials. The rain began to lash down as the hospital came in sight, so I ran for the entrance.

As I passed through the doors I felt better immediately. Better, almost happier in a way, despite everything that has happened here. I was glad of the warmth, and of the noise and the brightness. For a second I stopped and marveled at the commotion, people coming and going, nurses and orderlies at work, and I realized that I had come to like the place.

"Fox," said one of the nurses as she passed, and smiled and nodded to me.

I smiled back and got to work.

It was a quiet shift, but there were two pieces of interesting news.

I could tell something was different on the ward as soon as I arrived.

"Have you heard?" one nurse said to me. "About Sister Maddox?"

"She's gone!"

"She's gone to France."

"I know," someone said. "We were as surprised as you are! Apparently she felt she wasn't doing enough here. She got herself sent to France, to a hospital in Rouen."

Maddox had seemed such a hard, uncaring woman. Maybe that's not such an uncommon thing in the medical profession, but perhaps we were wrong about her. She didn't tell anyone she was going, and left without a word to any of her staff. More and more nurses are making their way out to France to the big hospitals, in Paris, in Rouen, where Maddox has gone, or Boulogne, where Edgar was when he was injured. They have to volunteer, and then wait to be called up. I know Father's responsible for passing the applications of nurses from our hospital.

I've overheard him talk about things in France. Yes. He'd say, "Always watching, always prying." But that's how I learn.

The existing French hospitals were soon overwhelmed at

the start of the war, and many other buildings, like hotels and warehouses, have been put to use as makeshift hospitals. And all these hospitals need nurses, especially ones as experienced as Sister Maddox.

The other thing that I learned was even more of a shock.

On my way home, I saw a nurse I knew walking the same way as me on the other side of the road. We must have the same shift patterns, because I keep bumping into her. It was the nurse who had found me in the linen room with Evans.

I ducked my head and tried to pretend I hadn't seen her. I tried to hurry, but she skipped across the road to walk beside me.

"Wait!" she said. "I want to tell you something. It's about your friend. Evans. The Welshman?"

"Leave me alone." I kept on walking.

"No," she said. "No . . . listen. I thought you might like to know. He's making sense again. I mean, he's getting better."

I slowed down, and looked sideways at her, to see if she was teasing.

"Whatever it was you did, it worked. All the nurses are talking about it, about how you made him better."

I stopped.

"How do they know?" I asked. "Who told them?"

The girl blushed.

"Don't worry," she said, hurriedly, "It's just nurses' gossip. Your father . . . I mean, the doctors won't take any notice of that, they'll think it was what they did to him that worked."

"Maybe it was," I said.

She shrugged.

"Anyway," she said, "I just thought you'd like to know."

"Thank you," I said, and I meant it.

# 69

Last night I dreamt about the raven again.

It was a vivid dream, so lifelike that when I woke in the middle of the night, my heart racing, it seemed real.

I was flying. Flying high above a darkening landscape, and without any reason I knew I was above the plains outside the city of Troy. Was I seeing what Cassandra had seen?

The sun was setting. In truth, I knew that for the people on the ground far below me the sun had already set, but looking down from on high, I could still see the last cusp of the red sun slipping beneath the far horizon. It flickered once more like the embers of coal in a fire, then went out. Night came and wrapped the earth in its dusky wings. Darkness flooded across the landscape from the west, but somehow I could see clearly.

I whirled and soared like a bird of prey, and some distance away I could see the walls of the great city, the top of which bristled with feather-laden spear tips. But my attention was drawn to the fields beneath me, from where I felt a terrible pull of death, as if the departing souls of the slaughtered men were trying to take me with them.

I resisted.

I resisted and tried to pull up into the sky and soar again, but I could not. I began to plummet toward the earth as I realized it was impossible that I should be flying anyway.

The ground hurtled toward me, but somehow with infinite slowness, so that I had time to gaze at the horrors that unfolded there. All around was carnage, and bloodied bodies. Broken chariots and splintered shields were strewn across the plains as if cast there by a god's hand. Here and there a few men still wearily tried to put an end to each other, but this was a battle that was already dead itself.

I landed, and in mild surprise saw that I had survived the fall, and landed on my feet, my legs merely jarred from the impact.

It was then that I saw the raven. It was a huge bird, and at first I could only marvel at its beauty. The blackness of its feathers was perfect; a glistening, oily blackness set off by the charcoal gray of its beak. It fixed an eye on me and put its head on one side, and only then did I see what it was standing on, what it had been feeding on.

I thought I was going to be sick, but I couldn't look away. And then the bird spoke to me.

It spoke with the voice of the dead upon which it was feeding.

"You!" it said. "You alone saw the horror of war, and wept when we did not believe you."

I woke.

# 68

Thomas has come home.

It's so wonderful that when he walked through the front door I threw my arms around him to hide the tears in my eyes.

He laughed, and pushed me away.

"Sasha!" he cried, and everyone laughed, even Father, though there was nothing really to laugh at.

"You've grown," Mother declared.

Tom sighed.

"Don't be silly," Father said. "He hasn't grown. You shrank him in your memory."

I think Father might be right about that, but Mother was right too. There was something different about Tom. He wasn't any taller, but he was older. He had aged by more than the few months he'd been away.

Father stepped forward and put out his hand. Tom looked at it for a moment and then shook it.

It was the first time that they've ever done this, and I immediately knew what it meant. Father considers Thomas to be a man, and as I watched I smiled inside for what I hope it means.

# 67

Tom and I have been catching up today, swapping stories of hospital life.

We chatted as we helped Mother make Christmas pudding, rather late this year. This is one job she likes to do herself, and not leave to Cook. She bustled around the kitchen, getting Molly to fetch ingredients for her. She was busy, she seemed happy, and I saw that she smiled, listening to us talk as she stirred in a bottle of brown ale and a bottle of stout.

Father came home later and we had supper. It was quiet at first, and I felt nervous for some reason.

Father looked at Tom, a forkful of food in one hand.

"So, how are your studies, Tom?"

Tom's face lit up.

"Everything's going well," he said. "There's only a few of us, really, because lots of boys deferred entry to go to . . ."

He stopped.

Father nodded.

"Go on," Mother said. "Tell us about Manchester."

Tom shrugged.

"It's well enough," he said. "It's not as nice as Brighton, but the people are friendly. Well, most of them."

I could tell he was thinking of the white feathers he's been given. I knew more about that than Mother or Father because he knows it upsets them, though in different ways.

Tom talked for a bit as we ate. Then Father put his knife and fork down and looked at Tom.

"I'm sure that any son of mine could make a fine doctor," he said. "But I think you may not have the chance to find out for a while."

Tom's head dropped.

Father was talking about conscription. It seems more likely than ever that a bill will be passed soon.

"But if we start now, we can get you a commission in the medical corps, and then you can do your bit as well as do what you feel is right."

Father was trying to compromise between what he thinks Tom should do and what Tom wants to do, and I was amazed. Father is not a man who usually compromises on anything.

But Tom let his head sink a little further, and would eat no more supper.

# 66

I saw Evans today, and it's true, he seems to be better. I was wheeling a trolley between wards when I heard someone behind me.

"How are you, today, Nurse?" he asked, as if he made small talk like this every day of his life.

I smiled.

"F-fine . . . ," I stuttered out. "Fine."

"That's good." He stood smiling at me, waiting for me to speak.

"And how are you?"

As I spoke I saw from the corner of my eye that three nurses on the other side of the corridor were watching us with interest.

I started to wheel forward again, but Evans was talking to me now.

"Very well," he said. "Thank you, Nurse. Very well."

"You look much better, I must say."

We were still being watched, and I was afraid.

"Yes, yes," he said. "Wonderful what the doctors have done for me, it is."

I thought about what he had said, about the tests, the lights and being hurt.

"Everything's right now, is it? The tests . . . ? They didn't—"

"Oh, no," he said quickly, smiling.

I started to feel uneasy.

"But what you said," I persisted, "about feeling as though you had already seen things once before. What about that?"

He stopped smiling and stood up straight, stiff. For the first time I could actually imagine that he could be a soldier.

"I don't know what you're talking about," he said, and turned on his heels.

I looked at the nurses who had been watching and they pretended to be busy.

I wheeled my trolley on to the ward.

I feel let down. Of course it's good that Evans is better, and I feel guilty for even thinking this, but when everyone thought he was crazy I thought I had found one person who I could confide in. And now he denies we ever spoke of such things.

If I only took heart from a discussion with a man while he was mad, what does that say about me?

# 65

Tom and I went Christmas shopping today. It didn't feel quite right, because Edgar won't be home this year. Nonetheless, we must try to make Christmas as normal as possible.

After a fruitless and tiring morning we decided that parents are impossible to buy presents for, and took a shortcut down one of the twittens that runs off Middle Street, to shelter in a small café in the Lanes, even though it's an area of town Father doesn't like us to visit.

We ordered buttered toast and tea, and hidden away in a corner by the window, I felt safer and happier than I had for a long time. I had been occupied at the hospital, but with Tom, I felt truly safe. But tired too, and told him so.

"Why?" he asked.

"There's been so much going on."

"At the hospital?" he asked.

"Yes."

I stopped.

"There must be a lot to learn. Some of it must be pretty horrible, too."

I nodded, and sipped my tea.

I looked out the window at the narrow, twisting passages of the Lanes. I could see a small slit of sky above the rooftops. It seemed likely to rain again soon.

"Are you all right?" Tom asked.

"Yes," I said.

"But are you enjoying it?"

"I don't know," I said. "I haven't thought about it like that. But yes, I suppose I am."

He stretched a hand across the table to mine.

"Then what's wrong?"

I didn't answer.

"What's wrong, Sasha? I can tell something's getting to you. You're different from when I went away. Is Father being mean?"

I shook my head.

"No more than usual." I smiled. "In fact, he's been quite generous at times."

"So what is it?"

I looked at my brother, and then looked away. He was so kind to me, he always had been, and he was open-minded and clever. If there was one person I could talk to, it was him.

I squeezed his hand briefly, then pushed it away.

"I'm fine," I said. "Do you want some more tea?"

He was the one person who might believe me, but if he, of all people, reacted the way everyone else had, it would hurt more than I could bear.

# 64

When we got home, we found Mother and Father in the drawing room. They had a visitor: Miss Garrett.

Mother forced a smile as we came in.

"Miss Garrett stopped by to see you," she said, but Father cut across her.

"To have a talk about your studying," he said. I looked from Mother to Miss Garrett, who seemed uncomfortable.

"Sit down, Alexandra," Father said. "Tom?"

Tom shuffled awkwardly in the doorway, then backed out, nodding to Miss Garrett and closing the door behind him.

"Mother?" I said, and felt very small.

Mother looked at her hands and then at Father.

"We understand that your work has been poor recently," Father said.

"I only said–" Miss Garrett began, but Father interrupted.

"We are very disappointed."

It all started to come out then.

"Alexandra, you're an intelligent girl," Mother said.

"But you've been so distracted lately," Miss Garrett said.

I couldn't think what to say; I knew it was true.

"Miss Garrett says you borrowed a book from her," Father said. "Will you please go and get it."

I hesitated, wondering what all this was about.

"Sasha. Please." Mother said.

She looked so upset I wanted to shake her, but I went and got the book. Father took it from me and glanced through it.

"Why did you want this book when you haven't been paying attention?"

I frowned.

"I wanted to read the stories," I said. "I thought I'd better make an effort to catch up."

"The Trojan Wars?" Father said. "Achilles? Ajax? Helen and Paris?"

"Your recollection of the classics is admirable," said Miss Garrett, with false jollity. She misread Father's tone entirely.

"And Cassandra, too?" he said, his voice loud. "Is that it?"

I could see what he thought, but I didn't know what I could say. As usual, his mind was made up.

I shrugged.

There was silence for a long time.

# 63

Miss Garrett left shortly after that, making some embarrassed excuse and hurrying out into the evening with Mother fretting at her heels, pushing the copy of *Greek Myths* back into her hands as she went.

I really don't think she meant to get me into such trouble. She's not a strict tutor, and she means well. I think she was probably genuinely worried about me.

Mother dithered in the doorway, but Father wouldn't let her back in, telling her to find Cook and that he wanted his dinner soon. She saw the look on his face and went off to the kitchen.

"Father," I said. "I haven't done anything wrong."

"Be quiet!" he shouted.

I sat down and felt myself shaking.

"Why do my children insist on making a fool of me?" he said, but I knew it was not a question I should reply to.

"What did you talk about?" he snapped.

"I . . . Do you mean with Miss Garrett?" I asked.

"No, I do not, and you know I do not!"

I didn't understand, I really didn't.

"The patient," he seethed. "The Welshman."

"Father," I said, pleading, "nothing. I said nothing. He talked to me, I asked him how he was. That was all!"

"It was not all."

"I swear it," I said.

"You talked about his treatment. About me! Admit it!"

"No, Father, no," I said, tears running down my face.

"You talked about the tests and the electrical stimulations. About the *déjà vu* he claimed to experience. Well, it's all nonsense."

I said nothing. It was clear someone had told Father and there was no point denying it anymore.

"You have been living a fantasy life, Alexandra, a fantasy. You have been idolizing the neurasthenic patients like Evans, and filling your head with wild myths from books!"

He paused then, as if I was supposed to say something, but there was nothing I could say.

"You are nearly a woman now, Alexandra. Did you ever stop to think what effect your childish imaginings would have on someone who'd lost a relative? Pretending you knew it was going to happen? How distasteful! How disrespectful! To make a game from their suffering!"

"No, Father!" I cried. "That's not fair. It's not true. I haven't hurt anyone."

"Maybe not," he said. "But I'm not going to give you the chance. You are not to go back to the hospital."

"Father . . . ?"

"You heard me. I forbid you to continue nursing. That's over now. You will go back to studying properly and conduct yourself in a manner more fitting to a young lady of your class. And that is all."

He left the room, and a few moments later, I heard him leave the house, heedless that dinner was on the way.

I don't think he will change his mind.

# 62

A generation of men is like the leaves on the trees. When the winter winds blow, the leaves are scattered to the ground, but with spring, a new generation of men bursts into bud, to replace those that went before. But this is a harsh winter, the likes of which has never been seen before.

I think of the words from my dream, croaked to me by that evil bird on the battlefield.

*You alone saw the horror of war, and wept when we did not believe you.*

I don't fully understand what it is that I have done in Father's eyes. I don't understand what is so terrible, but I have been punished anyway. Not just with words, but with deeds, too. I am not to be allowed to continue nursing.

And all for something I did not wish for. A power which

has been given to me, to see endings, but to be unable to prevent them, or even to make others believe what I have seen. In idle fantasy you might think that to see the future would be a wonderful gift.

It's nothing but a curse.

# 61

It's nearly Christmas.

I haven't been to the hospital, nor anywhere near it. I have seen no more visions of the future, and yet still I feel fate swirling around me like leaves caught in those tiny whirlwinds that eddy in the autumn streets.

Today there was another coincidence. I was walking home from Miss Garrett's in Preston Park, and was surprised when a soldier coming up the hill stopped in front of me.

"Hello, Nurse," he said. "And goodbye, I suppose."

It was David Evans. The uniform stopped me from recognizing him immediately.

I struggled for words. I knew that it was perhaps because of what he'd said that I'd lost my position, but I didn't want to talk about that. It wasn't his fault; he probably didn't even remember anything about it now.

"Are you leaving?" I asked, though it was obvious. He had a kit bag on his back and was heading for the station.

"I am indeed," he said, smiling, as if it were the most natural thing in the world. "Got to get back to my mates. That's important. Stick together, we do. That's the only way."

I nodded.

"Yes," I said, "yes. Don't you have family to see first?"

"No family, no," he said. "The boys, the sergeant-major. That's my family. See?"

I nodded again.

"Well, better be along, got to get the train to Southampton. Catch a boat, you know!"

I smiled.

"One last thing," he said. "May I give you a kiss?"

I took a step backward, but I could see he meant no harm.

"If I tell the boys I kissed a girl as beautiful as you," he said, laughing, "they'll be green fit to burst!"

I laughed too.

"Very well," I said. "Are all Welshmen as charming as you?"

"Not quite," he said, winking.

He leaned down and kissed me quickly on the cheek, like an uncle.

As he straightened up again I noticed he was looking at me thoughtfully. At my eyes.

"What is it?" I asked.

"Nothing," he said, casually. "Nothing. I just . . . Well, anyway, I must be going now. Goodbye."

He slung his kit bag over his shoulder, and set off to the station once more.

I felt a little glow of satisfaction inside as he went, though

I never thought my first kiss would come from a Welsh soldier.

I was puzzled. He seemed to have made such a complete recovery from the wrecked shell of a man he had been when I first saw him. That didn't often happen with shell-shock, and I spent the rest of the day wondering what had made him better.

# 60

Christmas has come. It's Friday evening, and tomorrow is Christmas Day.

Earlier this evening, we sat in the drawing room, and all had a glass of sherry, even me. Mother asked me to play some carols on the piano, which I was happy to do for her, though my heart wasn't really in it. I played quite badly, but Mother and Father and Tom sang along and thanked me when I finished.

I can't help being sad that Mother hasn't tried to get Father to change his mind about my nursing. If only Tom could speak out for me!

His own situation is hard enough, with the tension between Father and him over joining the army. Tom wants to continue his training until he is forced not to. If he were to try to take my side, we both know it wouldn't help either of our causes.

We had a Christmas card from Edgar. I don't know how he managed to get time to send it. It's very jolly and shows some young ladies on a sleigh, wrapped in furs, with *Joyeux Noël* in ornate writing across the front.

It had come a few days ago, but Father kept it hidden as a surprise and read it out to us this evening.

> *Dear Family,*
> *I trust you are all together at home now in Clifton Terrace. I wish I could be with you, too, but you know that I must be here. Nevertheless I wish you all a Merry Christmas. We're hoping for a bit of a do ourselves, God willing, so don't worry about me. I must go now.*
>
> *Your Edgar*

Father put it up on the mantelpiece, in pride of place, moving a card from someone else aside to do so.

Mother was delighted.

"You were naughty to keep it from us," she chided Father, gently.

He smiled, and kissed her on the forehead.

"But it's the best Christmas present we could have had," I said, and everyone agreed.

Then we had a supper of goose and gravy, and went to bed happy.

I am tired now; it is late, and Christmas is here.

# 59

The nightmare I was dreading has started.

I don't know what to do.

I don't. I don't.

I woke early, but not with the excitement of Christmas morning. I woke in the grip of fear. And my heart pounding so hard it hurt.

A thought came into my head from nowhere.

The Christmas card. Edgar's Christmas card. I suddenly realized that after Father had produced it and read it to us, he put it straight on the mantelpiece.

I had not touched it.

But I have now.

I went downstairs, took it from the shelf, turned it over and read it myself.

That was hours ago. I don't even remember how I got back upstairs. I must have run here for safety, to my own place.

I don't know what to do.

I have the card in front of me, and cannot stop looking at it, at the writing.

Writing that is now stained with my tears.

I can still see what it says, in Edgar's writing, but it is what I heard when I read it the first time that has told me what I most fear.

The words are there just as they were before, when Father read them. But as I read them I heard Edgar's voice, and he was saying something quite different.

> "I must go now. I had a bayonet put into my back as I was doing the same to another man. I must go now. I am dead and I must go."

I heard it only once, but it was clear enough; the minute I touched the card a shock shot through me.

*I am dead and I must go.*

I have sat for hours, shaking and crying. I am too scared to do anything, to talk to anyone. It is light outside now, I can hear the gulls screeching dimly at the back of my brain, but I cannot move.

I can't even bring myself to get Tom, though I want him to be here more than anything.

I know I'm right, but no one will believe me.

What am I going to do?

\* \* \*

There's a knock at the front door.

I look to see what time it is. Later than I thought. It's gone nine.

It strikes me dumbly that no one knocks on a door at nine o'clock on Christmas morning.

I know who it is.

I hear Mother going downstairs.

Clutching Edgar's card, I open my door, go down the stairs, and reach the top of the landing just as Mother opens the front door.

I hear one word, spoken quietly, in a tone of terrible respect.

"Telegram."

That's all.

And then I hear Mother screaming.

She's screaming and screaming.

# 58

Though the events of Christmas morning are months ago now, I can still see them all as if it has just happened. In some ways I can see things even more clearly now than I could at the time, because then my vision was obscured by shock and pain.

Now there's only pain.

# 57

Tomorrow will be June the twenty-fifth.

It's six months since we heard that Edgar had been killed. It is five days more than that since the actual moment, but details are still hard to come by.

The telegram was brief and to the point, and to be honest, it didn't really matter at the time. But now I want to find out more about it. I want to know everything, though we may never know it all.

We had a memorial service for Edgar in early January, but there was no funeral because there was no body to bury. He was buried somewhere in Belgium, in a military cemetery.

A letter we had later from a friend of his, another captain in his battalion, said he had been killed leading a raiding party into the enemy trenches. He said Edgar had been very brave and the raid had been a big success.

But that's a lie.

Just as I had heard Edgar tell me he was dead, I had seen a horrible tableau of the moment.

The panic. The complete chaos. No one was brave, not Englishman nor German; there was only horror and fear and utter bestial panic as Edgar's party arrived in the wrong place, as they killed and were killed, and as a couple of lucky men managed to stagger back to their own trench, their only success being alive to report what a disaster the whole thing had been.

But I said nothing of that to anyone.

Mother and Father cling desperately to the idea that their son died a hero's death, as if it makes any difference. Death is death. But if it helps them to think that, then it is well enough, I suppose.

# 56

**S**ix months.

The longest of my life. We have been pretending, and pretending, and pretending, all this time. That life could go on, that the war would end soon, that Edgar would come home, that it isn't really happening.

Now we know the truth.

Mother is broken, Father is sullen, and Thomas?

Thomas has gone.

That is almost the saddest thing about Edgar's death.

Something changed in him that Christmas morning.

He didn't cry, not like Mother and me. Father shouted and cursed, but Tom went silent, immediately.

Now he is in France.

# 55

It was only a few days afterward, maybe not even into the new year, that Thomas told us he was going to join the army.

Mother took it badly, and begged him not to go, but Father . . .

I had thought he would have been overjoyed, even delighted that he had finally won the argument with Thomas, but he wasn't.

"Very well," he said, but his voice was toneless. "You should go. I am proud of you for coming to the right decision. You can make *us* proud and keep the memory of your brother alive."

I can't believe what Tom did when Father said that.

He hit him.

There and then, he struck him across the chin. Father stumbled back and sank into a chair, but what is even more amazing is what happened next.

Nothing.

I was ready for Father to explode, to beat Tom, throw him out, at the very least curse him. But he sat in the chair, looking like a tired old man, and rubbed his chin.

Tom glared at us all, then turned on his heel and left. As he went I saw drops of blood from his knuckles stain the carpet in the hall.

# 54

That moment, six months ago now, that lives on so vividly with me, was forgotten, or rather ignored by us all.

Tom went back to Manchester after Edgar's memorial, hardly saying another dozen words to any of us.

Not even to me, and I could hardly bear that.

One thing was clear, he intended to join up.

Father made some 'phone calls, and as with Edgar, he managed to secure a commission for his son, though Tom would be in the Royal Army Medical Corps.

Then, without warning, Tom arrived back in Brighton. Father had been trying to make contact with him for days, to let him know about his commission, and was a little annoyed when he just strolled into the kitchen through the back door one day in January.

"I'm leaving," he said.

We all looked puzzled; he had only just arrived back.

"I'm leaving for France."

"I don't understand," Mother said. "Father's got you a place in the RAMC, you can't be leaving yet."

Tom looked from her to Father.

Neither of them said anything; then Tom put his hand out awkwardly to Father. He left it there for what seemed an age, until finally Father took it and shook it.

"Thank you," Tom said.

Mother smiled.

"It'll be fine in the RAMC," Father said. "Much safer, but you can still . . . you know. Help."

Tom stepped back abruptly.

"No," he said. "You don't understand. I'm grateful to you for trying, for getting me the place. But I'm not taking it."

"What?" Father said, his voice pinched with disbelief.

"I'm not taking a commission. I've enlisted with the Twentieth Fusiliers, in Manchester, the Public Schools Battalion. As a private."

I saw Mother put her hand to her throat, and the color drained from her cheeks. I stood up and grabbed Tom, begged him not to go, but he wouldn't listen. I asked him what had changed, why he didn't want to be a doctor anymore, and a hundred other things, but he wouldn't talk.

Mother was trying, and failing, not to cry; Father stomped around the kitchen, starting sentences, then stopping them, hot under the collar.

"But Tom," Mother pleaded. "You'll be safer in the RAMC, and you want to be a doctor, don't you? Don't you?"

Tom looked at her, miserably, his lip trembling.

"There's no use in it."

That's all he would say.

# 53

He left in January. It's June now. Winter ended, spring came and went, and now summer is here.

The house is so quiet. Father is working longer hours than ever. Mother speaks of nothing but what is necessary, and I have been left to myself, day in, day out, going crazy.

I have far too much time to think, far too much.

I think about everything that has happened to me, and to my family, and it does me no good at all. I pray like the stupid little girl I am to be young again. For all this not to have happened. For Edgar to be alive and for Tom to be happy. I long to be a young girl playing in a summer's garden, but even that desire has bad memories. Then I understand how naïve I am. That past, that happy past, is gone. Long gone. I will never have it back. Now I can see what it is that put distance between me and my family. It goes all the way back to Clare. Mother was scared by it, and has spent all her time since then trying to keep at bay a future she didn't want me to face. Father disbelieved it, and withdrew from me, and Edgar took his lead from Father, as always. Only Tom kept some faith with me, probably just because he was too young to do otherwise than keep loving his little sister.

And that's the feeling I've had all this time. Guilt that I lost my family because of what I am, and that they lost faith in me.

One day, I tried to talk to Father about becoming a nurse again.

He seemed to listen, but he wouldn't agree. Then I made the mistake of reminding him that Edgar had said I should have the chance to be a nurse, and that I ought to be given the chance again.

It was a mistake to mention Edgar's name.

At the end of May it was my birthday.

I am eighteen.

In a few days time it will be Thomas' birthday. On the first of July he will be nineteen. I wonder where he will be. When he was in Manchester he wrote all the time, but he's silent now. Of course, it's harder for him to write than it was for Edgar. Edgar was an officer and had more privileges. Tom is a private, and all we have had from him are two or three postcards that the army issues. They have a list of banal phrases on them, and Tom just crosses out the ones that don't apply.

Both times he has crossed out all the phrases on the card except the first.

*I am quite well.*

And he has signed it. That is all we know.

# 52

I had had no more premonitions since the moment I touched Edgar's Christmas card, but last night the raven came back to me in a dream.

I heard the beat of its wings, drumming louder and louder. It came right up close to me.

Its wing drifted across in front of my face, so close that I could see the barbs of each feather. The wing swung like a huge black curtain across the stage of a theater, and lifted to reveal a thousand ravens swinging around the treetops of a blighted wood.

The ravens parted, and I saw a gun.

The gun fired, with a violent bang that shook me awake in an instant.

Just before I was pushed out of the dream, I glimpsed one more thing.

The bullet's target.
Thomas.
It hit him. He's going to die.

# 51

At last my time has come.

I know it from the foreshadowing of Thomas' death.

I don't know how, but as I lay awake shivering after the dream, I know it hasn't happened, and that maybe it won't for some time. It is definitely something that has yet to be.

I don't know why this is happening to me, or how it does. It feels as if someone is playing games with me, with my life, my destiny. Or with that of my family.

Finally I have the chance to do something with what I have seen.

I know it's no use to talk to my parents about it. They thought I was living with fantasies before. If I tell them I know Tom is going to die, they'll probably think I've gone mad.

I have to live with this curse now, the curse that is to know the future but never to be believed.

When the sight came to me before—for Clare, for that

soldier, for Edgar's friend, for those patients, for Edgar himself—it did no good.

What was the use? Edgar was dead, but I had no warning; I only knew a few moments before we found out from the telegram.

But this time . . .

This time is different. I've been given time to do something with what I have seen. And even if I am wrong, it makes no difference to what I've decided.

There's a big offensive due to start soon; the papers have been full of it. The British and French armies have been gearing up for something massive for months, or so we're led to believe. If that's true, then many men will die, but Tom isn't going to be one of them, because I'm going to stop it.

I've planned it all.

Although Father has kept me from the hospital, on several occasions I've bumped into nurses I know. We've chatted, and they've told me about the comings and goings. Lots of young girls have been volunteering to go to France as Red Cross nurses. The hospitals there are desperate for them.

I know where they sail from, and to, and where they go next. The boats leave almost all the time from Folkestone. Dover's too dangerous, so they sail from Folkestone, a bit farther down the coast. From there, the nurses head to Boulogne, or to Rouen.

And tomorrow, there's going to be one more nurse joining them.

I don't know where Tom's battalion is, but they're somewhere in Flanders, and once I'm there, it shouldn't be too hard to find out where.

Then I'm going to bring him home, and stop his death ever having the chance to happen.

If it's true that I lost my family, and that they lost their faith in me, then this is my chance to mend it all. I want to heal the rift between us, make everything all right again. If I save Tom, then maybe they'll understand me at last, and I will get them back.

I will save Tom.

It's my only hope. I must do it.

I must.

# PART TWO

# 50

I've been in France for nearly a week, and this is the first chance I've had to stop and think.

A week, but it feels like a year, so much has happened.

When I was on the ship, I thought vaguely that I would keep a diary of my journey in France, but I see what a ridiculous idea that was. There wouldn't have been time, and one week's experience of the real nature of the war is enough to make me want to forget everything I've seen, not make a permanent record of it.

It's Saturday morning, and I'm sitting in the canteen. All around me are the noises of the rest station, and the sound of trains. I can scarcely believe I'm here, in France. Soon I'll be moved to work in No. 13 Stationary Hospital, based in huts up on the cliffs, but I'm being given two weeks' experience in the rest station first. They say it will give me a taste of what I'm likely to encounter. I couldn't tell them, of course, that I don't intend to stay that long. As soon as I can find out where Tom is, I'll be moving on.

The rest station is part of the railway station, converted from rooms along the platform into a suite for ambulance work. We have a surgery and dispensary, a storeroom, and a staff room. We cook outside on large portable boilers.

The reason the rest station is here is because the wounded men roll right into our hands, in trains that have come down from close to the front line. We're the first port of call. We give the men something to eat and drink, clean them up and maybe dress their wounds. Then on they go, to hospital in Rouen, or a convalescent camp in Havre. If they're lucky, they might be heading for a ship home.

There's another thing that can happen. They can die in the rest station, and be taken away to be buried.

It's an incredible place, full of people throughout the day and night, full of noise and activity. All around, people are speaking English, which surprised me at first, but there are very few Frenchmen here. This place seems to belong to the British Army now, and the few remaining Frenchmen are either very old, or young boys. The rest are away. Fighting. Those who are here work as orderlies and porters, like the old man who runs the platform. He's in charge of his own little army, composed mostly of boys, and they work continuously, and efficiently. The station is now a station and hospital combined, and runs very smoothly, from what I've seen. There's even a tiny track on the platform itself along which runs a small wooden truck, to move supplies and medicine from one end of the platform to the other. All day long the Frenchman shouts at his boys, who scurry about on the truck, taking rides and fooling about when they think no one's looking.

I left Brighton last Monday. That was the twenty-sixth, but first I had to prepare my escape.

# 49

Escape it was. I knew there was no way to tell my parents what I was going to do. All I could do was post a letter before I left Brighton. It will scandalize them, and their acquaintances, when they discover their daughter has vanished, but I can't help that, either. This is a difficult world now.

On the Sunday before I left, I had to undertake the first part of my plan. A small mission without which none of what I have achieved so far would have been possible.

It was early evening. It was warm, though not bright, but Mother didn't bat an eye when I said I was going out for a short walk.

"Take a coat," she called from the kitchen. "It looks like it might rain later."

That was all she said, but how was she to know of the nervous beat of my blood?

"I've got one," I said.

I walked out of the house and turned down to the seafront, but soon doubled back by turning up Montpelier Road. There, I was lost in the throng of people taking the evening air. I made my way to the hospital.

I carried my coat over my arm; hidden underneath it I had a canvas bag, neatly folded.

Though my heart was racing, I knew that my best chance of success would be to act as relaxed as possible, to project an air of confidence. So as I walked through the doors I simply nodded at the lady on the reception desk. I knew her by sight, and she knew who I was.

I half smiled.

"An errand for Father," I said, by way of explanation, trying for all the world to sound bored and exasperated in equal measure.

I made my way up the central staircase, pretending to head for Father's office.

I did need something from his office, but I passed by its door. There was no light inside, as I knew there would not be. Father was out on the rounds with the other special constables, telling people to put their lights out.

I made my way to the end of the corridor, then came down by the back staircase to the end of one of the wards, and there lay my goal. The laundry room.

The hospital was quiet that evening, which was my good fortune, but even so, I checked up and down the corridor before I slipped inside.

For a moment I began to panic. The laundry room was full of sheets being washed, and blankets, and pillowcases. I could see uniforms, too, but they were the wrong sort. There were plenty of regular nurses' uniforms, but I needed a VAD one. In fact, I needed both an indoor uniform and the heavy brown outdoor uniform.

Frantically I began to hunt through the piles of clean uniforms, but couldn't find what I needed. In desperation I looked around and saw the basket for uniforms waiting to be washed. I rummaged through it and at last pulled out a couple of long gray VAD uniforms. Then I found various aprons, each emblazoned with a red cross.

A thought occurred to me. I held up one of the dresses, but I couldn't be sure.

I looked at the door; there was no lock on the inside. Instead, I wheeled a huge laundry basket over to the door and jammed it up against the handle.

Quickly I stripped and tried the first dress on, and was glad I had; it had been made for someone larger than me and I looked silly. I would be spotted in a moment. Fumbling, I pulled it off and stuck my arms into the second dress. It was fine. I pulled it off again, and put my own back on. I stuffed the uniform into the canvas bag, along with the cleanest apron I could find, and a couple of caps.

I couldn't see an outdoor uniform, and decided I would have to just wear my coat and risk it.

I pulled the laundry basket back into place, put my ear to the frosted window and slipped out again.

Still I saw no one as I walked back to Father's office.

I tried the door, and to my relief it wasn't locked. This was a hospital, not a prison, after all.

I hurried inside.

I stood there undecided, and then started to hunt.

I knew Father was responsible for passing and processing the volunteer nurses selected to go to France. On my last visit to his office, when we'd tried and failed to have tea, I'd seen a big box file on his desk that contained, I hoped, my ticket to France.

It was still there, labeled: JOINT WAR COMMITTEE, SERVICE ABROAD.

Inside were several bundles of papers, each one concerning a nurse. I began to leaf through them. The first few only had the preliminary applications in them—documentation that the nurse had put her name on the register to serve abroad. That she'd been notified of selection, that she'd applied for her passport, and so on. These were of no use to me. I riffled through to the end of the box. They were all the same. I tried to stay calm as I searched the desk, and then, in Father's Out tray, I saw another bundle, just like the ones I had been looking at. He must have been working on it on Friday night; it was a completed set of papers.

I grabbed it and checked it through.

The nurse selected was called Miriam Hibbert. I didn't know her, and I didn't want to, in a way. I was about to severely impede her means of going abroad.

Everything I needed was there. Her completed contract of service. The brassard arm band with its red cross. An identity disc. An identity certificate. A red permit that allows travel abroad.

And then the passport.

My heart sank. I hadn't seen a passport before then. Until the war started we didn't need them. I didn't know they had photographs. I looked at the small black-and-white image of

Miriam Hibbert. She looked nothing like me. There was no getting around it. How could I pass myself off as her, with that tiny picture to prove it was all a lie?

Not wanting to give up, I looked at the identity certificate.

The Anglo-French Hospitals Identity Certificate was a small paper document. And it had no photograph.

On it I read that it could stand in place of a passport where none was present. I didn't know quite what that would mean in practice, but my heart soared. The certificate had the most basic information on it. Name, address, age, height. Again my luck held. Miriam was just an inch or two shorter than me, at five foot six, and she was twenty-three. I could pass for twenty-three. Then there was a brief, rather blunt description of her.

Tall; round face; brown eyes. Medium build. Straight, dark brown hair to just above shoulder length.

It fitted me, apart from the round face and medium build. Well, I could tell them I'd lost weight. And my hair I could cut easily enough.

It was time to go, but just as I was sliding the papers on top of the uniform in my canvas bag, I saw a book I recognized on Father's desk.

On impulse I picked it up and slid it into the bag along with everything else.

The blood was still chasing round my veins twice as fast as it should, even when I was halfway home. All the way I expected to hear running footsteps coming after me, or cries of "Stop! Thief!" but none came, and eventually I began to realize that I had done what I set out to do. I had my passport for France tucked up in a canvas bag under my arm.

As I reached the Seven Dials I stopped in a doorway and took out the book.

Miss Garrett's copy of *Greek Myths*.

There was no doubt. There, on the flyleaf, was her juvenile signature.

The book had made its way back into my possession. Mother had pushed it into Miss Garrett's hands as she'd left on that awful night over six months before. Had she sent it to Father? She must have done, but why?

There was a piece of paper folded inside the book, and I wondered if it was a letter from Miss Garrett, explaining her reasons for sending it, but it was not. It was some official letter of Father's that he was using as a bookmark. And if he was using it as a bookmark, that meant he was reading the book. I put the letter back between the pages where it had been.

For the first time since I had decided to leave, I began to doubt myself.

# 48

I have the book with me now, as I sit in the canteen on this Saturday morning. It was a hazy start to the day, but it's clearing up now. In front of me is a bowl of porridge, and tea in an enamel mug. All around me are the smells of war and the smells of medicine. I've kept the book in the large pocket of my uniform since it came back to me. At first I saw it as an omen about home, telling me to stay. Then, more worryingly, I saw it as a link from me to Cassandra herself, and I was scared by that. But in the end I decided that it could only mean good luck, that maybe Father was trying to understand me at last. So I brought it with me to France.

With a shock I suddenly realize that today is Tom's birthday. I look up and around me. No one is looking at me, no one knows who I am. No one here knows Tom. I have no idea where he is. For a moment I feel very lonely, but it passes.

I raise my tea to my lips and whisper.

"Happy birthday, Thomas."

Sitting here, feeling the weight of the book in my pocket, I allow myself to dwell on my last few hours at home.

When I got home with the uniform I went straight to my room. Father was still out, and Mother was sewing in the drawing room.

Going downstairs again, I forced a yawn, and muttered something about an early night.

Mother looked up at me.

"Fine, dear," she said, smiling weakly. "You need plenty of rest."

I didn't agree, but that's what I had been hoping she'd say.

"I'll take a drink up with me," I said, and turned to go.

Mother didn't answer, but dropped her head back to her sewing, straining her eyes by the light from the standard lamp behind her.

I was struck by the sight of her. She looked like a painting, a woman at her sewing in the half-light, her husband out in the evening somewhere, one son dead, the other away at the war. For the first time in my life I realized my mother was an old woman, and I felt like crying.

I stood gazing at her for a long time, but she was so lost in her thoughts that she didn't even notice. The feeling of sadness inside me welled up so powerfully that I thought I would crumble. I looked at her one last time, and closed my eyes, trying to fight the feeling that I would never see her again.

I closed the door.

I slept, and I slept surprisingly well, until, at four in the morning, my alarm clock went off right beneath the pillow under my head.

It was time to leave.

# 47

It may be summer, but it is still dark at four in the morning, and since Daylight Saving Time started back in May, it's darker for an hour longer in the mornings.

The darkness would help me later, but in my bedroom I fumbled for the things I'd prepared the night before. I had my case that I used for holidays, small but strong. Everything I needed fitted into it, including the uniform, wash things and Miss Garrett's book. I took all the money I had, as well as everything from Cook's housekeeping jar in the kitchen. I felt bad about that, but I knew Father would replace it.

It was a fresh morning. There was a train for Folkestone at five, so I had plenty of time, though there was something I had to do first. I hurried down to the station, praying that I would see no one I knew, but I needn't have worried. It was still dark, and besides, no one of my acquaintance, or that of

151

my family's, would be out at that time of the morning, a time only for thieves and tradesmen, or for people like me, with a long journey ahead.

At the station I headed straight for the public conveniences. There, I pulled off my clothes, and changed into the VAD uniform. I put the clothes I had been wearing and Miriam Hibbert's passport into the bag, and shoved it up on top of the cistern, where it was out of sight.

I pulled out a little mirror and the scissors I had brought, and considered my hair. It was straight, and easy enough to cut, though when I'd finished I saw what a mess the back was.

I tied my hair in a bun and hid the whole thing under my nurse's cap. I took my case in my hand, and left.

I waited at the far end of the platform for the train, and by five past five, Brighton was left far behind me. My journey had begun.

I thought of my parents, still asleep in their bed, unaware that with every passing minute I was a mile farther from them.

# 46

I thought I had planned my journey in detail, but on the train that morning I began to think of all sorts of new things.

I knew that the hospital ships sailed from Folkestone to Boulogne, but had I fully understood what I was walking into, I might not have been so brave.

Then there was the question of passports. I hoped the identity certificate would be good enough.

As the train rattled into Kent I remember thinking I might have to give the whole thing up, or I would be stopped and sent home, in disgrace. Maybe they'd even think I was a spy trying to get back to Germany. The papers had been full of stories of people being arrested as spies, although most of them were probably totally innocent.

I got off the train at Folkestone with little clue where to go or what to do, but then I saw another girl in a VAD uniform smiling at me. She came over. I began to panic. I should give the whole thing up, and go home to face the shame and anger of my parents.

"Are you lost, too?" she said.

I nodded.

"I was, but I've got it all sorted now. I'm off to Boulogne. Are you?"

Without thinking, I told her I was, and then, of course, she wanted to talk to me.

"What's your name?"

I hesitated for a moment.

"Miriam," I said. "Miriam Hibbert."

"Where are you from?" she asked, after she had introduced herself. Her name was Amelia, but she told me to call her Millie.

"Brighton," I said. I didn't want to be rude, but I couldn't afford to give too much away.

We made our way down to the docks, and soon we were in a queue of people, mostly soldiers returning to the front, all waiting at the gate in the docks. It was about midmorning by then, and the boat was due to sail at noon. It was a hot, bright day, and the queue was long. Millie smiled as the seagulls cawed and screeched above our heads. The boats in the harbor sounded their horns from time to time, and we could smell the salt in the air.

In spite of everything, in spite of my fear, it was thrilling.

Millie chatted as we shuffled slowly forward.

"How old are you?" she asked. "I'm twenty-three."

"I'm twenty-three, too," I lied, but she just laughed and I smiled. After that she chatted away merrily, and asked fewer questions. I learned a lot about her, without having to tell her much about myself.

She'd been working in London and decided she wanted "a bit of adventure," as she put it, so she had put herself forward for service overseas.

I realized from what she said about her home that she was from a very wealthy family, but found life rather boring. This was her way of having an "adventure" in a manner that her parents could not object to.

I watched Millie closely as we chatted. She was quite pretty, I thought, though some of her prettiness was down to having money to spend. I felt mean for thinking that, and tried to listen more attentively. She had a small round mouth with lips that flew as she nattered about this and that, and deep brown eyes, like mine. I decided I liked her, and I thought I could trust her. Not with the whole truth, but with some of it, at least.

"Millie," I said, when she stopped for a moment.

"Yes," she said. "What is it?"

"I have a problem, but I wonder if I can ask you to help me?"

"What is it?"

"It was so early when I left this morning, I forgot things. I forgot my passport."

"Oh!" she said. "Oh, no. And what about your letter?"

"Letter?" I asked.

"From your hospital? You need a letter of authorization for transfer from the commandant of your detachment at home. Don't tell me you don't . . . ?"

"Oh, yes," I said, quickly. "Yes, I've got that. And my identity certificate."

She looked at me, exasperated, but then smiled.

"Don't worry!" she declared. "I'll get you through. As for

155

your passport, well, either they need nurses out there or they don't!"

And she was right.

We got to the front of the queue to find a woman in civilian clothes but wearing a red cross on an armband. There was a sailor there too.

Millie had such an air about her as she explained my predicament and flourished my identity certificate that in no time at all we were making our way up the gangplank onto the deck. It seems that passport controls are much more about stopping people from coming into the country than letting them leave.

The ship was a vast thing, almost a liner, which had been converted into a Red Cross hospital ship. It was painted white with a large red cross on each side, and we learned that it spent its time crossing the channel, bringing the wounded home and returning with supplies of all kinds, as well as new nurses like us.

We set sail.

# 45

The crossing seemed to take a lifetime. Millie assumed that we were going to stick together, and I have to admit I was glad of her companionship.

Besides, without her I would probably have been on my weary way home.

It was a smooth crossing, but even so, I felt a little queasy.

"You'll feel better if we get some air," Millie said, and since it was a warm day, I agreed.

We found a sheltered spot on one of the foredecks, and settled down, using our cases as seats.

"I wonder if I can get us a drink," she said, and before I could answer, she was up and away. She is so bright and full of life.

"Watch my things, Miriam, please?"

I started, not yet used to my new name. But I smiled. She

made everything seem easy, and I wondered if maybe it was. Maybe life *was* easier than I made it.

She was gone a long time, and I took the copy of *Greek Myths* from my case and began to read.

Out of curiosity I opened it at the place Father had been reading, and felt a stab of regret shoot through me again.

Cassandra. He had reached a page that talked about Cassandra.

I read for a while, but the motion of the ship, the warmth, the fresh air and my tiredness all caught up with me. I must have fallen asleep.

At least, that is what I imagine, for only that can explain what happened next.

I was no longer Alexandra, in 1916, but another girl, long, long ago. I was on a ship still, making a fateful journey, but it was a warmer sea that my boat was crossing, and the boat was moving under sail and oar, not coal and steam. A ship that left the waters of the Hellespont, with the battered walls of Troy far behind, to head out across the Aegean.

As the ship reeled across the heaven blue sea, I suffered as that other girl suffered. Abducted from my home by the violence of a foreign king, I prophesied not only his death, but my own as well, and despite the heat I shivered at the pain of a storm of things foreshadowed and foreseen.

The worst of it, as ever, was that no one would believe me.

My every utterance was taken to be worthless, the rantings of a madwoman. Yet I *knew* the truth for what it was, and it was coming to meet me faster than I thought possible.

The seagulls wheeling above my head should have told me we were approaching the French coast, but as I gazed at them, they were transformed into ravens. They flapped blackly around the boat, calling to me, mocking me.

*"You should know the future only when it has come; to know it before is grief too soon given. All will come clear in the sun-light of the dawn."*

The boat drove on through the breaking waves.

# 44

By late afternoon the French coast was in sight. The sunshine of Folkestone had vanished, and a heavy rain beat down on us from a black sky. Our ship had to wait while a troop ship maneuvered in the harbor, and so it took slow turns up and down the coast for an hour or more.

When Millie had finally returned with a bottle of lemonade, she took one look at me and decided I was unwell. I think I was no more than tired, but she feared something worse, and dragged me into the ship's galley, where once again she had no trouble in making everyone do as she bid.

Before long I was sitting with my feet up in an officer's berth, a glass of ice water in my hand. This was not the quiet, unobtrusive arrival I had planned, but I couldn't stop Millie, and in any case, I was in something of a mess.

By the time the boat docked I had recovered, and then there was no more waiting.

We stepped onto Boulogne Quay, onto French soil. The whole journey had taken no more than twelve hours. As we made our way from the docks to the railway station, I wondered what was happening at home, in Brighton. My parents would have discovered that I had disappeared. It would be a day at least before my letter reached them—I had wanted to give myself that much of a head start in case they came looking for me—and even when they did get it, I didn't think it would reassure them very much. I knew they would be sick with worry, and yet I felt detached, not just by the distance between us, but by my sense of purpose.

That evening Millie and I were put into our detachment. There are a dozen of us in all, with a superintendent and a quartermaster above us, and a commandant above them. Our superintendent is called Sister McAndrew. She's tough, keen on discipline. When I told her I'd forgotten my outdoor uniform, she made me buy one from the stores.

She gave us each a booklet of rules detailing how we have to behave in France. I tried my best to look interested, though I can't shift the feeling that none of this really applies to me. My disguise is a means to an end; I'm only here for one thing. Then I remembered that if I'm caught I won't be able to find Tom, and I started acting like a nurse again.

I saw Sister McAndrew looking at me hard, but I told myself it was only my imagination. I am Miriam Hibbert now.

Millie and I have been assigned to No. 13 Stationary Hospital, but we will spend a couple of weeks learning general duties in the rest station at the railway station.

It has been a baptism of fire.

# 43

They all have it.

All of them.

The trench-haunted look. An appalling weariness behind their eyes. Every single man who has passed through the rest station while I have been here, and there have been literally thousands of them, has exuded an awful aura of . . . of what?

Is it horror? Or fear? Pain or fatigue or shock?

It is all of these things. They don't talk about the trenches specifically; you pick up hints and notions and hear stories and rumors, but none of them talk about it directly. Yet there is enough to form a terrible picture of what they have witnessed, what has been done to them, what they have done to other people. That's what made me realize what it is about them.

They have lost faith.

They have lost their faith in what it is to be human. And

so the smallest act on our part, not even of kindness, but of mere consideration, makes them so desperately grateful that it makes me want to cry.

I haven't seen much of Millie, although we're in the same detachment. We've been so busy that we've had no more chance than to nod and smile as we've passed once or twice. When I do see her, though, I'm still struck by her irrepressible nature.

As for me, I see death at every turn. I see these men like ghosts waiting to be born. Sometimes it's just a feeling I get as I am tending to one of them, a sad realization that I'm wasting my efforts in patching him up, because in another fortnight he'll be dead anyway. Sometimes I get a vision, horribly real, impossible to ignore. Last time it happened I nearly gave myself away. As I washed a soldier I suddenly saw corpse worms crawling across his face. When I blinked and looked again they were gone. I realized that it had been a premonition of his death in a field somewhere in Flanders.

I began to shake, but managed to control myself, and no one suspected anything.

In one way, that's the worst part of it. I've had to control my reactions to my visions, for fear of exposing myself. I'm assaulted by them almost every waking hour, and it makes me sick to admit it, but I've got used to it. Not completely, of course, but to a very large degree, I witness these walking ghosts and don't turn a hair.

If I do, I may lose the chance of saving Thomas.

# 42

Although we're VAD nurses in the rest station, and not regulars in one of the base hospitals, we've had more to do than mere domestic work.

Each ambulance train has been specially converted to hold over three hundred men on stretchers, as well as maybe another fifty sitting on cases. At times, when trains have been rolling into the station every hour, we've been inundated.

When men arrive here by ambulance train, they may have been washed and had their wounds cleaned by the nurses on board, if they weren't too busy. The doctors decide what will happen to them next: home, hospital here or back to the front.

Of course, most of them hope that their wound is bad enough to get them sent home.

"Is it a Blighty one, Sister?"

You hear those words all day, on every side of you. *Blighty* is a word picked up from the Indian soldiers; it's derived from their word for British things. The men want a Blighty wound, to get themselves a Blighty ticket, one of the little forms like luggage labels that we tie onto the wounded who are being sent home. On the brown card ticket is a diagonal red cross, as well as all sorts of information. The man's name, of course. His army number, regiment and the date and name of the hospital ship he'll be taking home. On the other side is the diagnosis, details of any treatment to be given en route, his age, his religion, his length of service.

And the sister will be gentle with them, or maybe joke with them, anything than say bluntly that they're going back to the war.

"A Blighty one? No!" she'll say, laughing. "Not that scratch!"

And when he complains, she'll maybe add something.

"Still, you never know, if you hang around here for three or four days, maybe the medical officer will have too many tickets to carry and we might persuade him to get rid of two on you!"

Two tickets, of course. For they are never issued except on the assumption that when the man is better he will be coming back to France to fight again. He may be injured, but that doesn't mean he's left the army.

In spite of myself and my intention to find Tom and leave France, I find myself being drawn in by the wounded men. It's not possible to remain impervious to the anguish all around. Already in my short week I've seen many cases of shell-shock. In these cases, the diagnosis on the tickets will say one of two things: shell-shock, or neurasthenia. I can't see the difference in the men themselves, and I believe it's really down to the view of the medical officer who writes the ticket. In brackets after the diagnosis, there is one of two letters: *S* or *W*. *S* is for sick, as in from dysentery or pneumonia; *W* is for wounded, when they've been hurt in action. For the shell-shock cases, sometimes they put *S* and sometimes *W*, as if they can't decide if they're sick or wounded. It may seem a small difference, but it will mean a lot to the men when they get better. For wounded men receive an army pension; sick men do not. It makes me wonder at how easily the doctors seem to make these decisions.

# 41

I haven't managed to get any news of Tom's battalion. The postcards he sent were as good as useless. The men are not allowed to say anything about where they are, in case the letters fall into the hands of spies and give away secret army information. But Tom knew he was heading for Flanders before he left, and I don't have any reason to suppose otherwise. If his battalion is still there, then any wounded would almost certainly come to Boulogne, though there's a small chance they might be taken by canal to St. Omer, and then Calais.

I've tried to check the regimental badge of every wounded man I can. Sometimes it's easy enough despite the mud, but sometimes . . . sometimes the uniforms are not just caked in mud, but ripped to ribbons as well. From the barbed wire in no-man's-land. Then it's very hard to see anything, maybe hard even to tell which bit of clothing it is you're removing from your patient.

I've found no badges from the Twentieth Royal Fusiliers. In a way that's good news, for though it means no news of Tom, it also means that maybe his battalion are in reserve, and not fighting at the moment.

I say I've had no news of Tom, and that's true. But I've seen him.

Last night I had the dream again, in which I see him being shot. It was just as real as before, but briefer, and chilling in its detail.

The raven was there, cawing at me, mocking as usual. I saw the gun that will kill Tom. It was so clear I could feel the cold metal of the gun barrel heat up as the bullet spun down it.

Tom was surrounded by huge rough spikes sticking out of the ground, up into the air. I couldn't work out what they were, and everything went hazy.

It's Saturday morning, and I'm drinking my tea and trying to shake the vision of the dream from my head.

It's the first of July. Tom's nineteenth birthday. It's actually pretty quiet on the station today, and in the rest station, but all morning, rumors have been running around that something big is happening.

Down the valley, in the Somme.

Those who claim to know say the big push has come, and that very soon the wounded will start arriving in numbers hitherto undreamed of.

So far, though, it's just distant thunder.

# 40

The last few days have flashed past like the blurred view from a speeding train.

How quiet it seemed on Saturday morning. It wasn't long before that peace was shattered and we knew it had merely been the calm before the storm.

The big push had finally come.

Although many of the wounded are taken to the base hospitals at Rouen, directly down the line from the Somme valley, just as many of them come up to us via Abbeville or St. Pol.

Millie and I were on the same shifts, and that day alone we must have processed a thousand men through our rest station. Next day was twice as bad, and there's been no respite.

It has been a continual onslaught, and it amazes me that we've coped, but we have. All day and night we take men in on their stretchers, direct from the train, clean them up, move them on. We load the trains with supplies for their next journey: clothes, cases of sterilized milk, butter, eggs, biscuits, meat extracts, cigarettes.

Over and over and over again, until we are not even conscious of our actions anymore. There are men everywhere. Bodies asleep in every conceivable corner of the station. And we keep working until every last one has been seen, and the station is quieter again. Then the next train arrives.

I've barely had a chance to think of Tom. Of course, at first I worried continually, and all the while expected to see him being carried into our suite. I've heard of stories like that. One of our nurses saw her own brother being brought in. He had died on the train. It might seem extraordinary, but with the thousands of men coming through here, sooner or later things like that are bound to happen. She was inconsolable, but next day she was back, working again. Her world had changed, but it changed nothing. She still has a job to do.

After a while, I stopped thinking about Tom, though from force of habit I kept checking regimental badges, and I've seen none from the Twentieth.

Then, yesterday, Tuesday . . .

It was a horrible day, rain lashing down in angry bursts. The sky was brutally dark, and it was hard to believe it was July. We could hear thunderstorms inland. At least, we thought they were storms, but sometimes we've heard the sound of the guns from the front. The big guns.

I handed a heavy bucket to Millie, and paused briefly to straighten my aching back, when the sister we were with crossed herself.

She was looking through the window of our surgery onto the platform. A shadow passed by. A dispatch rider stuck his head into the room, as if looking for someone. When she saw him, Sister looked away hurriedly, and bent her head to cleaning the rough wooden table we used to operate on.

He was gone almost as soon as he'd arrived, and Sister crossed herself again, shuddering.

"What is it?" I asked. "What's wrong? Do you know that man?"

"No," she said. "And I don't want to. Everyone knows who he is."

"I don't," I said. "What's wrong?"

She looked at me briefly, then started working again.

"Hoodoo Jack. That's what they call him. He's a bad wind and you should stay away from him."

"But why? What's he done?"

"It's not what he's done, it's what he says. Used to be a soldier. Then he started to know when his mates were going to get it. He was right once too often. Went crazy. He's a jinx. That's why they call him Hoodoo."

She crossed herself a third time, and would say no more.

# 39

I knew immediately that I had to talk to Hoodoo Jack, but two days passed before I got the chance. In that time there has been nothing but work. I am so tired. I looked in a mirror last night and hardly recognized myself. My face is sunken, my eyes are dull, my hair is lank, my skin grimy. My hands are sore from all the washing. Washing men, washing clothes, washing myself.

I saw my first gas cases yesterday. The first since . . . that man . . . in the hospital. Simpson. I tried not to think about him, but it all came back to me. What a different world the Dyke Road hospital seems to me now. Even its makeshift nature was luxury compared with the primitive rooms we work in here. The floors are scrubbed, but they're still bare. The walls are whitewashed, and we put flowers in jugs, and keep it all as tidy as we can, but there's no forgetting that the rest station is just four primitive rooms in a French railway station.

There were three gas cases. Two privates and a corporal from a Scottish regiment. Their skin was blistered and burnt by the gas, and one of the privates couldn't see. None of them could talk, but they didn't need to.

I saw it all from them.

The dark fumblings in the early dawn.

"Gas!" someone called down the line.

I could see their wretched attempts to pull their gas helmets on, and though they managed it in the end, they were too slow. The gas was borne in on a westerly wind, clinging to the ground, seeping into every crevice, unseen. The corporal got it worst because he stopped to help his two young soldiers.

As he did so, he could hear his sergeant shouting at him.

"Always put your own mask on first. You won't be able to help anyone if you're dead!"

He heard his sergeant's words, though his sergeant had been dead two weeks by then. But he couldn't help it. He had to help the privates, they reminded him so much of his own boys at home. Thank God, at home.

I didn't see any more. I couldn't move. I was useless for five minutes, till Millie hissed at me. I'd never seen her angry before.

Afterward she told me. Sister McAndrew was staring at me from the door. I forced myself back to work. I cut the men's clothing, and prepared them for departure to No. 13 Stationary.

And they were gone. Another three among the thousands I have seen. But I hope to God that poor corporal sees again.

\* \* \*

The others don't seem to complain, so I dare not. I know I'm not really a nurse, but no one else knows my secret, not even Millie. I've always wanted to be a nurse, but I know now I was naïve. I had no idea what it would be like. I can't do this.

I can't tell anyone, but I long to. To grab someone and scream at them that I'm not a nurse, that I don't know what I'm doing, that I'm not strong enough to cope with all the horror around me. That I want to go home.

But I cannot. I think of Tom, and I cannot.

# 38

Later on, after the gas cases, I went out with Millie. The canteen was full of noise and people, and though our legs were crying out for us to sit down and rest, we took a mug of tea out onto the platform.

"Let's walk," Millie said.

The station is massive, busy and noisy around the center of the platforms and the buildings, so we headed for the far end of the platform. It's from that direction the trains roll in from the front, and yet, for the time being, everything was quiet.

Something made me think of Edgar. I was angry with him; he'd said I was useless and weak. Then I felt guilty because I remembered that he's gone.

I thought of Tom. It's almost overwhelming sometimes, and I don't know which is harder to cope with. The fact that

Edgar's dead, or that Tom's still alive, but could be killed any day.

Millie and I had nearly reached the end of the platform. The rails ran off in front of us, away through Boulogne, away into the countryside, through towns and villages, through cuttings and clearings, until somewhere, the track must come to an end maybe just a mile or two behind the front lines. I could smell cordite, though I have never seen a gun fired in my life; I could hear the shouts of battle.

Suddenly I realized Millie was gazing at me.

"How old are you really?" she said.

"I told you."

She looked at me, dropped her head to one side.

"How old are you?" she said, gently.

"Seventeen."

"And you're not a nurse, are you? Not really."

For a second I tried to act offended, surprised, but there was no point. She knew.

"No," I said. "Not really."

"Who are you, Miriam?" she asked, "What are you doing here?"

"My name's Alexandra," I said, slowly. "I've come—"

"No!" she said, suddenly. "I don't want to know."

I must have looked hurt, because she softened then.

"I mean, it's probably better if I don't. I can guess anyway. You've come here to look for your sweetheart, you want to get married before he . . . before . . . well, something like that."

"Yes," I said. "Something like that."

Neither of us spoke then. A minute passed.

I looked at Millie and smiled.

"How did you know?"

"Just a feeling. You're too young, though I don't think anyone's too worried about that. And your nursing. Have you had any training at all?"

I shook my head. "I was a VAD for a while. I've spent some time in hospitals. My father—"

She held up her hand again.

"Don't tell me," she said, but she was smiling. "In that case, you're doing really well, but to a trained eye it's obvious once you stop to look."

There was no point denying it, but her words cut me. I thought I'd been doing well, but if it was that obvious I was an impostor, my chance of saving Tom could be snatched away at any time.

"I'll help you, if I can," Millie said.

She put her hand on my shoulder, and without thinking I turned into her arms. I cried, quietly. Then I pulled away.

"I'm ruining your uniform," I said, and we laughed, though it was a short, bitter laugh. Her uniform was already a mess from the day's work, the gray flannel stained with red blood, bright and fresh.

"Millie," I said, "you won't say anything . . . ?"

"No," she said. "I won't. *Miriam.* I believe you're here for a good reason, and anyway, you're helping the wounded. Don't be too hard on yourself, you're doing a good job. But I've noticed, and it's only a matter of time before someone else does. I have to tell you, I think McAndrew's got her eye on you. Be careful."

I nodded, and tried to smile, but I couldn't. I physically couldn't.

"We'd better get back to work," she said.

We turned to walk back to the hustle and bustle of the rest station.

A train was rolling in.

# 37

Seven ravens fly about my head.

Whirling, whirling, their gun black feathers beat the air, making a drumming in my ears that doesn't stop, but is transformed into the sound of cannon fire.

Their beating becomes more frantic, until, as I gaze upward, a single black feather falls down to me, spinning like a sycamore seed on its way to earth.

The feather falls straight toward my face, and I try to lift my hand to catch it, but my arms will not move from my sides. The feather strikes me and brushes gently across my eyes.

Everything goes black.

I am sitting down. I can move my hands now and I feel a desk in front of me, like a school desk, but I am drowned in blackness.

From somewhere in the darkness, someone is suddenly shouting at me. It's hard to recognize the voice because the words are Greek. I think it must be Miss Garrett, but then I realize who it is.

It's me.

The other me wails the words, as if she is a demon, shrieking each line with barely a breath between.

She screams the last word at me.

*The Iliad*, I think. That was from *The Iliad*.

"*Iliad*," I say.

Yes, I know that answer. Please don't ask me another.

But she is shouting and screaming at me again.

"*Who wrote it?*"

"Homer."

Don't ask me another.

"*Why is it dark?*"

"Because of the war," I splutter out, hurriedly.

I got that one, but please don't ask me another. Please. Because I don't know that I can get another question right.

And then?

And then—

She is screaming at me again.

"*Why is there war?*"

I have no answer.

"*What does it mean?*"

I have no answer.

"*And the raven?*"

"What?" I cry out, tears streaming down my face.

"*The raven! What does it mean?*"

"I don't know," I sob.

\* \* \*

I don't know, I don't know, I don't know.

There is a flash of light through the darkness, and a moment later a terrible bang, and I burst from my nightmare, sweating, crying, panting.

But alive.

# 36

Hoodoo Jack.

I don't know what I was expecting, what I was hoping for, but it wasn't this.

I asked around, as innocently as I could, though to be honest no one suspected my interest in Jack was anything other than food for gossip.

He had turned down a commission as an officer, but had become a corporal. Something happened to him and he ended up as a dispatch rider. Dispatch riders get away with a certain degree of freedom, even though they have messages to ferry around. Maybe that suits him better, being on his own much of the time. I understand that.

Every evening, I've lingered after my shift, hoping he would come by again. This evening, as I was leaving, barely able to keep my eyes open, I saw him walking down the platform, straight toward me.

I stopped in my tracks, and stared at him until he was close enough to touch. Then I realized I was being rude and looked away, embarrassed. He must have seen me, but he took no notice and walked past.

I turned.

"Jack?" I called, quietly. "Excuse me."

He didn't even turn his head, but walked on into the rest station.

I felt a fool, and then I felt angry, and then I decided not to let the chance go.

I waited for him to come back, and I didn't have to wait long.

I went straight up to him.

"You're Jack, aren't you," I said, firmly.

He still ignored me and kept walking. I ran after him.

"Hoodoo Jack," I said.

He whirled round, and for a moment I thought he was going to hit me. He didn't have to; his eyes did enough damage.

I don't know what I'd been expecting. He isn't middle-aged yet, but he isn't as young as lots of the men I've seen here. There's something about him that doesn't fit. Something that says leave me alone. And whoever's in charge of him hasn't pulled him up on his stubbly chin, or filthy boots. His face is round, his eyebrows are thick, and his skin is dirty.

"I'm sorry," I said. "I just—"

"Don't call me that," he snapped.

"I'm sorry," I said, again.

He didn't reply, but brushed past me.

I followed.

"I'm sorry," I said, yet again. "I just want to talk to you."

"Very funny," he said, not slackening his pace.

I scampered along beside him. We'd reached the end of the station. I guessed he was heading for the gate, where I could see a motorcycle leaning against the railings.

"Wait," I said. "I want to talk to you. Really."

"That's what they all say," he spat out. "Then, when I've told them a few stories, they have a good laugh."

"No, I—"

"You're all the same. Stupid, ignorant little bitch of a nurse."

"No!" I shouted.

He stopped, and for the first time, looked at me.

"I'm not a little . . . bitch," I said. "I need to talk to you."

He was a few strides from his motorbike.

"Wait! Please!" I was getting desperate.

He reached the motorcycle and swung his leg over it.

"I see things!" I shouted, not caring if anyone else heard.

He hesitated, briefly, looking at me for a second time.

"Please believe me," I cried. "I see things. I need to—"

But my voice was drowned by the roar from his engine as he spun it to life. He twisted his wrist and whirled away from me, dragging the back wheel around in the dust, and then speeding from the station.

"Please," I said, though by then he was long gone.

# 35

It's Thursday evening. It's been raining all day, and I am exhausted. The business with Hoodoo Jack was the final straw. I know he'll be back soon, he's an RAMC rider and is around Boulogne all the time, going from hospital to hospital. I'll try to speak to him again. He can only tell me to go away.

Millie's sneaked off into town with a couple of other nurses, though if they're caught they'll be sent home.

I don't want to take the risk. Millie didn't protest when I said I didn't want to come. She could see I'm dead beat.

"Get some sleep," she said. "You need it."

Then she gave me a kiss on the forehead, as though I was her little sister, and left.

I'm lying on my bunk in our billets in Wimereux, but I don't want to sleep. Sleep only brings dreams.

I think about the day.

The men. The pathetic men.

There is nothing noble in a suppurating, festering wound, and I wish Father were here to see that.

Then there are the cases of hand and foot wounds. They say lots of these cases are probably self-inflicted. Sometimes soldiers shoot themselves in the foot during a raid, hoping it will give them a nice safe ride back home. Some of the nurses treat any men with these injuries contemptuously. But no one knows how they came by their wound; whether they're lying or not.

In the stationary hospitals they say men put dirty coins into their wounds to stop them from healing, so they won't have to go back to the fight. I don't know if that's true.

Today I treated a man who had two fingers missing from his left hand. I don't know what happened to him; I saw nothing. But if things were so bad he was prepared to shoot a couple of fingers off to get out of it all, then I can only feel pity for him, and shame. The shame of it all.

As the men arrive from the front, we have to sort the wounded and to try to keep them from dying before they get their treatment. We are so overstretched here that there are not enough doctors to go around. Things were so bad at one point that Millie and I were sorting the dying from the nearly dead. Those who had a chance from those who had none. Life was leaking away from many of them, I could feel that, but we had no way of knowing which man needed treatment immediately, which could wait. We had to decide for ourselves, there was no one to tell us.

Sometimes I got a vision from the man I was treating, and that made me wonder if there was any point in helping them at all. What is the point in saving someone now, for them to be killed in a month's time? But then I realized. If I decide to pass by a man because I know he's going to die soon anyway, what does that say about what I'm trying to do for Tom?

We are playing God, but we are weaker gods. Imperfect, unknowing gods. Gods that get things wrong.

But at the time we thought nothing of the sort. We did our best, I suppose, judging from their coldness which soldier was too far gone and which might have a chance.

Day after day we cut off bandages to reveal stinking wounds that have rearranged the whole idea of a man's body. A picture comes to me as I lie here in bed.

I see myself gazing mesmerized at the chaos, the men on stretchers on the floor, the heaps of discarded boots and mud-caked clothing, the cheap blankets, the smashed bodies and filthy bloodstained bandages. An unbearable stench rises from the appalling horror that waits underneath the cotton wool, and at one point the only equipment that I had for dealing with it was a pair of forceps standing in a glass jar half full of meths.

I'm just a girl in a nurse's uniform, but that doesn't mean I know how to save these men, and they—they are men in uniforms, but that doesn't mean they know how to die.

# 34

Time is running out.

That's true for me, it's true for so many out here. I hope it will not be for Tom, but I don't feel like praying. Although I wouldn't say it aloud, I don't think God is listening anymore.

My time is running out. My money is running out.

The *V* in VAD stands for voluntary, with good reason. We don't get paid. That's why VAD nurses are from wealthy backgrounds, or have private means of some sort.

I looked at how little money I have. Fortunately I don't need much here, but McAndrew made me buy an outdoor uniform. Of course we are fed, we have our uniforms and a roof over our heads, but that's it. If I leave here to find Tom, I'll have very little to live on.

Nor do I really have a plan for finding him. I've been here nearly two weeks, and haven't found a single soldier from his regiment. That was as far as my plan went.

And Sister McAndrew is on to me.

Thank heaven for Millie.

I don't know how she does it. She has boundless energy. I heard her come in late last night from the trip to town. She told me this morning that they found a café where there was music playing, and dancing. There were some Tommies there, who asked her to dance, but she refused. Instead, she danced with the young French waitress, and they laughed and laughed until her father, who owns the café, told the girl to start waiting on the tables again.

Despite that, she was up for duty on time, whereas I could hardly drag my aching limbs from bed after another night of wretched dreaming. And she was ready for McAndrew.

We were seeing to another batch of men.

Sister McAndrew was with Millie, me, and a couple of other VADs.

She took one look at the men, and then barked at me.

"Nurse! Nurse Hibbert. Fetch the Harrison's."

I didn't have a clue what she was talking about.

She rounded on me.

"Did you hear me, nurse? The Harrison's pomade. Now."

I dithered.

"You do know what it's for?" she asked, her voice slowing. I could sense her suspicion.

Millie cut in, saving me. She was playing innocent, I could see.

"It's for the lice," she said. "Isn't it? Sister?"

McAndrew glared at her, then at me. Before she could open her mouth I decided to speak.

"I just don't know where we keep it," I said.

"I do," said Millie. "I'll go."

Millie, bless her, left for the store cupboard.

McAndrew gave me another hostile glare.

"Where did you do your training?" she asked.

"I . . . the Dyke Road in Brighton," I said. I had to go along with what I knew about Miriam Hibbert. I had no choice.

"For how long?"

I saw my chance.

"I had the three months minimum," I said.

"It shows," McAndrew said, eager to take the easy jibe that I had offered her.

"I just wanted to come and help," I said, trying to sound as pathetic as possible. It wasn't hard.

And then Millie was back with us, and started chatting to McAndrew about her days in London as if they were old acquaintances.

She saved me.

This time.

# 33

After my narrow escape with Sister McAndrew, I saw Hoodoo Jack passing the window of the dressing suite. I looked at Millie.

"Cover for me? Please?"

I begged her with my eyes not to question me.

"Don't be long!" she called, but I hardly heard her.

Jack slipped into a room farther down the platform, and I followed him.

He was on his own, waiting to deliver a packet. He turned as I came in.

"You," he said, without obvious meaning.

"You remember me?" I asked.

He grunted. "I'm mad, not stupid."

There was silence.

Then I broke it.

"I see things, too," I said. "I see when men are going to die."

He looked at me with such disgust and hatred that I felt I might wither on the spot.

The door flew open.

It was a captain; beyond him I saw other officers sitting around a desk.

The captain glanced at me, but didn't bother to ask why there was a nurse in his quarters. The place is a hospital of sorts, after all.

"That all?" he said to Hoodoo Jack.

"Sir." He nodded, and handed over the packet.

The captain tried to take it from Jack, but he wouldn't let go. His fingers had frozen around it. I saw Jack staring at the captain for a second, maybe two, no more.

"What are you doing, man?" snapped the captain, and Jack shook himself.

He muttered something under his breath, then, pulling himself together, saluted messily, turned, and left the room.

Without knowing what I was doing, I grabbed the captain by the arm.

"What on—?"

It was enough. I let my fingers slip from his tunic.

"Thank you," I said, quietly, for I had seen all I needed.

I ran after Jack. I don't want to think of him as Hoodoo Jack, though. Not now.

I caught up with him.

"You saw that?" I said.

"Go away, girl."

"You saw it. I saw it too."

He hesitated before answering.

"You saw nothing."

"You saw what I saw. The captain. Lying dead in a shell hole, with the back of his head gone."

"No!" He shouted at me now, so loudly that I could see people around us staring.

I hadn't realized it, but we were already back outside the suite where I was supposed to be working. Millie stood in the doorway.

"Get in here," she whispered at me. "For pity's sake, before McAndrew comes back."

Jack had gone.

I slunk in and got back to work.

Then—was it only an hour ago?—he came to me.

I'd finished my shift, and was walking out of the station to catch a lift in a truck to our billets up on the hill at Wimereux.

I heard the low growl of a motorcycle behind me. I turned and saw, yes, Jack, coming up behind me at no more than walking speed.

He drew level, and I stopped walking.

"Do you know when?" he asked. "When he's going to die?"

He was talking about the captain, the captain whose arm I'd touched. Whose death I'd seen.

"I . . . I don't know," I said.

I was afraid that the slightest wrong move on my part would send him away, but he stayed.

"Tomorrow," he said. "By this time tomorrow, he'll be dead. Everything else will be just as you told me."

It was enough to know that he believed me.

"Do you still want to talk?" he asked.

"Yes," I said. "Yes, I do."

"Then get on, and we'll find somewhere quiet."

He nodded at the metal luggage rack behind his seat on the motorbike.

"No . . . ," I said. "I can't. We're not allowed to . . . If anyone sees me, I'll be sent home."

"Fair enough," he said, and pulled his goggles down over his eyes.

"No!" I shouted. "I'll come. But let's get away from here quickly."

I got on, put my arms around his waist, and prayed to heaven and hell that no one would see me.

# 32

I don't think of him as Hoodoo now. Not now I know he's a person. A person just like me. Hoodoo is a name superstitious people gave him. A horrible label that helps them to think he's a freak. Well, if he's a freak, so am I.

I don't know exactly where we went.

We rode out of Boulogne and into the rain. I had to pull my long skirts up to sit on the bike, and the seat was a tiny plate of metal.

"Hold tight!" he shouted from in front, and I clung to him as tightly as I could.

We rode through some ugly villages, heading inland, until we came to one slightly larger, but no less down-at-heel.

"No one will know us here," he said.

Not for the first time it crossed my mind that what I was doing might be very unwise. But I had no choice.

He stopped outside a seedy-looking café. They call them estaminets. Inside it's sort of a bar, but they cook basic food, too. I had heard of them but never been in one. It looked awful. There was a beaten old piano in one corner, but no one was playing it.

The place was busy, but not full.

"Don't meet anyone's eye," Jack said. "And keep your coat done up. Nurses don't come to places like this."

He pulled me along to a table by a wall in the quietest corner.

A young girl came over. I tried not to look at her, but I couldn't help it. She was very young, and very dirty, and when she spoke there were gaps in her teeth. She wiped her nose on the back of her hand and looked at Jack.

"Monsieur?"

"*Du vin,*" he said. I didn't dare open my mouth to protest, and I knew my English accent would give me away even if I spoke French.

The girl sloped off, and came back after an age with a jug of red wine and two glasses.

"*Vous mangez quelque chose?*" she asked, but Jack waved her away, which was a pity, because I would very much have liked something to eat, even if it was the ropy stuff I could see on other people's plates. Especially if I was going to have to drink wine.

Jack poured us each a glass and I glanced at the other people in the room. Locals, I guessed, all old men, and a couple of boys; the sort with something wrong with them, or else they'd have been away fighting. There were soldiers at another table, but they took no notice of us. I didn't want to know what they might be thinking.

"How long?" Jack said.

"I never understand what you ask me," I said, trying a smile. He didn't smile back.

"How long have you been seeing things?"

I shrugged. I thought about Clare. But that was so long ago, and it had only happened once, then.

"Almost a year, maybe," I said. "How about you?"

"Pretty much from the start. Since I got here."

He emptied his glass, and refilled it straightaway.

I took a sip of mine, to show I could if I wanted. It was vile stuff, but that didn't stop Jack.

"It was nothing at first. Just a tingling. Like an itch from a mosquito bite. So faint you might be imagining it."

"You were a captain then?"

"Who told you that? No, I was never a captain. I turned down a commission, because I wanted to be one of the men. We're all out here to fight, and I didn't see why I should be safer than the boys just because of my background.

"I was a corporal then. But even corporals aren't supposed to indulge in that sort of thing. Superstitions. Of course, we lads in the trenches, we live by them. And die, too.

"We all have our little routines, for good luck. Which sock goes on first, maybe. Or something from a dead mate, a watch, perhaps, that sort of thing. And it's bad luck to say something good without grabbing a bit of wood right away. The ones that are left alive think that just goes to show that their superstitions are working, and the ones that are dead can't argue back that theirs aren't."

It was clear he wanted to talk now.

"So what happened, then?" I asked. "When did it start to change?"

He finished another glass of wine, and I began to doubt that there was any chance of getting back to Boulogne safely.

"The itch became a scratch one day."

He tipped the jug up, drained it, then waved it in the air. The young girl brought a full one over.

She eyed us curiously, and I looked away. I drank some more—it seemed to help.

"All of a sudden," he said, "the itch was a scratch. It scratched me so hard that I jumped to my feet. And shouted."

"What did you shout?"

" 'Williams has got it.' And the other lads in the trench looked at me as if I was a madman. 'Sit down,' they said. 'Nerves getting to you?' they asked. 'Happens to us all,' someone said. And then, five minutes later, the news came down the line. 'Lieutenant Williams is dead. Got his spine ripped out by a nose cap.' And that was that.

"I stood there, feeling sorry for the lieutenant. But it was no shock to me, you see, because I'd known it was going to happen. The lads stared at each other. I noticed that, straightaway. They looked at each other, but none of them would look at me. And that was just the first time. . . ."

"What happened?"

He didn't answer, but gazed at his wine, as if it were a looking glass.

"I'm sorry," I said, after a while, to fill the silence.

"It's all right," he said. "What about you? How does it happen for you?"

I told him how it had started slowly, like his itch. How it was coming clearer each time. I told him about the hospital, back at home in Brighton. I told him that people had seen things in my eyes, though I didn't know what.

I told him about Clare, and then I told him about Edgar.

"What's your name?" he asked.

"My real name's Alexandra," I said. I could see no point in lying to him.

"Alexandra," he said, carefully. He seemed to be thinking. "And no one believes a word you say?"

I shook my head. I knew that if I tried to speak, I would start crying and maybe never stop.

" *'And soon you too will stand aside, to murmur in pity that my words were true.'* "

He was quoting at me, and I knew where from. Miss Garrett's book had not been wasted after all.

My heart was racing. He knew about Cassandra.

"And now?" he said.

Now, I thought. Yes, what now?

"Let me put it another way," he said. "What are you doing here?"

I hadn't told him about Tom.

"There's someone I have to find. I've seen his death."

"Your boyfriend?" he said, without sympathy.

"My brother. My other brother."

He laughed at me then, and I didn't like it.

"Do you believe it hasn't happened yet?"

I nodded.

"I know it," I said.

"And what are you going to do?" he asked. "You, a girl, against the whole of the German army, and the British one, too? You're going to have to defeat them both to get him out of here!"

He cursed bitterly, and drank his wine.

I pushed mine away. I felt like throwing it in his face.

"I don't know what I'm going to do. I saw his death. I know it hasn't come yet. I'm going to try to find him. I'm going to tell him what I've seen, and I'm going to get him out of here. And no, I haven't the faintest idea how!"

I broke off.

People were staring at us. At me.

Jack looked at me, but more gently than before.

"I'm sorry," he said.

"That's all right. . . ."

"I'm sorry," he said, "but you don't understand. There's nothing you can do."

"No," I said, "I'll find a way—"

"No," he said. "You don't understand. If you've seen his death, then that's it. It's going to happen. You've seen the future. You can't change it."

His words cut me badly. I suppose I had known this deep down all along, but had tried to not let it surface. Now it was out in the open, and I couldn't ignore it.

"All those other times. You have seen deaths, and they have happened, because they were the future. What makes you think it will be any different with your brother? That's how it is. You should go home before you get yourself killed. Or worse. What are you going to do? Dress up as a man, as if this is some kind of fairy tale, and find him in the whole of the front line?"

I could feel tears falling from my face onto the table now.

"But that's—"

"Awful?" Jack said. "Terrible? Terrifying? Appalling? Which is it to be? Because I've been through them all, and still can't decide which. The future is written, and there's nothing you can do about it. The future is written in blood. Your brother's death, yours, mine. All written and waiting to happen, and not a damn thing you can do about it!"

He flung his hand at the jug, which smashed against the wall. The last of the wine flowed across the rough surface of the table, and I could not help seeing it as blood that had been shed.

A large old man came across the room toward us. He looked angry. I guessed he was the owner. I could see the young girl peering at us from behind the bar. The soldiers, too; one of them stood up, sensing trouble.

But Jack averted it all.

He rose, took an extravagant bundle of francs from his pocket, and put the notes on the table, avoiding the wine.

He held his hands up to the man, and shrugged, showing that we were leaving. Seeing the money, the man smiled back.

As we went Jack spoke to him.

*"Je suis desolé,"* he said.

And in my muddled state, I couldn't remember whether that meant "I'm sorry" or "I'm desolate," though I knew what Jack meant, in truth.


Jack seemed to sober up quickly. Maybe he was never anywhere near drunk, but he brought me back to Wimereux, where it was Millie's turn to be appalled at how late I was.

"Alexandra," she whispered to me, through the darkness. "I heard McAndrew talking about you. She was talking to our section superintendent. I didn't hear what they said, though. I just heard your name. Well, they said Miriam, but you know what I mean."

I was too tired to care.

\* \* \*

I'm lying in bed now, trying to remember everything Jack said. As he stopped the motorcycle and helped me to the ground with a gentle hand, he spoke to me, softly.

"Alexandra," he said. "Try to understand that there's nothing you can do. The future has already happened. We're just waiting to live it."

"Well, then," I said. "In that case, it's my future to try to save Tom, whether he dies or not."

Jack smiled, thoughtfully.

"You're a wise girl. It took me years to get to that point. Very well, then it's my fate to tell you this. Your brother's brigade is in Flanders. Around the La Bassée canal. You can't miss it. There's a new crater near Givenchy called the Red Dragon that you could lose St. Paul's Cathedral in. But you'd better hurry, no one stays in one place for too long around here."

And he sped off into the darkness, his engine roaring loud enough to wake the dead.

# 31

I dream.

I dream of Jack, his pale blue eyes, and I can see that once there was life in them, that once they showed joy. I see him as a young corporal, eager to please, prepared to work hard.

It's gone now, that blue fire in his eyes; they are eyes that have seen too much death and are dying from it themselves.

But not entirely.

I cling to the fact that even Jack, who has had all belief ground out of him, had enough spirit left to set me on my way to Tom.

I'm coming.

# 30

Five days have passed since that evening with Jack, the longest five days of my life.

I thought I was coming to find Tom, but the war had other ideas. In a way it was the war that saved me, and the war that betrayed me.

The day after Jack told me where to find Tom I got even more definite news of his battalion. I had still not seen a soldier wearing the uniform of the Twentieth Royal Fusiliers, but I also knew that had there been any I might have missed them. There were still as many as thirty trains a day arriving loaded with wounded.

We were stretched beyond exhaustion that Saturday, as we had been all the previous week. Most of the casualties were coming from the south, from the Somme, but there were one or two trains from the east, from Flanders, and that was where my attention was now fixed.

From the east there finally came the message I had been waiting for, but it was a grisly one.

A train rolled in from Bethune about nine o'clock that Saturday evening, and I set myself to help unload the wounded. There was such chaos and confusion along the platform that no one noticed that I should have finished my shift and left by then.

I saw what I had been waiting for.

He had died on the train. A private of the Twentieth, a public school boy who didn't even look as old as Tom.

Shamelessly I cursed him for dying before I could question him, ask him where he'd come from, where the rest of the men were now. And whether he knew Tom. But he must have. I know that Tom's battalion is a small, closely knit one. It has a poor reputation because it's very new, and it's formed only of boys from public school.

But the boy in front of me would be answering no questions.

Sisters and nurses were staggering wearily from the carriages; orderlies were lifting the stretchers onto the platform. The men who could walk were shuffling down to the rest station.

I would have to be quick. The dead boy lay on a stretcher on the platform. It was obvious he was dead, but everyone was too busy worrying about those still living.

I put out my hand and touched his white face. I hate to say it, but I have seen so much death now it leaves me cold. If I thought of every mother of every soldier waiting at home and praying, I'd break down. It's the same for all the nurses. We have become immune.

Nothing. He had gone, and whatever life is had gone with him. I felt nothing, saw nothing, heard no words.

Then I felt ashamed of myself, and came away before anyone noticed that in spite of my immunity, I was crying over a dead boy I'd never even met.

# 29

I went back to our billets, and slept.

Things were closing in on me last Sunday, though as I reported for duty that morning with Millie, I had no idea how fast.

It was another ominous, cloudy day.

Trains poured in constantly, and once more we waded through a sea of wounded men, and their bloody bandages and muddied uniforms. Cutting, washing, daubing, wrapping.

Then we heard that there were shortages of nurses and doctors aboard the trains. It meant nothing to us at the time. There's a shortage of everyone and everything everywhere.

Later that morning Millie heard that she was going to make a run on an ambulance train to Amiens and back. It meant she'd be away for hours, the best part of a day, in fact, and then I was scared. I needed Millie, I needed her looking out for me, covering my back, keeping an eye on McAndrew.

It wasn't to be. Around lunchtime, she left on the train for Amiens. I didn't even see her go, or have time to say good-bye, because I was waist deep in mess in the rest station. At the time I just felt sorry not to have seen her go.

I had no premonition. I didn't know then what has happened since. I had no idea what was going to happen to me later, and it made me aware of something I had not considered before.

In all the things I have seen, and witnessed; in all the fore-shadowings, I have yet to see anything about myself.

# 28

The war saved me.

It was about ten o'clock on Sunday evening. I had been working for nearly fourteen hours without a break. I scarcely knew what I was doing.

Men came into the rest station, without ceasing. Man after man after man. Tall ones, short ones, thin ones, young ones. A few older ones, but not many. By then they were all the same to me. I hate that. When I got to France, I cared about every man, and I saw each as an individual with his own story. Now they're just men, and I treat them all the same. I have become blunted to them, I can no longer feel for them. But I sense their terror as a single huge monster.

Occasionally I see death in front of me on a living man's face, but even that no longer shocks me. I have seen it so much.

But every death reminds me of Edgar, and reminds me of Tom.

Suddenly I was plucked from the slow hell of the rest station dressing suite.

"Hibbert!"

I was so lost in my work, so exhausted, that I heard the name called maybe only the third time.

"Hibbert!"

Dimly I wondered who McAndrew was shouting at; then I saw the other nurses looking at me.

With a sickening fear I realized that it was me she was calling.

"Come with me," she snapped.

McAndrew walked briskly down the corridor until she reached the superintendent's office.

"In here."

I went in, expecting to find someone waiting for me, but the room was empty.

McAndrew closed the door behind us.

"Who are you?" she said, her voice quiet now in the closed room.

I hesitated, tiredness fuddling my thinking.

"Miriam," I said. "Miriam Hibbert."

"Don't lie to me," she said, again quietly. She pulled a piece of paper from her pocket. A telegram.

"Just so you know there's no point lying," she said, flourishing it in my face. "I wired the Dyke Road on Friday. I've just received this reply. They say Miriam Hibbert is in England, some problem over her papers, it seems. So who are you?"

I was speechless.

All around me, and yet as if from a great distance, I could hear the noise of the rest station, of the railway station that it still was. I could hear shouts along the platform outside, the hiss of steam from the engines.

"So, you refuse to speak, do you?" McAndrew said. I couldn't help noticing that she seemed to be enjoying this drama. "Well, I have warned the commandant of my suspicions. I'm going to fetch him now."

She opened the door, taking the key from the lock. She paused, and looked at me.

"They shoot spies, you know," she said, her voice full of threat.

Then she closed the door and locked it behind her.

A spy? Surely they couldn't think I was a spy?

Of course they could. I was silly and weak. I could almost hear Edgar telling me so. I had got into something way over my head.

Breathlessly, I waited.

I had no idea how long I waited, but as I said, the war saved me.

Outside on the platform, I heard a train getting ready to roll out of the station. Shouts came from the head of the line.

I heard footsteps running.

"Come on," shouted a voice, teasingly. "We'll go without you!"

McAndrew may have locked the door, but I suppose the police game was new to her. Either that, or it never crossed her mind that a young woman would do such a thing as climb out of a window, even a young woman who's a spy.

But there was a window from the office onto the platform, and it was not locked.

I opened it a crack, and saw an RAMC doctor hurrying for the train.

"Bethune, then!" he shouted, leaping aboard. "Here we come!"

Bethune.

From that moment on I didn't think.

Everything I did, I did with complete calm, and I swear not a further thought ran through my head.

Bethune. The train was heading for the casualty clearing station in Bethune, the nearest point to the La Bassée canal.

I opened the window fully, and looked up and down the platform. There were people everywhere: wounded soldiers, nurses, RAMC, orderlies. I ignored them all.

With a loud hiss and a heaving of pistons, the train started to move. As if it were the most natural thing in the world, I pulled a chair to the window, sat on the ledge, swung my legs over and dropped to the platform. I walked steadily but without panicking toward the train, and was in time to step calmly onto the last carriage as it passed me.

Avoiding any chance of being seen from the platform, I opened the carriage door, and went inside. I came face to face with a VAD sister, and although she was a sister, she looked only a few years older than me.

"Hello," I said, smiling. "They sent me along too."

She nodded.

"I nearly missed my train," I added, trying to make her laugh.

She smiled, but it was a thin, unfriendly smile.

"Very good," she said. "We need all the help we can get. Have you been on an ambulance before?"

I shook my head.

"Then I hope you learn fast."

The train picked up speed, but was still traveling quite slowly, and I knew it probably wouldn't go much faster. Many of the trains are a mixture of carriages from different French railway companies, and I've heard that the tracks are patched up in places. It isn't safe to go very fast.

I settled down for the journey, with failing hope and little knowledge of what might happen to me, but I was sure of one thing.

There was no going back.

# 27

"What's your name?" the sister asked me.

"Alexandra," I said, without thinking, but if the sister wondered why my face suddenly flushed, she didn't say anything.

"We use surnames here," she said.

As she waited for me to reply, it occurred to me that maybe it wasn't such a bad thing to have given my real name. If anyone was coming after me, they would be looking for a girl called Hibbert.

"Fox," I said. "Sorry, Sister."

She was a tall, well-built woman. From the white eight-pointed star on her apron, I saw she belonged to a St. Johns VAD unit, but I saw other nurses with the red cross on their uniforms, like me, and relaxed. But it made me realize there were so many tiny things that might give me away.

"There's not much to do on the way," Sister said. "It's the journey back that . . ."

She trailed off.

"Well, you'll see."

"How long does it take?"

"Hours. It's barely fifty miles, but you see how slowly we're going. It's a long train, can't go that fast. Then sometimes we have to stop and wait for the line to be cleared. Or if there's an air raid."

She called to the other nurse in the carriage.

"Nurse Goode, this is Fox. Show her the ropes. She can help you with the brechots. Then you should both try to get some sleep."

Nurse Goode came over to me as Sister made her way through the connecting door to the next carriage.

"What's a . . . ?" I hadn't even heard what she'd said properly.

Goode smiled.

"A brechot? See where the stretchers go? The brechot is the rack that holds them. We have to check they're all ready, with sets of clean sheets for when the men are brought in."

I nodded.

"She's not so bad," she said. "Sister, I mean. She meant what she said about getting some sleep."

After we had finished, we went along to the carriage at the end of the train set aside for nurses. There we lay down on the low bunks, and slept our way toward Belgium.

Toward the front, toward the war.

# 26

The lights in the carriage were low and the blinds were drawn so that no light would show to enemy aircraft. This was a newer train, I could tell, because the lights were electric. The carriage even had radiators warmed by steam from the engine.

I lifted a blind, and peered out into the night. I could see nothing. No stars, no moon. I could only guess at the shape of the countryside through which we were moving.

The train rattled on, click-clacking over points from time to time, rocking us slowly into oblivion.

But I could not sleep, and I needed to talk.

Goode was snoring gently opposite me.

I felt bad, but I couldn't stop myself.

"Wake up," I said, shaking her shoulder gently. "Wake up."

After a while, she opened her eyes and lifted her head.

"What is it? Are we there?"

"No."

"Then let me sleep, will you?"

"Please," I said. "I'm scared."

She sat up.

"I know," she said. "So was I, first time."

"How many times have you done this?"

"Once."

"How close do we get to the front line?"

"Depends," Goode said. "Bethune Casualty Clearing Station. I think it's just a couple of miles out to the front at the moment. But listen, when we get there, you'll be so busy, you won't have time to be scared."

I looked at my watch.

It had gone midnight.

"Go to sleep," she said. "We'll be there soon enough."

She couldn't know about what was happening to me, about Tom. I wondered if we'd really be there soon enough.

I lay down on the bench seat again, taking my apron off to use as a pillow. It was softer than it had been—it had not seen starch for a long time by then—but still, it didn't make for comfortable rest. I had been working since early that morning, and I could stay awake no longer. My mind began to drift, but not at random. I felt my mind drifting out ahead of us. I was on high, looking down at the steaming train, churning through the dark French air. Occasionally the driver would stoke the boiler and I saw the orange flash of fire from the coal in the furnace.

If I looked I could see all the way back across the sea to England. Over the water, past the piers, to Brighton. Into my home. I could not see Mother and Father, I had no sense of them. I wondered what they were doing. I knew they would be worrying about me, but they would have no idea where I had gone.

Then, from somewhere ahead, I saw other, different flashes of light. After each one came a thunderous rumble. I drifted on, far ahead of the train now, and began to feel the souls of those who had died and were dying.

It scared me because I thought I was still awake. I pulled my mind back from what lay ahead and tried to form a plan. I had come straight from the rest station, with only the uniform I was wearing, with no money. When we got to the CCS at Bethune, I knew it would be pandemonium. There would be a chance for me to slip away if I wanted, but where to? With no money, and no idea how to find Tom.

And what about the men? I wasn't supposed to be on the train, but I was. If I was looking for Tom, it would mean turning my back on men I could help.

Somewhere along the line, I did sleep, and I dreamt. The sound of the train rumbling became the sound of wing beats. And there in my dreams, as I expected, the raven was waiting for me.

I was almost glad to see it, because I needed it to talk to me. I needed it to tell me what it meant, but it said nothing this time. It hopped around on the stump of a blasted tree, and flapped its wings. It cocked its head on one side and opened its beak, but no words came. It mocked me with its silence.

It told me nothing, and I woke, cursing it, still unable to understand why it keeps appearing to me.

And then I realized the train had stopped.

# 25

As I lifted the blind on the carriage window for a second time, my hand was trembling. It was early morning, and a weak dawn light spread across the landscape.

I felt more alone than I have ever done in my life. We had trundled through the night, traveled east, inland, and reached the railhead at Bethune, being used as the casualty clearing station. It's a squalid little place, a drab provincial town suddenly made important because a war has happened to come by. I was watching the scene at the platform when the door of our carriage opened, and Sister came back in.

"Right, you two. This is it. Look sharp."

I forced myself to think. I had to decide what to do, and I had to decide quickly, but I was tired, and before I knew what was happening, the first of our men were being carried in on their stretchers.

The smell hit me first. They were fresh from the battlefield and reeked of death and disintegration. But as Nurse Goode had said, there was no time to be scared. And there was no time to make choices. I had to help get the men stowed aboard. As soon as our carriage was full we began to cut their uniforms from the worst wounds where possible.

As I worked I began to talk to the men. After the initial shock I gathered my wits. I had to take this opportunity because if I went back, my time would have run out.

I asked each man I tended about Tom's regiment, but no one knew anything about it.

I felt desperate. Already the train was taking on new supplies of water and coal; as soon as we had everyone loaded we would be setting off back to Boulogne. I would just have to slip off the train and take my chances.

Then one of the last men aboard heard me talking to another soldier.

"I'm trying to find out where my husband is," I was saying, thinking that might move someone enough to talk to me.

"You said he's in the Twentieth Royal Fusiliers?"

I turned and saw a man in the top of the brechot behind me. He was in a mess, but he seemed sensible enough.

"Yes," I said. "I know they're around here. I heard they were at the Red Dragon crater. Do you know where that is?"

"The Twentieth?" the man asked again. "They're in Thirty-third Division, aren't they?"

I shook my head, desperately. I didn't know what he meant.

"Thirty-third," he said. "Look. You see that man there?"

He nodded through the window. There was enough light sweeping across the platform now to see well enough, but there were a lot of men, and I didn't know who he meant.

"Him, the corporal. The short one. He's in the Royal Welch. They're in the Thirty-third, too. Ask him."

I saw who he meant.

The train gave a powerful lurch as the engine was uncoupled and started to move to the other end for the journey back.

I jumped from the train onto the platform, and ran to the corporal from the Royal Welch.

I grabbed him.

"Do you know where the Twentieth Royal Fusiliers are?"

He turned and his eyes widened when he saw me.

"The Twentieth. Have you seen them?"

He said nothing, still too surprised to speak. I saw him look over my shoulder, but I kept on, begging him to understand, and finally he did.

"The Twentieth," he said. He voice was just like Evans'. "Yes. They were with us. But the whole division has moved, we were relieved a couple of days ago. I'm the last of the Royal Welch. I got stuck. The rest of the boys have gone, and the Twentieth would have been with them."

I felt sick, almost too sick to speak.

"Where?" I said, my voice failing. "Do you know where they've gone?"

He shook his head, and I thought it meant he didn't know, but that wasn't the reason.

"The Somme," he said. "They've all gone to the Somme. It's all quiet here now. That's where they need the men. What's all this about?"

I was in completely the wrong place.

In a daze, I was aware that the corporal glanced over my shoulder again.

"I think someone wants to talk to you."

I turned and saw in front of me two burly-looking sol-diers, wearing the red caps that I knew marked them as mili-tary police. A third stood by the steps to the train, talking to the sister who I'd met on board. She was pointing in my di-rection.

"I'm not a spy," I said, but it was no good.

They weren't listening.

# 24

They're too busy to know what to do with me. That's what it seems to come down to.

On the face of it I'm just a crazy girl who got herself dressed up as a nurse, but there's always the possibility I'm a German spy. I wouldn't be the first. And if they think that I am and they prove it, then I'll be shot.

I can't speak a word of German, but then, I'd pretend not to, if I was a spy. So I might be a spy or I might just be a nurse who's gone a bit mad, or I might not be a nurse at all. The trouble is they're too busy to find out which. A young woman does not travel around freely in a war. Even nurses are confined to certain times and places: in hospitals, in billets, on trains. I didn't know how to be a nurse in a war well enough, and so I was discovered and traced eventually.

I was brought here, to this army base.

I have no idea where I am. I'm being kept in a tent, which

doesn't seem much of a prison, but then I suppose they're not used to having female prisoners. Anyway, there's always a guard on the door, so I can't go anywhere. And even if I could, what would I do?

I was brought here on Monday. I've been interrogated by all sorts of people; there have been cables and 'phone calls, I know, but they still don't know who I am. For the time being I think they've given up.

I've told them my real name, and that I'm not a spy, and that my father is an important doctor and if they shoot me they'll be in awful trouble. But that's all I've said. I hope it's enough.

The worst thing is thinking about Tom.

I have felt nothing of him for days, and I fear that it might be too late.

That it might be over.

# 23

I've had the best part of three days to sit and think.

I've been thinking about Tom mostly, but Edgar keeps coming to my mind too. I've had a glimpse of what he went through, and it makes me angry and sad to think of it. What it did to him, how it made him and Tom fight. And all of us. It pulled us all apart.

Still I have felt nothing of Tom. No dreams.

At first I was able to talk to the guard on duty outside the tent. He was obviously mystified about having to guard a young woman, and seemed happy to talk, although nervously at first.

When I told him I wasn't a spy, that was good enough for him, and then he spoke about himself, the war, and anything I put into his head.

He patted his leg, which didn't move properly, and said

he was glad not to be at the front anymore, but that he hated the job he had now. He said he'd guarded more than one man on court martial offenses, and that last week he'd had to watch over a private before he went to the firing squad.

I didn't believe him at first. I couldn't believe we were shooting our own men, but he said the boy had run away from the battle when an attack was on. That was desertion, and the punishment was death.

Then someone must have noticed that he was standing inside the door of the tent and not outside, because he was replaced by not one, but two surly soldiers who said nothing to me no matter how hard I tried to get them to talk.

Since then I've spoken to no one.

# 22

Before my friendly guard was replaced, I asked him about the Somme.

He'd heard that talk was spreading about some of the engagements, but his knowledge was scant. He'd been in the trenches himself, last summer.

"Where?" I asked him.

"Place called Neuve Chapelle."

"Was that where you got wounded?" I asked.

He shook his head.

"No," he said, and laughed a quick, short laugh. "I was a proper hero in the trenches. Neuve Chapelle turned into a right fiasco, but I was a real hero. I went on five raids. Never got hurt. Not even a scratch."

He told me about the raids. Four or five men and an officer would creep out through our wire at night, armed to the teeth. They might be just having a look at the enemy lines, they might be going to try to kill Germans.

They'd crawl on their bellies over the mud, around the shell holes, right up to the German wire, sometimes through it, freezing if a flare went up over them, then on again when it went dark.

"The first time I went . . . ," he said, and then gave me such a look, I knew what he meant. He was scared fit enough to die from it.

"But I went back, and back again, with my stick. . . ."

"Stick?"

"Oh, yes," he said, cheerfully. "We made a lot of our own weapons. We're supposed to use bayonets in the trenches, but that's no good on a night raid. So we make all these things. Like a policeman's truncheon, say, but with spikes like you don't want to see. Some lads prefer a good big knife. Easier to use when you get into a trench."

I didn't say anything and he changed the subject.

"But that's not how I got my leg. That was an accident. We was having a demonstration of a new grenade. Up to then, we'd been making our own bombs. We'd get jam tins, and pack them full of nails and the like, and the charge. The explosive charge, yes? Not very reliable.

"So there was a new bomb they was showing us. A metal canister, packed full of shrapnel. There's this corporal showing us. He's supposed to throw it over a heap of turnips, but his aim is off and it falls short. We all dive to the ground, like crazy, like we're going to get it.

"Then there was a bloody great bang, and a load of turnips flying through the air. Everyone bursts out laughing, and gets up. Then I tries to get up, and found I couldn't. Bit of shrapnel. That was the end of my time at the front."

He laughed.

Later, I thought about him on his raids, with a weapon in his hand. Presumably he had killed at least one man. Maybe several. He was a friendly man, he seemed very ordinary, kind even, but he didn't seem to be bothered by what he'd done. And when he got to the German trenches he must have met German soldiers, who would have killed him too, if they could. I wondered if either Englishman or German had the slightest idea what they were killing each other for.

# 21

Each night as I lay down to sleep in the tent that has become my prison, I hoped to sense Thomas. He seemed to have gone quiet on me, but at last he is back.

With no one to talk to, no one near, I'd had no premonition in days, not even a hint of that itch Jack spoke of. Although I hate it, and dread its coming, when it suddenly vanished, I felt lost without it.

Then, last night, I dreamt.

There was Tom. He had his back to me, he was walking away from me. He was in the countryside somewhere, in a wheat field on a beautiful rolling hillside. Away on the horizon was a lush green wood, in the full glory of summer, the trees thick with leaves.

I could only watch; I felt like a mere observer, unable to take part in this dream.

Tom held his right arm out to one side, and then I saw the

bird perching there. At first I thought it was a bird of prey; he held it as if it were a falcon. But then he gave his arm a gentle lift, and the bird took wing, and then, of course, I saw it was the raven.

It flapped lazily into the air, and wheeled around, coming back toward me in a wide circle, just to let me know that it knew I was there. The raven flew by and I heard it flapping away behind me. Then it must have turned, because it came forward again.

It passed me, then passed Thomas, too, and headed toward the wood. The wheat withered and died where its winged shadow fell. As it flew on up the hillside, the blight spread with it, and the hill became a quagmire of sticky mud, pitted with shell holes and strewn with the wire.

Then the bird reached the lovely wood, which mutated before my eyes into a square mile of splintered trunks and stumps. Those were the strange spikes I'd seen before, and not understood. I knew them now for what they were: a wood that had been murdered. Killed by days of shelling.

It was another nightmare, but my spirits rose nonetheless. I am used to horror now, and the dream told me something I needed to know.

Tom is still alive, because I saw him in my sleep last night. More than that, I sensed him as a living being.

There is still time.

# 20

There is still time.

But I'm trapped.

Two guards outside the tent.

I had to do something to get out. I looked at the back of the tent. Only a tent, after all. Very soon they would surely move me to a proper prison somewhere, and then I would truly be stuck. I decided to wait until dusk before trying anything.

The day dragged so very, very slowly, but at last, the light began to fail. Through the tent flaps, I could see that there was now only a single man outside. They must have decided that two was a bit much to guard one girl.

I watched the soldier, what I could see of him, for a long time. He didn't move—at least, the back of his right leg and the right side of his back remained motionless—and I watched him for more than half an hour.

As usual, outside, I could hear the noises of the camp. Men calling orders, vehicles rumbling by, shouts, some laughter.

I took another look at the guard, and crept to the back of the tent. I did it slowly. I used my watch, and made myself take ten minutes over it. I lay down on the ground, and taking a deep breath to try to calm myself, I peered under the flap.

All I could see was grass and more canvas. There were other tents nearby. Maybe if I could get out I could lose myself among them.

With a slippery wriggle I forced myself under the tent wall. I was halfway under when I realized that the pegs were too close together. I was stuck. I gave an almighty heave with my shoulders and slid out from the canvas.

"Just how stupid do you think I am?"

I rolled over and looked up into the face of my guard.

I spent the rest of the night lying on the bunk in the tent, staring at the canvas, tears rolling down my cheeks. In the distance I could hear the sound of big guns.

I called Tom's name over and over softly to myself, hoping he could somehow hear me, though I knew he could not.

# 19

Now the tent is far behind me.

Early this morning I was woken by what I thought was a rumble of thunder. Then I heard the murmur of voices outside. I could only catch snippets of the discussion.

". . . move her . . . Etaples."

I couldn't hear the reply, just a tone of dissent, but I knew then that my chances of escaping were over.

The discussion outside continued.

"All right. Wait here. . . ."

Then silence, followed by the sound of retreating footsteps.

A second later, the flap of the tent was pulled open, and a large soldier came in, ducking under the low doorway.

I stood up to meet my fate, and then, as he raised his head, my heart leapt.

Jack.

Before I could say anything, he put his finger to his lips, and gave me a look that told me he wasn't meant to be here.

"Do you want to get out of here or not?" he whispered.

I nodded dumbly.

"Put this around you," he said.

He swung off his greatcoat and handed it to me.

"We don't have much time. My bike's outside."

"But h-how did—?" I stuttered, confused, half asleep.

"Not now!"

It was still early as we put our heads out into the camp. No one was around. Our guard had vanished.

And there was Jack's motorbike, its engine the only warm thing in a cold, dew-laden summer morning. Condensation dripped from the tip of the exhaust into the damp grass. Never had a thing looked more beautiful to me. I did the greatcoat up. It swamped me. I pulled the huge collar up and around my hair. I could hardly see, and hoped that that meant no one could see me inside.

"Hold on tight," Jack said as we climbed aboard. Once again I rode sidesaddle, and we roared away, passing out of the camp so quickly I barely saw the place where I had been held captive.

Now we are somewhere in the French countryside. Jack told me the camp was just outside Bethune. We drove as far as a village called Dieval on the main road; then Jack turned off onto roads that are only farm tracks. He said it was too dangerous to move on the main roads.

I wondered how he knew where he was going at all, but he seemed to know everywhere, without even using a map.

When I asked him about it, he laughed.

"It's my job!"

He's spent months riding all over the same small area of France, here and there and back again, avoiding trouble, learning the best routes. I suddenly felt safe, for the first time in weeks.

# 18

We headed to the south of Bethune, into the deepest countryside. We found a small stone hay barn at the back of a wood, and rested there.

At last, I had the chance to ask Jack all the questions in my head. He seemed quite amused by it, and I felt he was somehow different from the last time we had met.

As we spoke we sat on a cattle trough under the eaves of the barn. We felt safe; there was no one around. In front of us was a landscape of great beauty. It had been a misty start to the day, a typical summer's-morning mist, which had turned into a drizzle of rain.

"Lovely, isn't it?" Jack said. "Reminds me of home a little."

"Where's that?" I asked.

"Hereford. I grew up on a farm. It rains there in the summer too."

He smiled. As the rain eased off, wood pigeons began to

call to each other in the treetops above us, but there was no other sound besides the dripping leaves.

"The fields, the woods, the low hills. But just think. If we got on my motorcycle and rode twenty miles that way . . ."

"What?" I said.

"They say it's the closest thing there'll ever be to hell on earth."

He paused.

I thought of Tom. Of Edgar.

"What's it like?"

He shook his head. The same shake of the head that the Royal Welch corporal had given me when he said "The Somme."

"We've destroyed it," he said. "All this. All that you can see here is gone. There are few trees, no grass, no buildings, no birds. No creatures but the rats and lice."

He didn't talk about the men who were dying, and something made me not mention it. I didn't know why, but he seemed more upset about the landscape than the men.

"Mud, and wire. Mud and wire, and holes in the ground. If we keep digging long enough maybe we *will* find hell."

"But when the war is over, it'll grow back," I said.

"When the war is over?" he said, shaking his head again. "You haven't seen it. Nothing could ever grow there again. Nothing."

We were silent then, and thinking I might have upset him, I changed the subject.

"What were you doing in Bethune?" I asked. "The chances of you just finding me . . ."

". . . were nil," he said. "That's because it wasn't chance. I came to find you."

That surprised me for a start, but I should have known. He had planned everything.

"You're big news in Boulogne," he said, grimly. "Quite the celebrity. Some say you went mad over your husband. Others have you down as a German spy. I even heard one story that you're a Russian princess, though God knows what they think you would be doing here!"

A Russian princess. With a sick stomach I thought of Mother. Where was her little Sasha now?

"Don't look so worried," he said. "You're safe enough. For now. The more nonsense talked about you, the harder it will be for anyone to get to the truth. And only you and I know the truth, don't we?"

I thought of Millie, but I had even lied to her.

"Yes," I said, "but I still don't understand . . ."

". . . how I found you?" he asked, but that wasn't my question. My question was, why?

"When I heard the stories in Boulogne, I knew immediately you'd got yourself into hot water. It wasn't hard to find out where you'd gone, so I got myself a job riding to Bethune. Swapped a run with another rider.

"I watched the camp yesterday, but I wouldn't have known where you were if you hadn't tried your escape by the back door."

I felt embarrassed at the thought of it, but Jack shrugged.

"You tried. You're a brave girl, that's for sure."

"But how did you get the guard to leave?"

"It was easy. He'll be in trouble, but I don't suppose they'll be too bothered finding you. I came up to him, told him I was to move you to a prison camp. He looked doubtful, but I just kept on. It's amazing what people will believe,

239

if you believe it yourself. I suppose he was confused because no one's had to guard a nurse before!

"I brought a sealed envelope. Waved it at him, said it was my orders, but if he wanted to check he'd have to take it to the officer commanding.

"So I gave him the envelope and he went. I offered to guard you while he was gone. He even said thanks!"

Jack smiled and I laughed.

Above our heads there was a rustling in the treetops, but it was just some birds flapping in and out of the shadows. We watched a pale sun peer through the last of the mist in the field in front of us.

I looked down, and saw a raven right in front of us, no more than twenty feet away, hopping toward me, cawing.

I screamed, and fell to the ground.

# 17

When I woke it was dark. Pitch-black. I felt straw under me, and from the way sound died around me I knew I was inside the haybarn.

"Are you awake?"

It was Jack. He was somewhere away in the darkness. I could smell petrol from the bike, the dryness of the hay and that was about all.

The rest of what happened came back to me. I remembered seeing the raven, and falling to the ground.

I think I was coming in and out of consciousness, sleeping, waking, dreaming, waking again, in such a state of confusion that I had little idea what was real and what was not.

"You've been in a bad way," Jack said. "It was the raven, wasn't it?"

"I'm just tired," I said. "And hungry too."

But he was right, it was the raven. A common-enough

bird, but the shock of seeing it had sent me into a hallucination of fear and dread.

I saw things.

I don't want to think about the things I saw, but when I finally woke up, Jack seemed to know.

"You can feel them, too, can't you?" he said.

"What?" I said, finding my voice. "Who?"

"The dead," he said, simply. "They pull at me when I'm asleep sometimes."

I nodded, but it was dark, and Jack couldn't see.

"I really am hungry," I said.

"I know," he said. "I went to try and find a farm while you were asleep, but I didn't want to leave you for long. . . . Have some water and we'll find food tomorrow."

He shuffled toward me in the dark and I heard him lighting a match. In the flickering light, I saw the barn around us, stacked high with hay, and Jack's face in front of me, grimy, and worn deep with lines. His pale blue eyes seemed lifeless.

"Quick," he said, holding his water bottle in one hand, the match in the other. "Before it goes out."

I took the drink gratefully, but the bottle was nearly empty.

"Tomorrow," I said.

"What about it?"

"I must find Thomas."

The match went out and plunged us back into darkness.

"No," Jack said. His voice was dry, and quiet. I knew he was holding something back.

I didn't answer, hoping he would say more, but he didn't.

"What do you mean?" I asked.

Suddenly I felt scared, sitting alone in the middle of the French night with a man I didn't know. A man whom most people considered mad, at that.

"I said, no."

"But what else are we doing here? Why did you help me get away if not for that?"

He lit another match, studied my face. I glared back at him, my breath coming heavily.

"I got you out because I didn't want anything to happen to you. I want you to go home to England. I want you to be safe."

"But Tom—"

"Is dead already."

"No!" I cried. "That's not true."

"If you've seen him killed then he's as good as dead. There's nothing we can do to change the future. Don't you understand that yet?"

"No!" I shouted. "He's not dead."

"Not yet!" Jack shouted back.

He cursed as the match went out.

I began to cry in the darkness.

"You don't understand," Jack said. "Why don't you understand? The future's already done! How else do you and I make sense of what we see? What you have seen will come to be, and there's nothing you or I can do to change that."

"I thought you had changed your mind," I said, through a mouthful of tears. "What I said that night. That we have to play our part anyway. I thought you understood that. I thought you'd come to help me play my part. I can't simply let him die!"

Jack said nothing, and I listened to myself crying, and hated myself. Edgar was right. I'm just pathetic. Weak.

"Alexandra," Jack said. "Don't cry. I'd like to help you. Don't you understand that? I got you out of Bethune because I want to help you. But there's nothing we can do. . . ."

"If he was your son, would you let him die?" I sobbed. "I've already lost one brother. I can't watch it happen again. If I hadn't been given this curse, then I wouldn't know any different. Maybe that would be easier. But I can't help it. I have seen Tom and I am going to try to save him. I'd like to say I can do it without you, but I can't. I know that. I need your help."

Still Jack was silent.

"Why are you helping me?" I asked. "Why set me free, when you don't want to help me save Tom?"

"I want to help you. I said that."

"Because I remind you of someone?" I said, spitefully. "Is that it? Your daughter? Your wife?"

"No," said Jack. "I'm not married. There's no one like that."

"Then why?"

"Because, Alexandra, you're the one person I've met in this war whose life I might be able to change."

"So you *do* think lives can be changed, then?" I asked.

Jack was silent.

There was silence for a long time, but in the end I convinced him. I don't really know how. I know Jack is a man who had all belief and hope taken from him long ago. But something I said seemed to make a difference. He lit a third match in the silence, and shuffled over to me. I didn't like him coming that close, but I couldn't say so. I thought it wouldn't be wise to anger him again. He was so near to me that I could smell him, his unwashed skin and clothes. His face was deadly serious.

He looked deep into my eyes, and he was so close I could see the match reflected in his. He put out a shaking hand toward me, and stroked my hair, just once. I closed my eyes and tried not to shudder.

When I opened my eyes again, he was sitting away from me, his eyes closed, his head bowed. He was motionless, as if deep in some dream.

The third match went out.

"I'll help you," he said.

# 16

Jack is sleeping, but I slept enough in fits and starts during the afternoon and am not tired.

I do not want to sleep again, in case I see those things, those dead people again. I cannot prevent one thing from surfacing in my mind, however. Amidst all the terrible things I saw, I had another sight of Tom.

I saw the gun that will kill Tom, and I flew with the bullet, spinning, spinning toward him. I was so close to it all, I could smell it. I could taste the powder from the cartridge.

The bullet struck his chest, and I followed only a moment behind.

# 15

The last two days have been a lifetime.

I think it can barely be thirty-six hours, in fact, since we left the safety of the haybarn, to where I am now.

Where I am now.

From what I can see in the valley below me, this can be only one place.

The mouth of hell.

# 14

We left the barn early.

We were both awake to hear a deafening chorus of bird-song in the wood behind the barn, but though the birds were singing, it was a desolate morning, with a lowering bank of cloud above us. A mild drizzle gave way to maybe an hour of insistent rain, but we left anyway, because we were hungry.

"We'll head for Doullens," Jack said. "We can find food there."

I suddenly worried that maybe Jack was going to change his mind about helping me find Tom, but I needn't have.

"Doullens is quite a big town," he said. "There're a couple of railheads there. Supply dumps. And at least two casualty clearing stations, that I know of. There're lots of people. If

248

your brother's division came through, we might find someone who's seen them."

We rode on the motorcycle across the wet French countryside. It was hard going. The roads we chose were small ones that had been subjected to less traffic, but nevertheless, the thin tires on the bike cut into the mud at times, and we nearly got stuck twice.

By midmorning we came over the crest of a low hill and saw an ugly little town in front of us. Jack brought the bike to a standstill as the lane we'd been using joined the main road into Doullens.

He seemed to be weighing things up.

"Jack . . . ," I said.

He looked at me, and I knew what he was thinking. Even from this distance I could see he was right about the town. It was busy, full of people, soldiers. A hive of comings and goings. I looked down at myself. Still in my uniform, though soaked with rain and mud, with Jack's greatcoat wrapped around me. I would attract attention immediately.

"You're going to have to stay up here," he said.

"No . . . ," I said, but I knew he was right.

"We passed a copse a couple of miles back," he said. "That will have to do."

It felt awful to have to turn around and retrace our steps even a hundred yards, but I told myself that until we had news of where Tom was, it made no difference which direction we went in.

Jack left me at the copse.

"Stay hidden," he said. "I'll be as quick as I can."

I scrambled into the trees until I thought I was out of

sight, and turned in time to see Jack and his motorbike disappear.

I sat down in the wood, and began shivering almost immediately. The rain had stopped, but I was wet through.

Above me in the sodden treetops, birds jumped and shrieked noisily. I looked up, fearing what I would see. Even the thought of the raven was nearly enough to push me again into a terrible vision of the bird that kept stalking my imagination and my dreams.

I hoped Jack wouldn't be long.

# 13

Maybe a couple of hours later Jack came back. I heard the hum, and then the throb of the motorcycle engine, but I waited until I was sure it was him before walking to the edge of the trees and showing myself. Having sat in the cold for all that time, my legs didn't move properly, and I feared he might miss me as I staggered out, but he had seen me, all right.

"Not a bad place," he said.

"Any news?" I asked.

He shook his head.

"Sorry. Nothing."

I felt panic rising, and had to fight to control it.

"It doesn't mean anything," he said. "We'll go on to Amiens. It's most likely they were entrained to Amiens, if they're heading up to the Somme. Someone there might have seen them. Be hard to miss a division on the march."

"Why don't we just go straight to the Somme?" I asked.

Jack laughed, then stopped abruptly when he looked at me.

"If it were that easy . . . ," he said. "We can travel quite fast back here. I know it seems slow, but at the front . . . no one goes anywhere quickly. The roads, if there are any, are thick with mud. And the front is full of people. Don't forget that. The closer we get to the front, the less like this it will be. We haven't passed anyone else all morning, have we? I could just about get away with it—I am a dispatch rider, after all. But you . . ."

I saw what he meant.

"We'd be stopped in no time," he said.

I nodded.

"So we need to know exactly where he's gone first."

I thought I might start to cry then, but Jack reassured me.

"Don't worry. We'll find him."

I wished I shared his belief.

"Breakfast," said Jack, swinging a bag from his shoulder. "Or is it lunch?"

"I think it's last night's supper," I said.

The bag was large, but I was disappointed to find that it was not all food. After he pulled out a loaf and some soft cheese, the bag contained only clothes.

A uniform.

"What's that for?" I asked.

"For you." Jack nodded. "Put them on. We might pass you off for a soldier from a distance, and besides, they're dry and you're not."

We ate.

"I thought you told me once that this isn't a fairy tale. That I can't dress myself as a man and get away with it."

252

"I said a lot of things," he said, and turned his back. "But it can't hurt, anyway. Get changed, then we'll head for Amiens."

I tiptoed a little way back into the wood, and pulled off my nurse's uniform. As I reached for the clothes Jack had brought me, I saw with revulsion that there were holes and bloodstains in the tunic. I wondered where he had got them, but it was obvious, really. He had said there were casualty clearing stations in Doullens. I saw the regimental badge on the shoulder of the tunic, but didn't recognize it. It meant nothing to me.

I pulled the clothes on, waves of different feelings washing over me. I realized how comfortable I felt in my VAD uniform, how I belonged in it. I knew who I was. As I dressed myself in a dead soldier's clothes, it made me feel fragile and weak. I saw my pale girl's skin slip inside the rough cloth of the uniform, and almost laughed at the stupidity of it all. I didn't belong in this world.

The uniform was too big for me, but not by so very much. And then, as I was turning the trousers up, a vision came to me and I knew it was how the man had been wounded. A wound from which he had later died.

I was wrapped in the soldier's dead world, and could not shed it. I had to wear these clothes if I was going to find Tom. I looked at my nurse's uniform on the wet earth of the copse.

I picked it up and made my way back to Jack.

"What shall I do with these?" I asked.

"Leave them here," he said. "Come on. We should go. The heat from the bike will warm you up again, at least."

Something felt wrong to me. I couldn't just drop my

uniform in the mud. I folded it up neatly, and made a small pile, finishing with my apron with the red cross uppermost. I placed it at the foot of a tree just inside the copse, and then turned to Jack.

"Let's go," I said, and swung my legs over the parcel rack of the bike properly, now that I was wearing trousers.

We left.

I squinted into the wind as we rode.

After a few miles, I imagined the dirty, stolen uniform that had become mine for a short while, lying in a wet French wood. Then I suddenly remembered that I had left my Greek book with the uniform. In the rush I'd forgotten all about it. I imagined what someone might think if one day they found a nurse's uniform and a small book of Greek myths in English on the edge of a French wood. Would they ever guess even part of the story behind it?

It was too late to go back for the book, and as we rode I couldn't help but feel I'd lost my lucky talisman.

# 12

Below me, as I sit here waiting, I take the occasional peep down into the valley. My eyes grow wide at the sights I see. The men. Thousands of them. The guns. Hundreds upon hundreds of big guns. The horses. The tents, the equipment, the cooking wagons, the ambulances. In a muddy field in the middle of France.

I think back to the last steps of our journey here, through smashed villages and rolling open downs, to this awful, awful place.

"You don't look much like a soldier," Jack said as we stopped to rest.

"What do I look like?" I asked.

"Nothing," he said. "You're too pretty to be a man, even under all that mud. And too thin. But you couldn't be a girl. Who'd think that? And there are some young boys out here.

Very young. The ones that lied about their age so they could come."

I shrugged.

"You don't look like anything," Jack repeated. "Your hair. That's the problem."

I had tied my hair up behind me, but I knew again he was right. Even though I had clumsily shortened it once before, and even though it was wet and dirty, there was just too much of it.

Jack fished around in the pannier on the bike, and pulled out a knife. A big, sharp knife.

He didn't have to say anything.

And I said nothing in return.

I took off the greatcoat and laid it across the seat of the bike so it wouldn't get any muddier. Then I stood before Jack and bowed my head.

Jack lifted the knife toward me, and took a tress of my hair in the other hand. He cut, and all too easily I watched my hair fall in clumps around my feet. I remembered having my hair cut as a little girl by Mother, and smiled bitterly to myself at these so different circumstances. And if a few tears ended up with my hair in the French mud, no one but me knew it.

"I'm no barber," Jack said, after a while. It seemed to be taking forever. The big locks had come off easily, but as he got closer to my scalp, it was harder work, and he had to saw the hair off with little jerking motions.

At last it was over. I felt my head, and couldn't believe it was mine. My long flowing hair had been replaced by short, clumsy spikes, an inch or so long, no more.

"It's just as well we have no mirror," I said.

Jack opened his mouth, then shut it again.

He looked at me sadly.

"Sorry," he said. "You're still too beautiful to be a soldier."

I turned away, embarrassed. I wished he wouldn't say things like that. When I turned back, Jack was pumping the starter pedals of the bike. It roared to life, and he held out the coat for me again.

"Getting low on petrol," he said. "We can't afford to mess around."

Around us the landscape had changed. As we skirted the edge of Doullens we had come into a different type of countryside. The land now was more open, rolling downs crisscrossed with fields, and fewer trees. Bleak. Even the mud clogging our wheels and our boots was different, a sticky gray paste that tugged at us, slowed us down.

Jack had decided that we could risk the main road to Amiens.

"Just keep your head inside that coat if we pass anyone."

But we saw no one. It was as if the world had ended, and everyone was dead except Jack and me.

On the main road we had made good time to Amiens, but as we neared the city Jack once again steered away from the place itself.

"Where are we going?" I shouted over his shoulder.

He shouted something back, but I couldn't hear what he said over the engine noise. It made no difference. I had to trust him in everything now. I had no other choice.

Finally we began to see people. I clung desperately to his

back and hid my face as we passed a column of soldiers marching into the city. Trucks rolled here and there, and I even saw a red cross on one and knew it was a motor ambulance.

The bike stopped.

There was a river in front of us. Not vast, but wide enough, and smooth flowing. A stone bridge spanned it.

"That's the Somme," Jack said. "Across the other side is a place called Longueau. If they came down from Bethune by train, this is where they'll have come."

We crossed and came to Longueau, to the station, which was just about all there was of the place.

We parked the motorcycle by the wall of the station. It was late afternoon, and although it's July, the sky was heavy and gray and the light was bad.

"Right," Jack said. "I'll do the talking. You stay with the bike. If anyone asks, you're a new dispatch rider and I'm teaching you the ropes."

"Is that going to fool anyone?"

Jack hesitated.

"No," he admitted, looking at me. "No. Just pray no one comes near you."

Jack trotted up the steps into the station. As I waited I tried to look nonchalant, and turned my back on the world if anyone came by, pretending to fiddle with the engine on the bike as I had seen Jack do. I thought it would probably do no harm to get some of the mud off it, and was so busy doing this that I didn't notice Jack had come back.

"Cardonette," he said, quite quietly, but I could see he

was excited underneath. "They marched from here to Cardonette. Four days ago."

"Four days?" I cried.

"Not so loud," Jack hissed. "They're hundreds of men on foot. We're on a bike. We can catch them up."

# 11

Cardonette turned out to be back the way we had come; in fact, we had passed within a mile of it earlier. But we weren't to know that.

It was evening by the time we got there, and with night falling I felt less conspicuous. We risked riding right into the heart of the village, passing by a tented village of soldiers in the fields as we did so. I craned my neck and strained my eyes trying to see if I could recognize anything that might lead us to Tom, but Jack told me to keep still.

"Have you any idea how many soldiers there are out here? How many units? How many battalions? If we have to find a needle in a haystack, then at least we need a clue where to look."

So I waited outside while Jack went into an estaminet for more information.

He came back very quickly.

"This is it?" I asked.

"No, but we're getting there," he said. "The Thirty-third were here, and with them, the Nineteenth Brigade. Your brother's battalion is in the Nineteenth."

"But where have they gone?"

"A place called Daours. It's back down on the Somme, near where it meets the Ancre."

"Can you be sure they were here?"

"Oh, yes," Jack said. "They remember them well here. The locals were forced to give their houses as billets for the soldiers. They don't like that. They have every reason to remember them."

We were getting closer to Tom, but not close enough.

"When were they here?" I asked.

"They left on Tuesday, three days ago."

"Then we have to hurry," I said.

"No," said Jack. "It's getting late. We're tired. We'll find a bed here and go on in the morning."

"No!" I said.

"Alexandra—"

"No," I said again. "We have to go on. I'm not tired. It's not that late. And it's much safer for us to travel in the dark, anyway. You know I'm right."

And for once, Jack had to agree.

So we moved on, to Daours.

# 10

We rode into the night.

It seemed the whole world had shrunk to just us. The two of us: Jack and me. Or maybe the three of us: Jack, me and the motorbike. Maybe I am tired, maybe I am going a little crazy, I thought as we trundled on the bike through the darkness. But without the bike I would be as lost as without Jack.

The bike's headlight shone dimly in front of us, and Jack was afraid of that, to show a light in the dark, but there was little we could do. It shone ahead of us, just enough to see the way as mile after mile of narrow mud-laden track went by under the wheels, while I listened to the sound of the engine rise and fall as it plowed through the varying ground.

I was sore, sore from holding Jack; my arms felt like lead around his waist. Sore from holding the bike between my legs, sore from sitting on the tiny metal plate.

It was very late by the time we reached Daours, and we repeated the whole performance. While Jack asked around in the village in his excellent French, I lolled on the motorbike, and ignored anyone who came my way.

The news was bad.

"They were here," Jack said, "till Wednesday afternoon. Then they marched on to Buire."

"How far is that?" I asked.

"About another ten miles," Jack said.

I got ready to argue with him, but I didn't have to.

"Come on," he said. "We'll find him, I know it."

"You mean, you've seen it?" I asked, but Jack shook his head.

"No," he said, turning away. "No. I just think."

I wanted to lie down and die. Every bit of me was tired, we had finished our food long ago, and I was ready to give up, but I couldn't. Tom was driving me on.

We got back onto the bike again, and slowly crawled out of Daours toward Buire. The night deepened around us, and through it I saw flashes of light ahead of us.

"Lightning?" I shouted to Jack over his shoulder, but he shook his head, and I understood.

Guns. Big guns were firing ahead of us, though not a sound could be heard over the noise of our engine.

We rode on and I gripped Jack grimly, and in the night and the haze in my head, I saw ravens sweeping through the darkness on either side of the bike. I shook my head to clear the vision, but they wouldn't leave, and I don't know if they were real or not. I shut my eyes and tried to think only of

Tom, but whenever I managed to bring him to mind, he was replaced by Edgar, laughing at me, waving a fistful of black feathers in my face.

We reached Buire in the dead of night.

Jack cut the engine and we looked at the sorry little village. A church was its most noble feature; otherwise, it was a mess of small terraced houses and the odd grander one.

Finally I was in the thick of people. Despite the late hour, the village was astir with hordes of soldiers, and more amazing to my eye, horses. Lines of cavalry wound their way around either end of the village, the horses plodding slowly and wearily in some places, proud and fine in others. I stared as a line of Indians made their way past us on horseback, their pointed beards and turbaned heads an almost unbelievable sight.

No one took the slightest notice of us. Everyone was busy doing something, going somewhere or just being too tired to wonder at a dispatch rider and his passenger in the middle of the night.

Once more Jack made some enquiries, and once more the news was tantalizing.

"They were here this morning," he said. "They left before noon for Meaulte."

"How far?" was all I could manage to say.

"I've never been there," Jack said. "It's about six miles. The road's easy enough to follow, but I've no idea how long it will take."

I couldn't believe we were so close to Tom, that we had traveled in a day what it had taken him four days to march. I said so to Jack.

"They stopped for a day or two here. Another day and we'd have met them."

"So . . . ?" I asked.

"So they'll be in Meaulte now. They'll be there tomorrow. It's six miles. We can take the chance to rest here."

I began to protest, but Jack stopped me.

"I can't go on. Alexandra. Please trust me. They'll still be in Meaulte tomorrow morning. We can leave at dawn and then we'll find Tom. But we need to get some rest first."

I was ashamed of myself, but in truth, a part of me was happy to agree with Jack, a part of me that was tired beyond belief and exhausted in mind as well as body.

There were large numbers of soldiers in tents in an old orchard on the edge of the village. We kept away from them, but found a small hayloft nearby. There was just enough room for the two of us.

As I went to sleep I heard the sound of guns. The atmosphere seemed to change around us, seemed to tense, as the low boom and rumble of the barrage reached us from the front line.

But Jack noticed none of this, and was already snoring by my side.

# 9

With night came the raven dream.

The dream of Tom, the dream of the bullet, and once more I watched, paralyzed, as with infinite slowness, and in precise detail, I saw the gun fire. There was a bright flash, followed by a loud bang. The bullet hurtled toward Tom, ravens' feathers whirling around him as if caught in a tornado.

The bullet left a curious trail of cordite behind it, a thin smoke that became unnaturally thick, and began to block my vision. I was blinded by it, until just as the bullet hit Tom, I lost sight of him altogether.

When I woke this morning, the world was shrouded in mist.

# 8

The mist was thick. So thick I could barely see twenty paces ahead.

I woke first, and shook Jack by the shoulder. I have no idea how early it was, but already there were sounds of the encampment stirring and I wanted to be away. I thought of Cassandra, and of the end of her journey. Her story ended in a pool of her own blood on the steps of the palace in Argos. I knew my ending would be very different from hers, and almost as if I had been bereaved, I knew that she was no longer with me.

The mist, at least, seemed a friend, and hid our progress as we climbed down from the hayloft and wheeled the bike out of the village without starting it. There was no point in adding to our problems.

We weren't alone as we left the village. An almost constant stream of wounded and prisoners approached from the opposite direction, and Jack decided we may as well start the motorcycle again. It looked stranger pushing it than riding it. And the less time anyone had to look at me, the better.

Once or twice I would fancy that someone was looking at me too closely, but no one said anything. Everyone was too busy to worry much about a strange boy on the back of a dispatch rider's motorbike. I suppose the truth is that no one actually looked at me. They just saw another boy in a uniform.

At last we came to Meaulte.

The mist was still heavy, but we could see that Meaulte was another drab town. It had a dejected air about it as we rode through. A utilitarian, slightly sordid sort of a place, with only its church to be proud of.

And it was there that I thought it was all over.

Jack could find out nothing. Although the place is only a mile or two behind the front, there were still lots of locals in the village. They resented the presence of the war in their world, and the presence of the army.

"Up until a fortnight ago, the front line was just ahead," Jack said. "The big push has moved it farther east. These people are still scared."

I couldn't blame them, but I was desperate to find Tom.

"You said they'd be here," I said, angrily, though I knew I'd have been lost without him. I would have got nowhere.

And now, as it is, I seem to have got nowhere anyway.

I am just sitting, waiting, on the edge of death.

# 7

Jack continued to ask around, and finally found an answer, but not the one I'd been hoping for.

He came back from a queue of men at a delousing machine standing at one end of the village. I could tell immediately that it was bad. He didn't have to say anything.

"They've gone," I said. "They've gone, haven't they?"

He nodded, a brief, small gesture, but one that dealt me a massive blow.

"Yes. Before dawn. No one knows where, except that they were headed for the front. Left most of their kit behind. They're heading for it, all right. Could be anywhere."

"But where?" I cried.

"I'm sorry," Jack said. "I'm sorry. I don't know. No one seems to know."

"What do we do?" I cried. I couldn't admit we were defeated. It couldn't happen.

"Someone must know something" was all I could say.

"It's chaos, Alexandra. Nothing's clear. There's fighting everywhere. There's been a big mauling in a place called Mametz Wood. I was talking to the lads over there, they're some of the survivors. We've got control of it now, and the fighting's moved on to some villages beyond. Bazentin, Delville Wood, High Wood. They could be anywhere."

Something struck me, and I don't know why I bothered to say it, but if I hadn't, then it might all have ended then and there.

"That's strange," I said. "Why does it have an English name?"

"What?" Jack said.

"High Wood. Why does it have an English name?"

"That's just what the army calls it. The French call it Raven Wood."

Raven Wood.

I went cold.

Jack saw; I must have gone as white as death itself.

"What is it?" he said. He grabbed my arm, thinking I was going to faint.

"That's it," I said. I trembled. "That's where he's going. High Wood."

Now I know what the raven means, now at last I can answer that question from my dreams.

I know what the raven means. It means death.

It means High Wood.

It's where Tom is going to die.

# 6

I am waiting now, on the edge of a place called Death Valley. That's not its real name, just one given to it by the soldiers. Some of them call it Happy Valley instead, which is supposed to be a joke, but how anyone can laugh here I do not know. Yet they do. I've seen them.

Jack knew I was right. He trusts my vision as I believe in his.

As soon as I saw the connection with the raven, it was obvious, and so we made our way here. I was feeling utterly desolate. We were surrounded by men on all sides, streams of troops marching to the front, or staggering back in ragged lines. Once Tom's battalion has gone up to the front itself, I will be unable to reach him. My only hope is that I can get him away before that happens.

We left Meaulte and rode on clogging mud tracks through the remains of other villages, one of which had only its church tower left standing. I don't know what they were all called, but a place called Fricourt was no more than a vast pile of rubble, with buildings that looked as if they had just collapsed and died.

Farther on, small copses of trees lay around us, some intact, some just fields of broken stumps. Jack explained that the front line ran through the area until the big push began a fortnight ago. There's been lots of fighting here, and I cannot describe the things I have seen that prove that fact.

Dead men lie at the side of the road.

Jack rode on, and though I stared, they were soon behind us.

Suddenly there was a strange whistling hum in the air, and seconds later we were at the edge of a storm. It was not a storm of nature, but one of machinery and artillery.

Explosions ripped the ground ahead of us, and Jack frantically pulled off the road.

"Five-nines!" he shouted. "Get in that ditch and keep your head down!"

He didn't have to tell me. We flung ourselves from the bike and cowered on the ground until the barrage stopped.

It didn't last long.

"Are you all right?" Jack asked me as he got to his feet.

I couldn't answer; I was too stunned to speak.

I nodded. We moved on.

Then the bike gave out.

We had been struggling through oceans of mud. The chalky land around us is covered by a thick clay, which had been churned into a gray-brown paste that binds and sticks.

The faithful Triumph had worked its way deep into this

mud at the bottom of a hollow, and no matter how much Jack tried, we could not shift it.

We got off, and tried to push it free, Jack revving it all the while, but I only managed to lose my footing and fall face-down in the mud.

Some Scots were passing. They laughed at me, but I didn't care. No one could recognize me now, I thought, and two of them came over and lifted the bike free with Jack's help, but we had only made our way a little farther when it ran out of petrol.

I was too tired even to cry now, and we stood staring at the useless bike, lying on its side like a dead animal in the mud.

With a strangely unnatural speed, the mist began to clear, the sun burning it off in a matter of minutes, and we could see it was going to be a hot day after all.

We saw we were surrounded by the dead. Bodies lay here and there, uncared for, unburied, almost unnoticed. I tried not to look at them, but couldn't help staring at the huge corpses of horses that lay among the human dead.

The old front line was ground covered with debris, with old and new shell holes, rifles, clothing and all sorts of other equipment strewn around and abandoned. I found it hard to take in. Even the word *desolation* comes nowhere near describing what I saw. It was a twisted and broken world, made by men.

More wounded came by. Going forward, streams of soldiers were marching, and more Indian cavalry trotted past on horseback.

Then, standing, staring in despair at the bike, I looked up at the file of men passing us, and I saw Tom.

Jack saw me start, and before I could call out, clapped a hand over my mouth.

The movement was enough to catch Tom's eye.

I barely recognized him, and as he stared back at me, as he stared straight through me, I realized that he didn't recognize me at all.

Jack stepped back.

"Tom," I said, mouthing the word at him.

Then he knew me, and a look of terror and wonder spread across his face. I saw what he saw. A thin, gangly boy, covered in mud, with rough shorn hair. And who looked a little bit like his sister.

He came over to us, glancing nervously back at the line of men he should have been marching with, and at Jack, and at me.

As he came closer I could see he finally believed it was me. "What?"

That was all he said, and I could not speak.

"Why?" he said. "Why are you here?"

He glanced again at his battalion, but no one seemed to be bothered that he had fallen out. In fact, it seemed they had reached their destination, for just ahead in a low curve of land, we could see the start of a huge encampment of men, guns, equipment and horses. Battalions of men were camped around on all sides.

"Why, Sasha? How did you get here?"

He glanced at Jack, then back to me.

"I've come to take you back," I said at last.

"You've . . . what?" Tom said, perplexed, his face dark.

"I've seen what's going to happen to you," I said. "Tom,

you must believe me, I've seen what's going to happen. You're going to be killed if you don't come away. You're going to High Wood, aren't you?"

"How do you know that?" he asked, scowling.

"Tom, you have to believe me. You have to, no one else does, but it's true. You're going to be killed."

"Oh, God," he said. "Why can't you understand?"

He reached out to me.

"Go away, Sasha," he said. "Go home. Get this stupid man who's brought you here to take you home again. I don't believe you. I don't believe you, because it's not true, and even if I did, I wouldn't leave. I can't. I belong with these men. I can't run away because my sister tells me to, and if I did, I'd be shot anyway!"

He stopped; then he turned and looked at his battalion, which was nearly out of sight at the head of the valley.

"I must go," he said, sadly. "Go home and be safe."

He went.


Jack and I argued over what to do, but in the end it was obvious. We had to go home. Tom wasn't going to come, and even if he did, he'd be shot for desertion.

All my hopes and plans lay in ruins. Everything I'd worked for. But I couldn't leave it like that.

I had to talk to him once more, and say goodbye properly. Then I would leave it alone like everyone wanted me to. I knew I couldn't risk being seen in the valley in daylight, and now that the mist had lifted, it was much too risky. We found an out-of-the-way crook at the top of the valley, a little hollow among some sickly-looking trees. Away in front of us was the valley, and beyond that, the awful sight of Mametz Wood. The whole place like a biblical scene of pestilence and death.

I begged Jack to go into Death Valley, find Tom and bring him to talk to me.

He agreed—grudgingly, but he agreed.

And that is where I am now, waiting for Tom, to say goodbye.

As Jack left, he lifted his tunic and pulled his revolver out from the case at his hip.

"Here," he said. "In case you get into trouble. Just squeeze the trigger. Don't pull. And keep your arm strong."

He really meant me to use it.

I knew what he was afraid of. If someone came across me, out here, away from the sight of the rest of the men, anything could happen.

I sat down in the hollow, using the greatcoat as a blanket, and waited.


And I am waiting still, for Jack to return with Tom.

If he doesn't, then what?

What if something happens to him? How will I get away then? I will be lost without him, and anything could happen to me. And if it does, my story will stop here, with me in this hole, clutching the revolver tight with every hour that passes.

My story could end right here.

5

# 4

# 3

I am blind.
I am as blind as a book with no writing on the page.

# 2

Blind.

Slowly, everything came back to me.

But it was a slow and painful recovery, a memory that did not want to come to mind easily, and did so like a difficult birth.

It has all been a bitter joke.

The hours passed, dragged by. Finally, I could stand the waiting no longer, and crept to the top of my little hollow in the trees, and peered down on Death Valley. I can only guess at how many thousands of men were massing there.

It was a vast waiting room, the point at which men and horses and guns were all being gathered in readiness for some terrible battle at the front. I watched streams of horsemen below me, the Indian cavalry again. I almost smiled to see them. Teams of guns were ridden up as well, and thousands upon thousands of men, all milling about in the open, as if it was an expedition and not a war.

I strained my eyes, desperate to glimpse Tom, or Jack.

More than once I thought about going down myself, but I forced myself back into my hollow and lay looking at the sky. I was starving, but what did that matter? There were more important things afoot than hunger.

I thought about Jack more than Tom for some reason. I understood that deserters were shot, and I worried that I had got Jack into danger. What if he was accused of desertion? He had been missing for two days now.

I couldn't bear the thought that I might be responsible for getting him shot because I had only been thinking about Tom.

And Tom. I now realized at last the misconception I had been living under. I'd wanted to mend everything by saving him, to make my family whole again—as whole as it could be, at least—but everything was in tatters.

I couldn't take Tom away, or he'd be shot for desertion too. The only way men got away from the front was with a decent wound.

I clutched the revolver so tightly my fingers ached.

Then, without warning, there was a scrape behind me, and two men came over the lip of the hollow.

It was Tom, and behind him, Jack.

I dropped the gun on the coat and jumped up to meet Tom, and put my arms around him.

We stayed that way for ages.

I cried, and so did he.

Jack stepped back, then sat down on the ground.

"You haven't got long" was all he said. He seemed nervous, agitated.

I looked at Tom, and at last I was pleased to see he seemed happy to see me.

"I can't believe you got here," he said, smiling.

"I've been nursing. In France," I said. "But I was just trying to get to you."

"You're amazing," he said. "It's hard to . . . But you're here, so it must be true."

"How are you?" I asked.

Tom shook his head.

"All right," he said. "I'm all right. Just tell Mother and Father that."

I must have looked strangely at him.

"What is it?" he asked. "Are they all right?"

"I think so," I said. "I don't know. Tom, I ran away. They don't know where I am. I did this for all of us, but if I ever get home they'll probably never speak to me again."

"Of course they will," Tom said. "And you must go home. It's wonderful to see you, Sasha, but you must get away from here. It's dangerous, for so many reasons. I spoke to your friend Jack. He's told me what you've done. He says he'll help you get home."

"Yes, Tom, but—"

"No, Sasha, no. I only came up here because Jack assured me you'd seen sense now."

"You don't know what I've seen," I said, angrily.

"Alexandra, listen, you have to drop all this talk about seeing the future—"

"Why?" I cried. "Why don't you believe me? Mother and

Father wouldn't believe me. Edgar wouldn't believe me. I thought you would, Tom. I need you to. You have to."

"It's not that easy to understand."

"Everyone thinks I'm a fool. Edgar died still thinking that. I can't take it from you, too."

"Edgar didn't think that, I swear," Tom said. "None of us do."

"How do you know what Edgar thought?" I said, bitterly. "The last time we saw him he was miserable and silent. You weren't even there. Then he went back to the war and was killed."

"No, Sasha, I did see him."

I looked sharply at Tom, incredulous.

"He came to see me in Manchester. He said he'd left Brighton a day early to come to see me. We talked like we'd never talked before. It made everything seem right again between us. I felt I understood him, and what he wanted to do. With the war. But he said it had changed him. It wasn't what he was expecting. He said it terrified him. He told me to go on trying to be a doctor. That there was more use in that than fighting."

I shook my head, struggling to understand.

"And he talked about you, so much. I know he was difficult with you, but he was proud of you, too. He loved you, Sasha. He really did."

I just stared at Tom.

"It's the truth. Then he went back to the war and he was killed, as you say. When I heard, I wanted to die too, and I couldn't think of any easier way to do it than to come out here. Do you understand? And I'm going to stay here until either I'm dead, or the war is over."

283

I felt utterly empty. I thought back to when Tom had changed his mind about the war, after Edgar died. Edgar had told him to go on with his training, but what had Tom said that day in the kitchen? Mother had begged him to go on being a doctor, and what had he said?

*There's no use in it.*

So he'd come to fight or die, instead. I would lose both brothers. I saw that now.

Tom turned to go. He hesitated, then came toward me, and put his arms around me. As he was breaking away he suddenly froze as he looked at my eyes. He saw something.

"God, no . . ."

Then he shook his head, pulling away, shaking his head as if to clear his vision.

"I'm so tired, I can't . . . I have to go now, Sasha. You understand that, don't you?"

And I had.

I had understood that he had to go, I really did. I knew there was nothing I could do, that he couldn't walk away from it all.

Unless he was wounded.

I think it was the weeks and days and hours of seeing and hurting and fearing and believing in Tom's death.

That was what made me walk to the greatcoat, and pick up the revolver.

It happened as slowly as it had in my dreams. But this time I saw everything.

I saw Jack's head turn, to see what I was doing. He began to stand, but I had already picked up the gun and pointed it at Tom.

Jack called out.

"No!"

Tom turned.

I pulled the trigger. The gun seemed to explode in my hand, and I felt a kick to my arm. I had tried to aim at Tom's legs, so I wouldn't hurt him too badly, but the force of the recoil sent the gun flying up.

A moment later, Tom lay bleeding on the ground, the trees above him still shaking from the gunshot.

"Oh, Sasha," Tom said. "What have you done?"

Blood began to pour from between his fingers as he held them to his chest.

Time stood still.

# 1

So, weeks have passed, and that moment is behind me now, but it leaves behind an awful fact: that it was I who shot Tom.

First, it is true that without Jack, Tom would have died.

As we stood in the hollow, and the reality of what I'd done broke through, I began to shake with fear. Those final moments are unbearable to think of.

Almost as soon as I shot Tom, a flight of shells began to twitter overhead. They landed nearby, with a soft plop into the ground, and no loud explosion.

I didn't understand, but Jack did.

"Gas," he said. "Oh, God."

Tom was barely conscious.

But somehow, we got him down from the hollow, and that's when I took the gas. I was lagging behind as Jack carried Tom toward the camp.

Suddenly gas was in my eyes, and my lungs, and though I was sure I was full of it, I must have had only a taste. Nonetheless, I was struggling to breathe properly. I staggered and fell well behind Jack. Another shell burst somewhere near me, not gas but explosive this time, and that's when I stopped seeing.

Amidst the chaos from the gas attack, Jack found some stretcher bearers and got Tom to the field dressing station. I stumbled along by myself, then felt Jack's hand. He had come back for me.

I heard voices.

"Poor lad, got a whiff," someone said.

"We'll sort him out."

It took me a while to understand they were talking about me. I must have looked so awful they really did think I was a boy. Jack told me later that I was a complete mess. My eyes were watering, my skin was gray. I was covered in mud from head to toe and coughing up great chunks of mucus and fluid from my lungs.

No wonder they didn't see the girl underneath it all.

We got away.

I didn't see Tom again. Jack says he was packed straight off to the ambulance train, and given his Blighty ticket with a good chance of making it. He had a nice clean bullet wound, not some terrible jagged mess from a piece of shrapnel.

I really believe he'll be all right. The visions have stopped.

In fact, for a long time, I had no vision of any kind.

Now I can see again, but like any normal person, nothing more.

\*   \*   \*

I was put on an ambulance train later, still unable to see, still fighting to breathe, and ended up in Rouen.

And there, as some friendly nurse cut away my uniform, they finally found out I was a girl.

Blind, I reached up and grabbed the nurse's arm.

"Whoever you are," I said, "please help me. I'm a nurse. I swear, I'm a nurse."

And bless them, they did.

I was put in a private room, and they nursed me back to health, and slowly, ever so slowly, my sight came back.

They said it was a miracle, but I knew I had to see again, and I did.


One day, I had a visitor.

I was sitting in the hospital gardens. It was a warm, hot day at the end of August, and I looked up to see a soldier walking toward me.

It took me a moment to realize it was Jack.

He was different. He was smarter. Cleaner. I had never seen him clean-shaven before, and his hair was smart too.

"Alexandra," he said, and put his arms around me.

I held him away from me and smiled.

"You can see again?"

"I knew I had to see you again," I said, and he laughed.

"Your hair's growing back," he said, as if it was the most amazing thing in the world.

"I've got something for you," he went on, and pulled a small package from his pocket. "I went back for it."

He handed me something wrapped in newspaper, and nodded at me. I opened it. It was Miss Garrett's book of Greek myths.

I began to laugh, with tears in my eyes.

"Thank you, Jack." I smiled. "Thank you. I said I'd take good care of it. Now I can send it back to her."

"It's a little worse for wear," he said. "A month in the rain."

I laughed again, and then he told me everything that had happened since the day we'd found Tom.

He'd got away with being absent from duty, he said, by claiming his bike had broken down in the middle of nowhere. He said they just about believed it because it was easier than trying to prove he'd deserted. And after all, he'd come back, and so hadn't deserted in the end, anyway. As for stealing me from the camp at Bethune, there was no proof that it had been Jack who had done it. They seemed to have let it drop.

"There's a war on," Jack said, grinning. "Much worse things to worry about."

We talked for hours in the sunshine.

It was wonderful to see him again, and he told me how much I'd helped him. He said he'd come to a new kind of understanding about his premonitions. That maybe what you thought you saw was not the *only* truth, but just *one* possible truth. Maybe you could change things to another, different truth if you tried hard enough.

Like I had, he said.

He said he still had visions, but they worried him less now.

"What about you?" he asked.

I told him that they had gone. That they had left me when I went blind, and so far had not returned.

But still an awful thought hung over me.

I had seen the very thing that had taken me all the way to

find Tom, and it was I who had shot him. Maybe none of this had to happen at all, had I not made it.

"Perhaps," said Jack. "But your brother would probably have got it anyway."

"What do you mean?" I asked.

"His battalion went up from Death Valley to High Wood a few days after we were there. It was a mess. They were annihilated. Almost none of them came back."

I thought for a while. I realized that I'd never really seen anything about myself. Of course, I'd had the raven dream many times, but never seen that I was the one pulling the trigger.

And somehow, I understood something else. Maybe it had to happen like this. Extraordinary as it is, I think this might be the thing that brings my family back together, in the end. Edgar is gone, but my memory of him is a happy and proud one now, and I know he felt the same about me.

Then something else came to me. I suspected something.

"Why did you agree to help me, Jack?" I asked. "After you got me out of Bethune, you just wanted me to go home. Did you see what was going to happen? When you touched me?"

Jack sighed.

"Yes. In a way. I couldn't believe it, but I went along with it. I wondered if there was a way out of it for you after all. I didn't say anything to you. What could I have said? But when I saw you aiming the gun . . . then I wanted to stop you, but it was too late."

After a while, Jack left me to my thoughts.

Before he went, we held each other once more.

"Do you see anything?" he asked, looking into my eyes.

"No," I said. Then, almost too nervous to ask: "Do you?"

"No," he said, smiling. "Just a long and good life. Be happy, Alexandra. You deserve it."

I waved to him from my bench in the garden as he turned the corner of the hospital, and vanished from sight.

And so I am left alone, but not alone.

I have decided to stay here.

I spoke to the commandant of the hospital here in Rouen, and told her some of my story, though not all of it. I told her I was a VAD nurse who had got into the danger zone, and that all I wanted to do was try to help men get well.

She asked no more questions. They need every pair of hands they can get out here.

One day, I might go home to my parents. I will write to them soon. I don't know what they will say, but for now, I am happy.

It's funny, but out here I often think of Clare, my friend from long ago. I'm not sure why, but maybe it's because I hope I'm making up for things at last, by helping with the wounded men.

Father didn't want me to be a nurse at all, and now here I am, in a war in France, doing just that. Maybe, like Edgar, he thought I wasn't up to it. But I realized a few days ago that I am. I went all the way to the front to find Tom, and though I was very scared, I did it.

I did it after all.

So I am happy. I am busy.

The bells are sounding.

Wounded men are coming.

And I must go. I have my work to do.

# Author's Note

This is a work of fiction. In order to give it credibility much of it is based on real places and events, but all characters in the story, both in England and in France, are fictitious. However, instances of reported premonition were not uncommon in the trenches, and the epithet Hoodoo is from a genuine case.

The French name for High Wood is not Raven Wood, though this is what Robert Graves asserts in his autobiography, *Goodbye to All That*. It was from here that I took the idea for Alexandra's visions, but I have not been able to find any other original source calling the wood by that name. The French word for raven is *corbeau*, or in the dialect of Picardy, *cornaille*, but the French name was *Bois des Foureaux*, or sometimes *Bois des Fourcaux*. (These names have no obvious translation, the former meaning maybe "waters of the kiln," but though the wood may have once been the home to charcoal burners, there is no river or stream running through it. I think the name is more likely to be a corruption of *fourchette*—the sweet chestnut trees were used by the local people to make pitchforks.)

Whatever the name of the place, it was here that the Nineteenth Brigade, with the Twentieth Royal Fusiliers among them, were heading in mid-July 1916. On Saturday the fifteenth they became part of the vast number massing in Death Valley, in readiness for their part in the assault on High Wood. Gas shells fell among them that morning.

On July 20, their turn came to go up to the engagement in High Wood, and the battalion was almost annihilated.

The official divisional record simply states: *Attack continued, extremely difficult to form précis of fighting.*

# About the Author

Marcus Sedgwick worked in children's publishing for ten years; before that he was a bookseller. He is also a stone carver and a wood engraver. His first book, *Floodland,* was hailed as "a dazzling debut from a writer of exceptional talent" and won the Branford Boase Award for a best first novel for children. *Witch Hill* and *The Book of Dead Days* were nominated for the Edgar Allan Poe Award for Best Mystery for Young Adults. *The Dark Horse* was short-listed for the *Guardian* Award and the Carnegie Award and was a *School Library Journal* Best Book of the Year. Marcus Sedgwick's most recent books are the thrilling companion novels *The Book of Dead Days* and *The Dark Flight Down.*